at last there is nothing left to say

matthew good

at last there is nothing left to say

matthew good

INSOMNIAC PRESS

Edited and designed by Mike O'Connor
Copy edited by Lorissa Sengara

National Library of Canada Cataloguing in Publication Data

Good, Matthew, 1971–

     At last there is nothing left to say

ISBN 1-894663-08-X

I. Title.

PS8563.O8327A9 2001   C813'.6   C2001-902152-6
PR9199.4.G66A9 2001

The publisher and the author gratefully acknowledge the support of the Canada Council, the Ontario Arts Council and the Department of Canadian Heritage through the Book Publishing Industry Development Program.

Some of the artwork in this book was generously provided by fans of Matthew Good. Artwork by Michael Cook appears on pages 9, 45, 48, 53, 59, 66, 82, 84, and 162. Artwork by Sugar Vashishta appears on pages 91, 127, and 130.

Printed and bound in Canada

Second edition.

Insomniac Press, 192 Spadina Avenue, Suite 403,
Toronto, Ontario, Canada, M5T 2C2
www.insomniacpress.com

For my father. In trade for his stories of India
and for Steve.

...now you watch me stagger on to another stage
you know I get run ragged before I earn my wage
and like a hungry maggot you know I like my meat
and like a careless faggot I don't care where I eat
I've been living to bad effect
I've been driven a nervous wreck
I've been given a place to rest
down near death...

—Tom Anselmi

Francis lived in a house that was built by his great, great grandfather in the middle of nowhere. Despite the fact that Francis wished very much to leave the middle of nowhere and move to a location considered by others to be somewhere, he did not. The house that Francis lived in was built by his great, great grandfather. It had been inhabited by a member of his family since its completion. And, in all that time, no one had ever thought of leaving it. Being that he was an only child, Francis felt obligated to remain in the house. So he did.

How Stupid the World? Let's find out.

A Joke Of You And Me. Joyous realizations of life on easy street.

timing is everything

There is no high like this high. You scour the drugstores, spending your twilight hours bumping into like-minded souls who want only to find something that works faster. The morning slides sloppily into frame each day, as if it were poorly drawn on some warped overhead projector. And all things, instead of themselves, represented by their particles and the symbols used to make them easy. I have been wondering about it. I have been sitting in the isles eyeballing the components, wondering what's to mix and what's not to. Surely something must work. Surely the whole world does not sleep to spite a pitiful few. I have been wondering about many things. I have been thinking of you.

We two are here on this island. We two, despite our lack of smarts, should have known better. We will struggle to find a way to escape this. Perhaps we will find it. There is no high like this high. I am better for having been here. The question is you.

How Stupid The World?
    You decide.
(Random excerpts from mail received at matt@matthewgoodband.com—July, 2000)
—You will burn in hell for your blasphemy. Jesus loves all people but I am afraid that he will never love you.
—I just spent the last couple of hours reading your manifestos. You make no sense. You should try reading some good books to get an idea of what people want to read. Like Danielle Steele books.
—Dear Mr. Good. You are a loud mouth and should be ashamed of not loving Canada. I assume that you have a problem with Canada since you didn't bother to even go and pick up your Juno awards at the Junos. Canadians are supposed to be known for being polite but you just give Canadians a bad name. I used to like your band a lot but won't listen to your CDs anymore because of your attitude. You should remember that bands need people to buy their records and that it is not in your best interest to make them angry.
    PS: Ian is hot.

—Why don't you just shut up about things you don't know anything about. Our Lady Peace is an excellent band and much more talented than you'll ever be. You haven't put out a good CD since Under The Table & Dreaming anyway.

That's why there was an idiot in 1-900-Idiot-Savant. To be honest, I really don't miss it much. I find that I have more time to blaspheme this way.

A Joke Of You And Me.

I have been told that I am missed. I have been told that I have become unentertaining in my old age. The difference between these two statements is that the latter is a common one amongst those who procure such journals as this to pore over various accounts of the fire-breathing sheepdogs and gibbons that I have trained in hopes of cornering the transcontinental personal courier market. The first I simply said to myself.

Is there a point to it all? A question for a million years, a million prior, and for all mankind unanswerable. As for these things, well, I used to believe that the benefit of the doubt was something that hope created simply to humour us into thinking that a commonality existed between all people. Arrogance exists when the presumption of greatness exceeds empathy, transforming the much touted principles of individualism into the creation of solitary existences. Individualism is arrogance in that it creates a void between individuals attempting to bridge the gaps between themselves. To possess uniqueness is useless without first having someone to share it with and, secondly, having the ability to appreciate it in others. But we have never been exposed to the factors of a divided existence. Until now, that is. We find ourselves in an era of absolute solitude, a state of being that has transformed individuality into something that no longer possesses the qualities of self-assurance and self-dignity. Instead it is something that is thrown about by people in an attempt to disguise their need for something altogether terrifying. The realization that others are needed to fill the gaps in themselves. In ages past this realization was quite clearly understood by most. Convenience has seen to it that the human infrastructure will be made to suffer in the wake of its own desire to be more expediently and easily catered to.

We are used. We are a society of used individuals who are coddled by the warm radiation of television and the voyeuristic thrills of cyberspace. We exist in a vacuum that has taught our children to complain about the rights of the individual while instilling in them the need to consume, to achieve, to

Disorientation

I'm so unoriginal. I've been hiding out hoping you wouldn't notice. I've been standing in front of your house with dynamite strapped to my body holding a large clock, waiting. Slumming so fantastic. Open your window. You can hear it if you listen hard. The ticking of your heartbeat, the rhythm of the traffic pouring down the streets. The mice scratching under the floorboards are safe to follow when the ship starts to sink. They'll be running in the opposite direction of the mad scientists. Towards Nihm, towards Nicademus, into the hazy summer sky-glow as the clock runs out. The score is tied so there's gonna be overtime. Sudden death. The pink pills are for your sanity. So lets go kids. Lets go...

The Better, Happier Me.

The Better, Happier You.

A Better, Happier World To Live In.

How is everyone out there in happy land?

You been taking your vitamins? You been

drinking lots of milk and saying your prayers?

You been good little boys and girls? Hmm?

You know Santa doesn't just check up on you

at Christmastime. He's watching all year

round. So you'd better be on your best behav-

iour. You'd better be looking both ways before

you cross the street and brushing your teeth

twice every day. Santa doesn't like little boys

and girls with yellow teeth. He sends them to

an unhappy land where fire falls from the sky

and rivers of blood cut through a harsh, bar-

ren, rocky wilderness devoid of plant life and

dominate. This occurs because we are on top of our game. It occurs because, beyond us, there is nothing save the view. Just the cheap seats to look upon and utilize for our own ends. My running shoes were manufactured in Pakistan by an eleven-year-old. An eleven-year-old who supposedly cares for nothing save the company's new *air-flow system* and whether or not it will help propel me to greatness as I dart from my apartment to my car, late as usual. The naïve have always believed that simple solutions exist to deter such things in our nature. Whether they be socialistic views or those of the extreme right, most fail to realize that the drug of power is stronger than good intentions. It matters little what you call it—capitalism, socialism, communism, democracy, gods and goddesses. It has been said that absolute power corrupts absolutely. If so, then a little corruption must go a long way. The danger inherent in believing yourself to be beyond corruption is that you must first believe that, given the opportunity, you could do better. This is impossible, of course, as absolute power corrupts absolutely, leaving a little to go a long way. Therefore, realizing that there is nothing to be done about it, it leaves your skin feeling refreshed and rejuvenated. Try some and you'll agree, there's no better brand than the one that was handmade by Chilean craftsmen from herbs and flowers grown on the slopes of the Andes. We have been lying to ourselves and getting away with it nicely. And so we should be. Welcome to the new world. Made in China for twenty-six percent less than we originally paid to have it produced in Pittsburgh. We hope you like it.

Everything is timing

I woke up this morning, it's been difficult as of late. I am convinced that I have been infected with an incurable malady. Everyone tells me that I am imagining it. So I have stopped listening.

I've taken to wandering my house in a three-piece suit, waiting for the doorbell to ring. I will be ready when they come for me. I have been ready for weeks. I have come to realize that if you spend enough time watching things that would have otherwise gone unnoticed, you will begin to realize that you are the keeper of a terrible secret.

Yourself.

Are You Ready to Rumble?

There's Chicago down there, all lit up. I'm on a plane. Moving.

Everybody gets a shit kicking. That's the rules. Everyone gets an overnight bag full of tiny bathroom products as consolation. Those miniature toothpaste tubes are extremely effective at capturing your curiosity. One has to wonder why anyone would put such a small amount of toothpaste in a tube. Probably because the brush that comes with it can only hold so much. Maybe someone just thought it would take your mind off things during your trip. Everyone is going somewhere. And along the way everyone gets a shit kicking. That's the rules. Look it up if you don't believe me. It's in the handbook.

The Earth is 93,003,000 miles from the sun. One more mile either way and history is undone. One less comet smashing into the Earth 63 million years ago and Godzilla is the mayor of Tokyo. The handbook doesn't say how far the Earth is away from the sun. Someone figured that out for themself. I like to think of the world as a giant, spherical Chia Pet. There's already a Chia Guy, a Chia Girl, Chia dogs and cats, and a variety of other Chia animals. So why not a Chia World? Just add water and wham: LIFE. If you think about it, maybe that's why it took so long for things to happen.

Before I continue I should clarify something. Someone recently wrote me and inquired if I was at all religious, due to the fact that I use the word GOD in some of the things I write. It should be known that my interpretation of the all-mighty usually includes all versions of God, whatever they might be referred to as. This is, by no means, an attempt to be politically and correctly mindful on my part. There are various aspects of many religions that I find interesting.

The most interesting aspect is that they all have several common fundamental principles. Such as: try your best not to kill other people, and love is a good thing so try using it in a sentence today, and there's hope after all—and my personal favourite—hey! You're forgiven!

Religion not only provides high drama, but moments of hilarity when you least expect it. In many ways, most major religions are dramedies.

Dramedy is a word that was invented in Hollywood, a location quite often confused with many aspects of an altogether elusive and unattainable afterlife.

I'm up in my beautiful, beautiful balloon. I've been watching a Japanese movie about dancing. Actually, the balloon isn't mine, it belongs to Canadian Airlines. I'm just borrowing a seat for five hours. We're over North Dakota I think. I can't really tell. I'm having fun with the FLIGHT ATTENDANTS.

animals (except for man-eating wolves and giant three headed vultures that can rip little boys and girls apart with their claws and teeth). So you'd better keep those teeth clean. You'd better be cooperative and obedient. You'd better be doing your homework, your leg work, your chores. I can no longer guarantee what will happen if you don't. They have a way of finding out if you're not happy. They have hidden cameras and informants dressed up like ordinary people. They smile all the time, as if setting some example for you to follow. Like there's an equation that you're supposed to memorize and use to attain that which all people strive to attain: inner peace, humility, civility, the pro-grammed ability to bend. Call it what you will.

I can't talk very well at the moment, so my inability to answer their dinner inquiries with resounding vocal responses has caused some tension.

I'm not sure why individuals who are easily angered tend to actively seek careers in the service industry. Better to join the military, I would think. At least there you can get pissed off and yell all day.

You're not allowed to call them stewardesses anymore. There's a law. I had the chicken. I dropped my cheese. Jack Daniels isn't good for throat ailments. Turbulence.

Everybody still gets a shit kicking though. Don't think because we're getting friendly that you're exempt. It's the rules. I didn't make them up, I'm just saying. One day I will open my mouth and nothing will come out. You will have forgotten this by then. You will have forgotten a good many things, I'm sure. I will open my mouth and the gears will fail. Just one more night, I'll say to myself, just one more night.

Through the smoke and the sweat there's this mass, this beautiful monster. There is no place I would rather be. One day I will open my mouth and nothing will come out. I will remember every word before that. Forever. Like a tattoo, like incurable cancer, like a dream. There are so many holes and never enough plugs. So many, many holes.

I hope you've enjoyed the flight. We look forward to serving you again in the future. The future. Tomorrow. The Earth is a long way from the sun. Numbers are unimportant in the end. But there's a reason why this crazy Chia Pet is floating around with a bunch of colourful frozen gases and huge, inter-dimensional wormholes. There just has to be. Maybe there was a bang. Maybe God's watering can has got some good stuff left. Maybe we should just get off our asses and buy a sprinkler. The handbook says that everyone gets a shit kicking. As to when? Well, that's the beauty of it. You never know.

There's Vancouver down there, all lit up.

WaterWorld II

I've decided to finance the making of *WaterWorld II*. I just finished reading the script and it's rough in places, but I think it'll do better than the first one. The story is about the children of the survivors that found Dry Land who've turned their island paradise into a *Lord of the Flies* kind of vibe. Lots of gory, unnecessary violence and such. The first twenty minutes is all blood and gore, actually. After that there's just a lot of unnecessary sex, betrayal, and explosions. Not exactly *The Bicycle Thief* or *Red, White*, and *Blue*, but what is these days?

I can't abide movies without explosions. They're just no fun at all. We're thinking about adding a scene where two secondary characters are having sex and get blown up in the middle of it. So you've got your nudity, sex, an explosion, and unnecessary violence all rolled into one three-minute scene. Shit, that could be the whole movie.

I just got off the phone with Steven Spielberg. He doesn't want to direct the picture. Even after my lengthy pitch about the horror, sex, and explosions. He kept babbling on about having small children and not wanting to be affiliated with a movie that's going to contain such scenes. James Cameron turned me down too. Same reasons and everything.

All big Hollywood directors are hypocrites. I bet you he makes *Terminator III* this year. Like that's not going to have a ton of violence and nudity. I can see it all now. The Terminator running around shooting flowers at elves riding unicorns. How lovely.

I think I'm going to use Sam Raimi. He was my first choice, but the writers wanted me to ask Spielberg and Cameron first. *Evil Dead, Evil Dead II*, and *Army of Darkness* were wicked movies. I think he's perfect for the job. It just doesn't make sense that people wouldn't want to make this picture. Nothing's made sense since *The Texas Chainsaw Massacre* as far as I'm concerned. Now that's art. You've got your power-tool-wielding psycho, your unsuspecting girl with big tits, your sacrificial-lamb types that get killed throughout the movie, and your gratuitous nudity and violence. There's even an equation that explains it. They call it a FORMULA movie. Check it out:

$$P+G(BT)+SLT+GN/V=\$\$\$$$

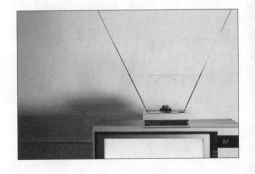

It's all there in simple black and white. It doesn't take a genius to figure it out. When you get right down to it, it's all about giving the people what they

They're watching and taking notes. They've got computer files, metal files, paper files, and the cabinets to keep them in. They're the ones that wrote the handbook. Everybody gets a shit kicking. You don't have a choice in the matter. They've brought in seasoned professionals to make sure that you get one. Everybody gets one. That's the rules. I didn't make it up, I'm just saying.

So be happy. Happiness is paramount. Your happiness is of the utmost importance. Everyone else has their own happiness to worry about. You just follow the program and keep reading the handbook. Everything will be revealed in time. But for now you just keep grasping for that gold ring, that blue ribbon, that dreamy picture-perfect-magazine you. It's want. Trust me, this is what they want.

Back to *WaterWorld II*, there are about 200 people living on the island. They've managed to defeat the rest of the smokers and now worship a statue of a golden half-fish, half-man god. The 200 people are divided into two warring factions who live on either side of the island.

So, one night, three boys from one group sneak into a costume party being thrown by their enemies. They drink, scope chicks, etcetera. But one of the boys spots this girl from across the room and immediately falls head-over-heels in love with her (or some superficial dream-like version of her that he's created in his own mind). They meet and start seeing each other in secret. Eventually their parents find out about the affair and all hell breaks loose. There are missile attacks and assassinations, torture and espionage. Distraught that their love is the cause of all this death and destruction, the two kids run away into the hills where they live in a cave for a couple of weeks. It's there that they discover the alien space ship.

During all the fighting we're probably going to throw in that sex/explosion scene I was talking about, as well as a small scene where the roof is blown off of a shower house and everyone comes running out screaming (à la *Porky's*).

As a subplot, there's also this little bald man that everyone likes who threatens to starve himself to death if both sides don't stop fighting. So when he begins to starve himself they stop fighting and start again when he agrees to eat.

I'm really not sure what's going to happen with the kids and the alien ship yet. Everyone's kicking around ideas, but we haven't got anything firm.

The two lovers eventually return to their villages only to get caught up in the war between their peoples. In the end the little bald guy helps the boy fake his own death, but the plan backfires because the girl really thinks he's dead and kills herself.

The boy wakes up and, after learning what's happened, kills the little bald guy and then shoots himself in the head. During all of this there'll be more explosions, sex, and violence as well.

Both kids are dead and everyone's pretty upset because the little bald guy's dead too, which leads to an uneasy peace between the two groups. This lasts long enough for the aliens to introduce a mind-controlling drug into their water supply, which turns everyone into their slaves. The aliens then activate a GATE back to their own world and take the slaves with them. And that's pretty much it. It'll all be quite dramatic of course, with a big score and all the usual merchandise.

The equations for this movie would look something like this:

$$B+G(BT)+W+E+GN(S)+LBG+A=\$\$\$$$

So there you have it. *Water World II*. A hit? I think so.

Take heed. The End is near.

in there somewhere. With your DNA, what you ate for dinner, and all those terrible secrets. You're in there somewhere, waiting to be reborn. The better, happier you. If you play your cards right the possibilities are endless. There's an equation for everything. For you, for us, for everything. Everything's been pre-arranged. Mostly for the better. Mostly for the worst.

The future of happiness is in your hands.

Do with it what you will.

Porno Safari

ACHTUNG!

This product contains elements of dirtiness. Pregnant women, Presbyterians, and those easily persuaded to climb inside of coin-operated tumble dryers should not ride this ride.

Collins Mini English Dictionary defines the following words as such:
Porno/*n., adj./Informal*/short for PORNOGRAPHY or PORNOGRAPHIC.
Safari/*n.*/expedition to hunt or observe wild animals.
Sausage/*n.*/minced meat in an edible tube-shaped skin.
Sausages/*n.*/many minced meat in an edible tube-shaped skin dealies.

There are many things in this life that cannot be helped or explained. Slappy Mutt Mutt found it difficult to swallow, but had spent a great deal of time considering the options and could come up with no other explanation. Slappy Mutt Mutt had spent years pondering it. What made it so confusing was all the alarmingly apparent exceptions.

1) Most things look pretty real.
2) Nuclear winter does not entitle you to a "second annual Christmas."
3) All things are comprised of protons, electrons, and neutrons which are, themselves, comprised of even smaller measurements of ridiculousness.
4) Ice cream will always melt on hot days.
5) Girls with big tits tend to have larger cabooses than girls with small tits.
6) X-ray vision glasses that are sold in comic books do not really work.
7) It is impossible to accurately calculate the trajectory of dinner rolls. (Especially in Hamburg, Turin, and Chelmsford—for some reason).

That said, Slappy Mutt Mutt had long since realized that most of life's constants were, on closer inspection, unpredictable. No matter what you might *need* to believe as being *the way it is*, nothing in this universe is definite. And that brings us to the whole kidnapping thing.

I'll be the first to admit that Slappy shouldn't have kidnapped the girl. But, if you really stop and think about it, he had no idea that he was going to do it. And there was little that I could have done to prevent it. I only went along because I was unconscious when the board was in session. I awoke to discover myself stuck in the middle of the Mojave Desert with a girl locked up in a cage.

If you are the sort of person who is easily disagreeable, I would suggest that you stop right here. This is not for you. To be honest, this is the kind of thing satanic high priests would find disagreeable. My mother was a dancer in a house of burlesque and she would not be pleased (to say the least). I was kind of intrigued by the whole thing. As vile as it might seem now, at the time it looked better than a banana split the size of Ojos del Salado.

Slappy had always been a bit of a reactionary. He was the kind of guy that wouldn't say anything about babies being killed, but kill one right in front of him and you'd never hear the end of it. Wholly mesmerized by an ill-formed compassionate teaching that is entirely based on unreasonable proximity. If you had to deal with the fact that there were children eating leftovers out of your garbage cans you would probably feel guilty. Guilty enough to be brought to action perhaps. Maybe you'd feed them. Maybe you'd just hack them into little pieces and toss them in your compost. Most North Americans have become quite desensitized to homelessness, for example. This is largely due to the fact that the homeless are so damn smelly and grubby lookin'. Therefore, proximity no longer has anything to do with it. Most North Americans tend to view *crazy people who talk to themselves on the street* as, well…crazy people who talk to themselves on the street, I would think. Schizophrenics, on the other hand, might argue that their illness is comparable to living one's life with their head stuck in a toilet that is constantly being flushed.

Most folks would not stop long enough to think about it. Most folks just wish such bothersome individuals would melt into the endlessness that is our great and desirable social landscape. Being that they are products of that landscape, the question remains: *where exactly should they be sent?* For if they are not to remain here, with us, then perhaps we are all destined for unceremonious exile. Having said that, know then that what occurred during those lost hours in the desert could be best defined as an experiment of sorts. It was an experiment to see what might occur if all the so-called sane people of this world decided to take the day off and just the crazies were left to mind the till.

Slappy Mutt Mutt had not always been a bad man. Like most people, he was once filled with emotions and thoughts of a pleasant nature. But things change, quite often for the worse to be honest. He had once been a good man. I did not know him then. I only knew the demonic Slappy who was, without a doubt, far more entertaining than his former angelic self. I'm sure.

I WANNA BE AN AIRBORNE RANGER

Freedom costs. It's kind of a hypocritical philosophy, really. We fight for the right to be free. We fight for the right to have a free-market system so you can buy anything you want, whenever you want, from whoever you want. We fight for the freedom of religious belief, though mostly we just fight amongst ourselves about that. Sometimes we even travel to the other side of the world to make sure that those less fortunate than ourselves can enjoy our special brand of freedom: video games, Coke, Pepsi, Jesus, and Taco Time. You have the right to eat tacos we'll say, and they'll smile and scream "FINALLY!" Some people even have the right to bear arms. Sometimes their kids get in on that right.

Sometimes people die for freedom and don't even know it. Funny how freedom works.

In the most perfect dream I will be sitting in a kick-ass lawn chair on a high plateau, watching the demise of Western Civilization. I'd buy a super powerful pair of binoculars, so as not to miss anything. I'd have a big cooler full of drinks and sexy chicks lounging around, rubbing my feet and shoulders. And I'd get new glasses, 'cause the ones I've got now are all scratched up. Better than a super summer blockbuster. No giant lizards, no aliens, no natural disasters. Just us, swirling towards the bottom of the bowl. I'll have some tacos and put on a t-shirt that says "finally."

I'll probably need some really good sun-

So there we were, five of us all told. The girl, who made six, doesn't count. She was safely locked within the confines of the cage called the *love-hold trap*, bound and gagged. That left Slappy, myself, Ernesto Valencias (the famous Honduran trapeze artist known for lighting himself on fire), Dr. Maurice, and Mr. Chips. The doctor was a rather peculiar sort of fellow. He couldn't have been an inch taller than 5'1", with a huge bushel of curly blond hair atop his head. He was a motivational speaker. During our foray into the wilds he did a lot of talking but failed to motivate anyone besides our captive.

There's history behind everything. The history behind our trek into the Mojave goes a little something like this...

It was a hot, dusty afternoon when I stumbled into town. People were sitting on their porches and waiting for the night to provide them with an excuse to be productive. Nighttime in the desert is funny like that. Much colder than most realize, the drastic difference between the two twelve o'clock markers is quite severe. Deadly heat during the day and vicious cold at night. Perfect for lizards and, for some unknown reason, elderly asthmatic Canadian golfers.

Slappy Mutt Mutt was born in the desert. He was raised in the desert, went to school in the desert, went to war in the jungle and returned to the desert, and (finally) opened an adult books and paraphernalia boutique in the desert. Besides the one year that Slappy spent in the jungle, he had lived his entire life in the desert. You know, I'm not quite sure what it is, but there's something about the desert that tends to blur the lines of social acceptability, like Las Vegas.

When Slappy was just a kid he used to live on the outskirts of town. His mother, Janice, worked in a roadhouse called the Three Suns. And although Slappy was under the impression that she spent her time at the Three Suns serving drinks to thirsty desperadoes, she was actually the one doing all the drinking. Janice was one of those rare prostitute-waitresses that rarely seems to have time to do either job properly. Either you get an unopened bottle of beer or half a yank. The woman couldn't concentrate. Years later, Janice would discover that she suffered from ADD. She would learn that she was dyslexic as well. And, as ridiculous as it might sound, once she chose to acknowledge and tackle these ailments, she was forced to come to terms with the fact that she had an IQ of one hundred and ninety-six. She was forty-seven at the time. She died two years later driving to Washington, where she had landed a job in one of those highly mysterious think tanks where people sit around all day and debate the pros and cons of things such as thermonuclear war. She accidentally drove her car into the back of a semi trailer parked on the side of the highway. She was doing ninety. She was putting on eyeliner. She looked great at the time.

But this wasn't the first time. Slappy was traumatized twice before the age of ten. The first time was when his father fell off the roof of the house while attempting to set up a Christmas scene after consuming a bottle of Wild Turkey. He fell and landed head first on the driveway. He was killed instantly. Two weeks later, Slappy's grandmother was shot to death by the milkman. From what I can gather the woman was quite unpleasant to most folks. After years of taking her shit, the milkman decided that he'd had enough. So he shot her nine times. The glorious bastard stood there and took the time to reload.

Coupled with spending a year in Vietnam, it was only a matter of time before Slappy cracked a bolt. He had spent the better part of twenty years living a life of mediocre filthiness in a town where people were too lazy to be bothered with the exotic entanglements of licorice whips, edible underwear, and love harnesses. Slappy's skull was just waiting for something ingenious to discover its dark, empty places. As it turned out, everything fell into place just as I strolled into town with an empty gas can. I would leave town two days later in the company of a would-be kidnapper and his faithful entourage. I would never see the gas can again.

It may sound almost too typical to be believable. But the truth of the matter is that I did indeed run out of gas in the middle of the desert. I had not planned it that way. I felt as if I had landed squarely in the first ten minutes of some disgustingly brilliant hacker film. It left me with little choice but to rummage around in the trunk for a gas can that at the time I could have sworn was bigger and head off in a direction best suited to the illusions of a hopeful outcome.

You won't find the town of Slappy's birth on any map. It's far too small for such recognition. Which must bring one to wonder why anyone in their right mind would open a XXX boutique in such a place. Slappy would later confess that he did it as an experiment in futility. I responded to that statement by walking into a wall three times in a row. The difference? Mine took under a minute. His took twenty years. It makes no sense.

I found myself in a one-road town filled with an odd variety of introverts, extroverts, mindless shapes, and the cackling ghosts of ill confidence. A town that had been frozen in the forgotten arms of the 1950s. Slappy, unlike many of his fellow citizens, had left that little town for a brief time. He went from

glasses and some super high-powered sun-block. It'll get hot, I'm sure. Maybe I'd have one of those kiddie pools to sit in instead of a lawn chair. That way I could beat the heat. The chemical wind will blow through my hair as I monitor the major news networks for further details and endless updates. The field correspondents broadcasting from within the flaming debris, conditioned to remain impervious to the dangers and drama unfolding around them. The earth bursting into flame. Little ships slipping picturesquely beneath the foaming waves. Hell hath no fury like a man sitting in a kiddie pool watching the end of the world who's run out of tacos. I'll have to remind myself to bring extra. The girls don't eat, you see, they're too worried about their weight.

And then come the missiles. Having spent the majority of my life living in a time of nuclear devices, I say launch them. I'm curious to see what all the fuss is about. Perhaps we can fire them all at India, France, and Pakistan. I'm open to suggestions. I'll play Pac-Man and Frogger while ICBMs plummet all around me like so many seagulls fed Wonder Bread mixed with Draino. I'll do the Safety Dance, the Electric Slide, the Macarena, maybe me and the girls will even line-dance. I'll put on a little Nina Simone and pour some bourbon. And I'll laugh, maniacally. 'Cause what the hell else are you gonna do. There'll be umbrellas in all the drinks, fireworks without warning labels, hundreds of rare T-bones, a million cigarettes, and plenty of pornography. 'Cause if

that place into the mysterious East where he shot at nothing and hid from everything. He returned to his desert time capsule and shut himself off. And that's where I come into it. He hit me with his pick-up, so there was little I could do about it.

It still boggles my mind to this day. How exactly does one get hit by a vehicle in a town with only one road? In a town where, even if the entire population owned a car, there wouldn't be enough traffic to warrant a traffic light. At the time I chose to blame Slappy's driving instead of my own foolish disregard. I stepped off the curb just as Slappy was turning the corner. I froze, he slammed on the brakes, and I was introduced to the outstanding arguments to the contrary pertaining to the existence of most things.

When I awoke I found myself in a saloon. It was rather empty as saloons go. That came as no great surprise mind you. According to several locals that I would speak to later that day, the town theatre had been showing *Logan's Run* their entire lives and none of them had ever seen it.

Semi-conscious in a saloon with five strangers. I would end up with four of them in the Mojave Desert with the fifth locked up in a cage, bound and gagged. They were, as stated earlier, Slappy Mutt Mutt, Ernesto Valencias, Dr. Maurice, and Mr. Chips. As my eyes opened, it was their faces that hovered above me like four angelic frauds. For there was but one angel in the room. And her name was Rosemary.

Now, it was easy to deduce that Slappy was in charge from the get-go. No one said or did anything without his strange, unconscious say-so. Everyone, that is, but Mr. Chips. Mr. Chips did not speak. From what I could gather he hadn't spoken since the spring of 1976. That's what Dr. Maurice told me the first time I attempted to make conversation with the eldest of our party. He said *"Chippy don't talk. He doesn't say a word. He hasn't spoken since May of 1976."* To this day I'm not sure if the story was true or not but the tale goes something like this. One night, in May of 1976, a local oil baron bet Mr. Chips one million dollars that he couldn't go for ten years without speaking. Mr. Chips took the bet and had not spoken since. At the time I didn't bother to do the math. I should have. It would have made the conclusion of that week all the more ridiculously entertaining.

I was quick to delve into the lives of the three men that still possessed the ability to verbalize. But as I was to discover, that merely gave way to hours of Slappy's never-ending analysis of the other two as they sat nearby, nodding whenever the occasion arose. Everyone seemed to give way to Slappy's "better judgment" about practically everything, not seeming to care how he went about painting their character. He went on and on about how Dr. Maurice could have been one of the greatest psychoanalytical minds of our time had he the strength to curb his appetite for young girls (especially those who were his patients). Dr. Maurice had once had quite a lucrative practice in San Francisco but was run out of town by the fathers of two young girls whom he had taken liberties with. Thankfully he had not been jailed. How, exactly, it led him to become a motivational speaker remains a mystery though. There wasn't anyone in that town worth motivating.

I met Ernesto in hell. A staunch Catholic, he viewed his time in the middle of nowhere as suitable punishment for killing his wife. Don't get me wrong, Ernesto wasn't a murderer by any means, but he blamed himself for her death none-the-less. You see, she had been sleeping with numerous other men while Ernesto was on the road with the circus. One night, returning home unexpectedly after suffering minor burns during a show, he caught her with one of her lovers on the kitchen floor. His wife, so distraught that she had been found out, promptly ran to the balcony, climbed the railing, and leapt to her death. The man, by the way, was Ernesto's half-brother Paolo Sanchez, the famed South American midfielder. The two of them had coffee while the police removed her body from the boulevard below.

After that, Ernesto decided to retire from circus life and wandered north in search of a suitable place to torture himself. Never one to go halfway with anything, his ceaseless exploration for the most despicable company in the northern hemisphere ended when he stumbled upon Slappy and Dr. Maurice dynamite fishing on nearby Lake Churapiña. As for Rosemary, I didn't really speak much with Rosemary until after Slappy had abducted her. But by then I did it more out of a sense of obligation than anything else. Her captivity was, after all, due to my overactive libido and naïve misconception that most people are not entirely mentally handicapped.

It was on the second day of my recovery at the saloon that everything went terribly wrong. I have, since then, been dumbfounded by my own stupidity in the matter. One must remember where one is at all times, especially if that locale is in or near any kind of desert. Because crazy things happen in the desert and no one ever hears about them.

In the small hours of the morning is when most things of this nature are born. So there we were, all three sheets to the wind, talking in circles, talking stupid-talk, when I came up with the extremely sinful notion of hitting on lovely Rosemary.

you're gonna go, go big. Like Stew used to say: "Big time, or no time at all."

That's freedom. Not some word in a dictionary. Not some corrupted thing bent to suit commercial purposes. Limitless freedom. Endless slow poison. No "tomorrow I'll go to the gym after work." Just sought after cancerous treats and spy-like glow-in-the-dark party favours. Naked riders, outrageous costumes, dangerous words blasted through megaphones, outlawed tunes played on outlawed guitars. A silence after a great noise. A thunder that's like so many violins and cellos. And then the ringing tones of a last, great chord. That's freedom.

MATTOPIA. Trouble Abounds in Wonderland.

Mattopia: a land where people could roam around freely in bikinis and *Star Wars* apparel. My island realm of the South Pacific would pay homage to some of mankind's greatest achievements. Of course the most significant of these would have to be the roller coaster. Others include water slides, futuristic tree houses, and a sewage recycling facility that looked good on paper but bad in reality. Having attempted to put my plans into effect I came across certain obstacles that proved too much for me. The cost alone exceeded one hundred and twenty-three million dollars. Then there were various problems concerning transportation to the island (due to the fact that I was unable to purchase the land that I

Knowing full well that she couldn't leave the saloon because she was the only employee and that she absolutely despised the lot of us with a hatred that could not be measured in even the cruelest of units, I decided to give it a go anyway. You see, Rosemary worked at the saloon because her father, an invalid, had been given the place by his father. Rosemary's great, great grandfather had built it during the late 1800s. Despite the fact that she reviled the customers and loathed working there, she couldn't bring herself to break her father's heart and leave town. She dealt with Slappy's shit by ignoring him. And, to her credit, she did a damn fine job of it. So much so, in fact, that Slappy and the boys rarely bothered to speak to her beyond ordering drinks.

So I found myself cross-eyed and slurring, sitting at the bar attempting to coerce her into a conversation. I will be the first to admit that my behaviour was less than appropriate. I should also have probably kept my voice down. Being that I am rather boisterous when intoxicated. I must admit, from what I can recall of it, Rosemary was a rather good sport about the whole thing. She must have endured my slimy verbal tentacles for the better part of an hour before she hit me in the head with the beer glass.

When I came around I was in the back of Slappy's truck. We all were. Rosemary was there too of course, bound and gagged within the silvery confines of *the love-hold trap*. I was bleeding from the head where she had crowned me with the beer glass and was in need of stitches. Her eyes, filled with panic and terror, looked into mine, attempting to make me realize that I was not yet a willing participant in her abduction. Perhaps she did it so that I might help her, I don't know. Truth be told, I was far too disoriented to fully grasp the severity of the situation. As far as I was concerned, at that moment, things of that nature were quite common in the desert. And who was I to say anything to the contrary? I grew up in a temperate zone.

Before I go any further I must explain the sudden appearance of **the device**. You see, Slappy wasn't altogether delusional when it came to his meagre existence in that little desert town. He had plans. One of Slappy's many hopeful flights of fancy was *the love-hold trap*. Designed as the ultimate in submissive-dominatrix aids, he hoped to one day mass-produce the cages and sell them to sex shops all over the world. The ridiculous thing about them was that they were just regular, ordinary cages. Anyone motivated enough to that extreme could easily make one themselves or purchase something similar from a kennel or pet store. But Slappy thought it ingenious. And there was just no convincing him otherwise.

It would seem that Slappy took offense to Rosemary hitting me on the head with that beer glass. His reaction to the incident was to gag her with a sock, wrap her head with electrical tape, tie her hands together with a bar towel, and march her out the back door to his truck. Leaving the boys to watch her, he then went back inside for me. Perhaps he had fantasized about the whole thing beforehand, perhaps he hadn't. It seemed to me as if the man was just looking for an excuse, any excuse, to do something that could not be so easily undone. So the first thing he did was to drive back to his house for the cage. After that he planned to drive into the desert.

It was near the end of the drive that I came around. What seemed like mere minutes had actually been almost two and a half hours. I was surprisingly sober. We all choked on the dust as Slappy sat alone in the truck cab, his foot weighing the gas pedal to the floor, his eyes fixed on some imaginary point on the night horizon. I just lay there and bled. There was nothing left for me to do. I was beyond altering the course of what was about to happen. I would regret it, I told myself, but it was better than the alternatives that had started the creep into my head. Someone was going to be left out there. It sure as hell wasn't going to be me.

What you are about to read is not pleasant. The truth, perhaps entirely foreign in this day and age, rarely offers tidings of goodwill. This you will learn as your clock ticks. The truth, though commonly misconstrued as something noble and empowering, tends to turn up more often than not sounding of hammer blows on coffin nails.

When we got out there, hidden away from the eyes of the world, lost in the windy cold of the desert night, we stood around pretending not to watch Slappy rape Rosemary. Then we pretended not to do it ourselves. Then, as if set on some diabolically irreversible course, we pretended not to do it over and over again.

Perceptions dictate truth? Most things seem pretty real to me, yet they are comprised of tiny little particle doo-dads. Does such information make them any less truthful? Is there even truth to the existence of such particles and like-minded miniscule nonsense? To properly explore the truth you must first discard the bullshit adage that "the truth *is* the truth."

I convinced myself that I hadn't done anything, despite the fact that I just had. Consumed by feelings of self-loathing, attempting to convince myself it was a crash course in how despicable behaviour can serve to further individual experience, I did my best not to outwardly crumble while I went about it all. Mistakes are made in every life.

I'm not exactly sure when we realized that Rosemary was dead. It was

had originally wanted). It seems the French have plans to do some nuclear testing on it. Either I'd have to find another location or wait a couple thousand years until it was habitable again. I chose to move. And that's when things started to get complicated. No airline in the world would agree to fly to the island. The nearest landmass was too far away to accommodate small aircraft so I was forced to add an airfield to the island's design. But following the failure of a last-ditch bid to get Bengali Air to service the destination I was forced to face the fact that it would be impossible to fly citizens in. This left me with only one option: sea travel. The nearest major port from which a passenger ship could sail was over nine days away. This then forced me to scrap the construction of the airport and begin constructing a docking area large enough to accommodate a ship of that size. True, the Mattopian naval docks had already been planned, but they were designed to be in a secured area that was off limits to international vessels. To make matters worse, I couldn't find any major cruise lines that would service the island. Like the airlines, they felt that it was too far out of their way. Due to the fact that Mattopia was only open to people with citizenship it wasn't considered to be a viable vacation destination. So I was screwed again. I briefly looked into buying my own ship until I realized how much it was going to cost. Leasing a ship would have been possible but without a

sometime the following night after a day filled with whiskey consumption, pretzels, and powdered donuts that someone finally realized she was cold. I was sitting against one of the rear tires of the truck, bottle in hand, oblivious to everything save my own hatred for all that I had allowed myself to become. I looked at her immobile body, wondering what it would have been like to wake up next to her or carry on a conversation about something mundane while she was in the shower. I did my best to convince myself that she was merely sleeping. And then I lost it and killed everyone.

It's a horrible thing to live in fear. Fear of the unknown, fear of others, fear of yourself. Better to become the master of those fears than allow them to consume you. After hours spent attempting to rationalize the most unforgivable thirty hours of my life, I decided that it would be best to stop trying to convince myself that I had simply slipped up. I had fallen, no question about it. So why not hit the ground hard and leave an impression.

Like any good desert dweller, Slappy had a gun rack in his truck. Two rifles were to be found on it. One was a hunting rifle, one was a shotgun. I ended up having to use both. After shooting Dr. Maurice and Ernesto with the shotgun, I was left with little choice but to use the rifle on Slappy. He had started to run. Now, as drunk as he was, he still made decent time. Being that I'm not entirely familiar with distances as they might pertain to rifles, I can't say exactly how far Slappy was able to go before I shot him. I used the scope. Once targeted, I steadied myself and proceeded to shoot him in the back of the neck. He was flung forward, rolled around a bit, and then lay still. It was that simple. All of it was that terribly simple.

Stranger still was that after having shot Slappy, I turned to discover Mr. Chips standing next to me, his head cocked to one side as if he were appraising my marksmanship. A round of uncomfortable seconds passed between us as I deliberated whether or not I was going to shoot him. He just stood there, his hands on his hips, looking out at Slappy's body, an entirely removed expression on his face. To his credit, he did not flinch. He didn't try to run either. Even when I turned towards him, the rifle held at waist height, my finger still on the trigger. He just stood there, calm as could be. I decided to let him live. I also decided to burn everyone. Everyone except for Rosemary. Her I buried.

Perhaps you were expecting something far more interesting. Let me assure you, there is nothing interesting whatsoever when it comes to such things. There is only the doing of it. The telling of such occurrences, though always touched with a bit of danger and mystery, never quite lives up to the true depravity of such actions. And therein lies the sickness that we embody as a species. Horrified by the fact and entirely mesmerized by fact sold as fiction.

Slappy Mutt Mutt was just a man. One man alone in a place without boundaries. One man left too long in the searing heat of imaginary inner workings with enough hours for them to conquer what little reality remained. I, too, am just a man. A man that did what had to be done to survive. I am not proud of what I did. I derived no pleasure from it. They say that from all things, no matter the outcome, something good emerges. I would agree. I am a much better shot than I used to be.

Having buried Rosemary, feeling altogether meaningless as if doomed to know the secret of things but unable to warn the world about itself, I turned to Mr. Chips and began to mutter something about the sheer insanity of us. Sitting down on the ground, I could think of nothing else but to put my head in my hands and weep. I have no idea why I did but it seemed the proper thing to do at the time. And that's when it happened. Eclipsing the sun, he walked past me and scanned the dry desolation before us. And that's when he said it. Shaking his head slightly he muttered—*"We are men never by choice...but apparently always by fault."*

Collins Mini English Dictionary defines the following words as such:
Hue and cry/*n.*/public outcry.
Nap/*n.*/short sleep. *v.*/napping.
Ran/*v.*/past tense of RUN.
Tombola/*n.*/lottery with tickets drawn from a revolving drum.
Wow/*interj.*/exclamation of astonishment.

Some say the world will end in fire,
Some say in ice.
From what I've tasted of desire,
I hold with those who favor fire.
—Robert Frost

decent return on its use I would have no way to make the quarterly payments. So that was that.

Near bankruptcy, and on the verge of a nervous breakdown, I was forced to scrap the entire thing. So now I've got this deserted island in a remote part of the South Pacific and nothing to show for it. I own the land outright, so I figured I might as well do something with it. And that's when it came to me (in the shower, of course). I tore down everything that I had built to date and sold it off to various impoverished countries and international scrap merchants. I then hired the world's best mini golf course architect and set him to work designing the most gruelling eighteen holes of miniature golf imaginable.

Drunk pilot seeks drunk copilot for unsuccessful transatlantic flight. Box #214

Kept thing. Keep the weapons warm. The monster I am, the monster I planned has lost control. And so go the slow days in the rubber house. I'm all whacked out on spooky pink pills and this thick stuff that tastes like glue. I'm back in grade two. Prison was a whole lot more fun than this lonely coloured palace of bottomless pits. There are no video games here. Just pop-up picture books about the outside world. They get you thinking after a while that it doesn't really exist. That it's just this fantastical place where the weather is controlled by pulling on little paper tabs. A place where a curious monkey and a tall man in a yellow hat live in a castle made of marshmallows guarded by bubble gum sentries. Where the wild things are is where I am. Subdued in wolf armour and a tinfoil crown. I got an army you see. The army's just me. And like Dr. Seuss I am rhyming for no reason, with the Dooers and Peepers, the Klingdanglers and Creepers. It's quite safe to say that I am well beyond thunder dome says everyone. There's no place like home. Fuck you Dorothy. In the bushes, in the tress, where the lions like to feed.

So this is it. This is the end of the end of the line. Far removed from the realm of cruel people, it's just us animals.

I was thinking about being a smart-ass when I came up with the plan. But now I'm not sure what the plan was supposed to be. It had something to do with the little people I think. I often dream of their tiny village when I sleep. It rains candy there. It hurts.

You've got to wear a special hat when it rains. It doesn't hurt as much then. Just on the shoulders, just on your knees and feet. But when it's sunny it doesn't hurt 'cause there ain't no candy falling from the sky. Just a permanent rainbow stealing graceful through the deep blue. And the little people don't work when it's sunny because their entire economy is based on collecting rain-candy (which they then export into the world of the big people who pay for it through the teeth). So when it's sunny they just sing their little people song and do their little people dance. And sometimes, not often, they bake enormous pies made of licorice and whipped cream. But that's usually only when they have special visitors, like myself.

So that's where I go. To the land of the little people. Sometimes I'll wake up and realize that I'm right in the middle of doing something like having a shower or brushing my hair. That's when the whole thing gets a little dicey.

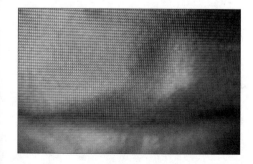

It's dicey because I only see the little people when I'm asleep. And if I'm asleep I can't be brushing my teeth you see. So it gets a little dicey and I have to have a bit of a nap

But besides the little people there isn't much happening here. Sometimes I talk to Herbert about the little people. Herbert is a skeptic. Herbert doesn't believe that the little people exist. Sometimes I show him my bruised feet to prove to him that candy-rain really hurts. And sometimes he gives me the juice to even out the black and blue. What're you gonna do? Argue? The juice is God when he's angry they say. So I don't like God much. He hurts more than candy-rain.

But it ain't so bad really. Mostly I just shut up about the little people and read the pop-up books about the outside world. I pretend I'm God and control the weather by pulling on little paper tabs. It doesn't rain candy in the outside world, so mostly I just keep it gray. A little water rain, now and again, for the trees is okay. But mostly I just keep it gray. Gray is an even colour and when you're even you don't get the juice. I used to do something before this though. I can't remember. I'd ask the little people, you see, but I don't speak their language. It's like luggage their language. Actually it's not, I just wanted to see what those two words looked like in the same sentence.

One thing I can say is that I've come to understand where people go when they're all out of the good stuff. They come here. And mostly they just play Perfection and Scrabble. You come across some interesting words when you play Scrabble in here. Words like Moto-go-go and Air Plane-pong. Once in a while you get to go into the immediate outside world and walk around in a field by the freeway. It's a bad place to lose your footing, so mostly I stay up top by the gate. It's my dream to someday make a run for it out there. There's bound to be something on the other side of that freeway. Mostly it's shrouded in mist, but sometimes, on clear nights, you can almost make out the other side. They say God lives on the other side of the freeway, so I guess the juice is over there too. But I'll take my chances. I can run fast. Maybe even faster than the juice. I dunno.

There's a man in the basement. The white-coats call him the Bury-man. They call him that cause he's the one that sends you to heaven after they squeeze you with the juice so hard your eyeballs pop out like they're Jiffy-Pop. He's got this big shovel that he uses to put you into the fire. And then you're gone. No one ever hears from you again if you go down to see the Bury-man. No one hears from you again if you get on the elevator and go below the M. Past that there's just the sub-basement and I hear there's people down there

Following that I had twelve small cabanas built, all of them equipped with modern fixtures, and linked them together with state of the art video phones. I then rented a plane, kidnapped twelve of the Dallas Cowgirls, flew to Los Angeles, got on a boat and sailed southwest. When we arrived on the island I burned the boat, drugged and brainwashed the girls, and played continuous rounds of mini golf using one Cowgirl at a time as a caddy. Since my arrival on the island I have played continuously for three weeks, three days, and seven hours. My goal is to play until I either drop dead or score a perfect round. That means that I have to get a hole in one on each hole consecutively. The odds of that happening, knowing how difficult the course is, are somewhere in the neighbourhood of 50,000 to 1. So there it is. If you guys see me on tour in the future then you'll know I pulled it off. If you don't then there's a good chance that I'm dead and twelve Cowgirls are going to give birth to the first generation of a new super race. A race of people that will dominate miniature golf for the rest of human history.

that don't even get to look at the pop-up books. They just sit in the dark until it's time for the juice and that's it. Maybe that's where the Bury-man is too. I dunno. I've never been. I don't want to go. They use words in this place that make no sense. Words like *friend* and *help* and *better*. I like *better* the best. Better means that you get to go to the other side of the freeway and they don't give you any juice. They say that God lives on the other side of the freeway. But God's in here doling out the juice. And if everyone's wrong and there ain't no juice on the other side of the freeway then I see no reason for God to be there. It must be a fine place though. I wonder if Moto-go-go counts in Scrabble over there? I dunno. I've never been. But I'd like to know. I've been putting pennies in a jar cause I heard you need them over there. Bad, bad pennies for your bad, bad cares.

So that's the way the day goes. Playing make-believe word games in a make-believe place. Some of the nurses bring their kids by once in a while when they can't find someone else to look after them. And it's funny 'cause they don't seem to think my stories about the little people and candy-rain are all that strange. They just nod and smile, like they wished they could come with me to the village and eat licorice-whipped-cream pies. And I know how they feel. No one believes the things they say either. But I don't think they get the juice. Only animals get the juice, that's what Herbert says. I'm an animal, not some cruel person. There's a difference you see. One is just a thing by chance and the other is a made thing. I still got some smarts up there somewhere. And when I find them I'm gonna make Herbert's ears bleed. Maybe just enough so he can't hear me tell him about the little people. Then he won't have any reason to give me the juice and I'll be juice free.

"Fuck you Herbert!" I'll say, and I'll dance around the room making funny faces and laughing at him.

I had a dream last night. But it wasn't about the little people at all. It was about the other side of the freeway. I dreamed that I could fly and I leapt from the window and flew out over the grass. Everyone woke up and stood at the windows looking at me flying. They all just stood there with their hands pressed against their heads looking stunned. And as I flew further from them everyone began to shake like they shake when the juice is moving through you and your body turns to concrete and Jell-O all at the same time.

And in my dream I almost go back, because I know they're all getting the juice 'cause I've escaped. But then I see the land on the other side of the freeway and I think to myself, "I'm going to go over there and prove to everyone that us animals don't need the juice so much." So I fly towards the freeway and that awful humming sound from the juice gets louder behind me. And as I fly towards the freeway I begin to see myself flying. And the closer I get the bigger I get. So I keep flying and I keep growing until I'm huge and right in front of myself. And then I stop suddenly and look myself in the eyes. And I realize it's just a big mirror. And then I see that another version of you and me is on the other side, like it's a big trick, one-way mirror. And we're being pelted by candy-rain. And we're loving it.

The Disneyland Bit

The world is a big place. Much larger than you think. In days gone by, while calculating the cosmos, one had to factor in the possibility that given the chance to go too far people might slip effortlessly off of the world and into the blackness of space. Painted in such an ancient light, the accomplishments of those aboard Apollo Eleven seem fraught with over-complication. Why bother when one could simply drift there in the belly of some armada?

Columbus knew the world to be a sphere. In all fairness, if I recall correctly, it was merely a belief on loan. Nonetheless, his refusal to see the world flat led him to the wondrous riches of San Salvador. Merely a stepping stone to a greater continent that sat

Step Right Up. There's Something Happening Here...

Like so many eyeballs glued to the sloppy remains of some car crash victim, it's safe to say that your double globes will find their way back here. I've been waiting for you to evaporate, like an assassin who realizes too late that escape was never assured but rather implied to heighten resolve. And therein lies the entertainment. The lion and the malnourished Christian playing back and forth. One too stupid to realize he can't win and one too realistic to allow him to. It perplexes me sometimes, the reasons for choosing which houses to trick-or-treat at and which houses not to. Within the most brightly lit lies the cold heart of some frail, old, discontented granny who has laboured ceaselessly to produce caramel apples with surprise centres. For all those years she put up with those damn kids running through her flowerbeds. Just one bite and you'll agree, modern medicine never looked so good. No tongue, no problem. If they can teach those stupid chimps to sign then you should have no trouble. So maybe you never did take the time to run it through your mainframe and you just hit every house you could. Treats, after all, are what it's all about. Eventually you'll wind up here. Everyone comes by sooner or later. Simply because I leave the lights off.

Another year, another fifty-two weeks wondering where fifty of them went. I've been better than this and I've been worse. But who's keeping score? Maybe I'm trapped in a jar, you're in grade six, and it's science period. Maybe I'm creepy and maybe I'm beautiful. Maybe you should just check your damn textbook and see what it says. Because I've been wondering about that myself.

5 Things to Remember While Intoxicated on Motion Sickness Pills. (Part 1: Condensed Research, 1989-1999)

Yeah, it's a tricky business all right. You've got to watch it when your stomach tells you to do one thing and your insatiable need to cut loose and go off tells you to do something else. You might find yourself waking up on some tennis court somewhere in hockey pants with some half-naked chick who's collapsed in a puddle of her own vomit on the other side of the net. I speak only from experience here kids.

There are always going to be good, solid reasons for not doing a variety of

extremely stupid things. Things like sitting in a lawn chair on your seventeenth birthday and drinking ten beers before deciding you have to ride your ten-speed to the store to get tomato juice. You should know better. But something in our nature disappears when inebriation takes hold. We are diminished in a way that mocks us and turns us into those people that stand sidestage during festival performances repeatedly shouting, **"PLAY SOME FUCKING HIP!"** You know who they are. They're the ones who have hockey hair but don't play hockey. They're the reason classic-rock stations flourish in this backwater country of ours. We could have been so much better than this if only beer wasn't our national pastime. But that's not the point. The point is NOT to abuse the secret powers of motion sickness pills. They look harmless enough, all beige and pleasant. But I assure you, they are not so benign. Take care to read the following research carefully. It might just save your life someday.

Research Key:

MSP shall represent "Motion Sickness Pill(s)" throughout. MSPI shall represent "Motion Sickness Pill Inebriation" throughout. DE shall stand for "Delusional Episode" throughout.

1) Sex and Motion Sickness Pills.

I cannot stress this enough: if you're going to abuse MSP and expect to have sex you'll be in for some pleasant and not-so-pleasant surprises. The upside to sex while suffering from MSPI only applies to males. There is a better than fifty percent chance that your staying power will be increased by at least eight to ten minutes. Unfortunately, due to the fact that I am not a woman, I cannot comment on any positives to the female sexual experience during MSPI. The negatives, on the other hand, are far more varied and troubling. There is approximately a forty percent chance that you'll succumb to the effects of fatigue long before anything even happens. There is also roughly a ten percent chance that you will have a DE involving the person you are with. This usually involves your partner appearing to be a giant lizard of some kind. There is also the possibility that sexual stimulation might be reduced if massive amounts of alcohol have been consumed along with the MSP. In such cases it is highly unlikely that you'll be able to stand or focus, let alone have sex with a living person. Corpses, on the other hand, don't tend to move so they're a little easier to manipulate. If it comes to sex with the dead I wouldn't worry about it too much. You'll probably be so out of it that you'll be expe-

waiting to be exploited by the minions of the Christ child, I've had this funny feeling of late that the inhabitants of those unlucky Caribbean isles wished the ancient notions of pushing one's luck held true. Go too far and drift to the moon. On the day that the world was discovered to be fraudulent, those peoples native to the Americas were the only ones made to suffer the arrogance of Genovese wanderlust . And now, despite the civilization delivered them, they can't play major-league baseball without sneaking out of their country illegally.

10 Things I Would Love to See but Know I Never Will.

1 Mars.

2 An all-nudist HANDS ACROSS AMERICA.

3 The day the Special Olympics becomes an *advertising-worthy* television event, instead of being guilt driven, broadcast out of pity, and McDonald's need to rent out orange-drink dispensers.

4 To wake up one morning, turn on the news, and discover that during the night Jerusalem was suddenly overrun and subsequently taken by the armed forces of Palau.

5 To endure an extinction-level event, survive it, and discover that the Bud Girls and I are the only people left on the planet.

6 To have the Playboy Channel hold Hedonism V at my house.

riencing a permanent DE and will most likely think you're manhandling Carol Alt. (Carol, dear, if you read this don't be angry: literary license and all.)

2) Operating Complicated Machinery and Appliances.

By far this is the most dangerous aspect of MSPI. Attempting to drive a car, work a washing machine, or bake cookies can turn into acts that rival the dangers of walking through a minefield. There is nothing worse for people suffering from MSPI than trying to drive a car, train, boat, plane, or zeppelin. The effects of MSP can vary in such circumstances but the most common ones are as follows:

a) Double vision.
b) Loss of depth perception.
c) Loss of peripheral vision.
d) The effects of altitude are diminished.
e) Having no sense of whether you are horizontal or vertical.
f) The delusion that you are Aqua Man.
g) You will most likely NOT look good doing it.
h) Onboard stereo manipulation while moving is unlikely.
i) Comprehending the difference between D, R, and P will be impossible. They will all appear to be the letter Q.

When it comes to operating household appliances you've got to remember some fundamental things. Electricity, heat, and extreme cold are usually involved (radiation and extremely fast-moving dangerous parts being a close second). You should note that the following effects may occur while attempting appliance use:

a) A complete loss of vision (but that's usually because you've simply forgotten to turn the lights on).
b) The inability to feel pain caused by extreme heat, such as sticking a hot iron to your forehead.
c) The inability to detect extreme cold or freezer burn.
d) The inability to properly manipulate door knobs, handles, or buttons of any kind.
e) The overwhelming desire to flip over the lawnmower while it's running and stare at the blades as they whip around.
f) Operating any kind of power drill or tool will usually cause seizures.
g) Locating ON-OFF buttons is near-impossible.

3) Speech and Motion Sickness Pills.

Most people have difficulty speaking as it is, let alone doing it while using MSP. It's safe to say that you probably won't be making much sense while under the effects of the pills. Although in rare instances, you might find yourself saying things that far surpass the intelligence that you display on a regular basis. In such cases I strongly suggest that you just go with it. Because let's face it, when are you going to sound that articulate again?

That said, ninety-nine percent of the time you'll probably encounter slurred speech and a complete loss of any vocabulary that consists of three syllables or more. This will reduce your ability to communicate to the lowest possible levels, leaving you with the mental prowess of a two-year-old. Such effects are bound to wear off in anywhere from four to six hours, though some people might experience a prolonged speech problem for up to three days depending on whether or not they've mixed their MSP with other drugs. If this occurs try to remain calm and, preferably, locked in a room without windows, sharp objects, or lava lamps.

Anyone who bothers to abuse MSP is going to have to live with the fact that speech difficulties are just par for the course. There's really nothing you can do about it, so just relax and try your best to nod and smile when someone says something to you. The fact that your inner monologue is just as poor as your outer one will be freaking you out enough as it is. So trying to make sense of anything will simply be a waste of your time.

4) The Effects of MSP Abuse on Personal and Working Relationships.

Make no mistake about it, it's going to be a rough ride. If you've come to the decision that MSP are going to be a permanent part of your life then you're going to have to deal with a few facts. First, you can forget about entering into, or remaining in, any kind of romantic relationship. There's just no way that someone else is going to be able to put up with your habit. There is always the chance that you'll stumble across a fellow MSP user and life will be grand, but it's unlikely. It'll start out alright at first. You'll just do it on the weekends and everything will seem okay. But as time passes your significant other will begin to notice some ugly changes in you and will eventually call it quits. So you're going to have to decide pretty quick: *the pills or the person?*

Hiding a MSP habit from co-workers will also be impossible. There's just no way to keep something like that hidden for long. So you've got two choices. Either you throw yourself down some stairs while on the job and get worker's

7 To see thousands of cars with bumper stickers that read: "If Jesus is the King of Peace, it's time for a little regicide."

8 Farm animals overrun a farm in England and build a giant windmill.

9 To invent a shrinking machine so that I might fuck Barbie and then steal her Corvette.

10 When juveniles wake up to the fact that they can go on gun-crazy killing sprees and will only be forced to serve eight months for it.

How's That Idiocy Coming By The Way?

I will destroy. You will obey. That's the way it has to be. You'll make the lemonade and I'll ensure that no other lemonade stand stands in our way. We will wear terrific panda suits. We will have a secret handshake. We'll stick to the plan. I will destroy. You will obey. That's the way it's going to have to be. Pouting about it won't change anything. Pouting about it will only make you look like an unhappy panda and we can't have that. So you should think before you speak. You should consider your options before you decide to become an unhappy panda. Because you don't want to know what happens to pandas that aren't happy. You'd best be careful.

Don't worry though. This is just us talk-

comp or start enjoying the benefits of welfare. There's no way you'll be able to function at work after a thirty-six-hour MSP binge. No one said that substance abuse was going to be easy. So, once again, you're going to have to make a choice: *MSP or employment?* Your call.

5) Mixing Your MSP With Other Substances.

It's a well-known fact that the effects of MSP start to wear off after a while if you're doing them straight. The next step is to start mixing them with other substances to elevate their potential. The most common mixer is alcohol, preferably hard liquor. Most hardcore MSP addicts will usually mix their pills with either whiskey or vodka. You should stay away from rum, gin, wine, and beer as these tend to make the ride either too rough or not rough enough. If you're new to the experience you should know one thing though: no MSP user ever takes more than one pill when mixing with booze. It's just foolishness. Well, the whole thing is foolishness really, so whatever.

When it comes to mixing MSP with other drugs I'm at a loss. It's an extremely dangerous practice to say the least. One of two things is going to happen in such circumstances. **One:** you're going to go way too low, or **Two:** you're going to go way too high. Let's just say that there's a difference between the normal MSP addict and those who are destructive. If you're going to bother making the most of an over-the-counter drug then why fuck about with ones that aren't.

When it comes to mixing with other over-the-counter drugs (and prescription drugs) here's a short list of ones that are okay (and may even enhance things a bit).

-Nyquil (never Dayquil)
-Zithromax (250 mgs and up)
-Zopiclone (preferably less that 7.5 mgs)
-Cefaclor (250 mgs and up)
-Ciprofloxacin (500 mgs standard)
-Co Actifed syrup
-Ether

How Debbie Parks Drowned in Cherry Jell-O

Strange things happen all the time. Even stranger things than this. Just last week they found some guy in Oregon in his bathroom with a garden hose stuck up his ass. He thought it felt good when he turned the water on. He forgot that the rules of pressure rarely conform to the rules of pleasure. So there he was. Dead. With a green garden hose stuck in his ass. When his wife found him she wasn't too sure what to make of it. She was extremely saddened because they had two kids and bills to pay and all that. And she was extremely saddened because she had a deep-seated thing for kink but thought her husband was one of those "by the book" kind of guys. You think you know someone and then one day you realize that all the while you could have been taking home plumbing to new heights.

That's not to say that Debbie Parks was a sex fiend or anything. Well, at least not when she was sober. Debbie was one of those young girls that suffered from what is known as "a split weekend personality." Most of the time she was just a regular high-school kid. But on the weekends she tended to turn into someone completely different. And that someone was so drastically different from her usual self that it led some to believe that she was easily influenced. That's how the whole thing happened. But let me make something clear right now. There's tragedy and then there's a tragedy. This was neither. What happened to Debbie was nothing short of the universal definition of "oddity." That's the only way to say it without sounding callous.

Debbie was known to be somewhat of a lush on weekends. It was one of those things that wasn't all that out of the ordinary for a girl her age. The weekends were for partying and everyone did it. Debbie's problem was that she was a horrible drunk. And by horrible I'm implying that she did things without thinking about them first. Most of the things were just stupid, crazy things that kids tend to do when they're plastered and feeling somewhat free-spirited. Things like truth or dare, streaking, skinny dipping, and the old "locked in the closet" trick. Debbie did them all and regretted it each time. Every Monday morning she'd walk through the doors at school and hear whispers about her weekend escapades. All the guys loved her because they could get her to take her clothes off in front of everyone at the drop of a hat and all the girls hated her because they didn't have the guts to. She wasn't a slut, contrary to the reputation people foisted upon her. Debbie had only ever slept with one boy. And that was when her family went to Disney World. It was one of those last-minute deals when you know you're never going to see

ing. This is just us coming together at the head. Like Siamese twins, like two happy peas in a pod. You would not like it if we were to do the other routine. There are no happy pandas in that one. Not at all. Just unpleasantness that I would rather avoid. So keep smiling. Always remember to keep smiling. There is nothing more pathetic than a sore loser. So keep smiling. Everything will take care of itself. Thank goodness.

I'm tired now. I am going to go to bed. I don't much feel like being your friend anymore. The good old days are gone. Best to get on board with the depravity of the here and now. The world consumes, the world revolves, the world will someday come to an end. If not by us, then pulverized by the sun.

the person again because you're too young, live too far away, and know in the back of your head that given time you'd probably become quite annoyed by them. So she was rather good about things of that nature. But that doesn't mean that she wouldn't get naked and slip into an outdoor hot tub filled with cherry Jell-O in the dead of winter now does it?

And that's exactly how Debbie met her end. Face down in a frozen, cherry Jell-O-filled hot tub. It's how the tub got filled with Jell-O that's interesting. You wouldn't have any interest in reading this story if it was simply about some poor girl that drowned. It's no different than some kids re-enacting *Full Metal Jacket* in the hallways of their school in some white, suburban enclave. You're glued to your TV because you think *"Oh my god! How could this happen? Why did this happen! Whose fault is it?!"* wa, wa, fucking wa. Three hundred people get hacked to bits in their sleep in some village in North Africa and it gets a blurb in the newspaper. But when something happens in the quiet confines of our perfect little world then it's a sure-fire sign that chaos is about to break loose in the streets and Satan is possessing the children. The only thing that it is a reflection of is our society's egomania. We figure we're so socially superior to everyone else that things of that nature should be uncommon. What we forget is that, like in every great society, the barbarians will one day be at our gates and we will slip quietly into the confines of some coffee-table book about ancient civilizations. And like those civilizations we were just as violently prolific as we were creative, ingenious, and compassionate. Because it all comes in a neat little package that has yet to be altered during our tenure on this rock. Welcome to life in the blind man's utopia. Retain ticket stub for possible refund.

But that doesn't explain how a hot tub got filled with Jell-O. It's quite simple really. All it takes is for your parents to go out of town for two weeks, filling the hot tub with clean, boiling water, adding multiple packs of cherry Jell-O, and allowing the freezing effects of mother nature to run their course. The secret ingredient, of course, would be the eight large bottles of vodka that you also threw in. Presto! Instant drunksicle. So the next thing you do is decide to throw the biggest party of the year and invite the whole school. As the night progresses everyone munches on the Jell-O and gets really hammered. This leads to all kinds of strange events, including the part where someone dares Debbie Parks to get naked and jump into the hot tub filled with the Jell-O. She's very drunk by that point and ends up going in rather awkwardly and with some momentum. This causes her to hit her head, but she pops up just the same with a big smile on her face and everyone cheers.

Debbie starts munching on the stuff while she's in there and eventually everyone decides they're cold and goes back inside. Debbie remains in the hot tub. Then she starts to feel a little woozy. Maybe because she's drunk, maybe because she's got a concussion. She passes out, her body temperature has melted the Jell-O enough so that there's some liquid in there and her head slips beneath the surface. And you've got yourself one frozen dead girl Jell-O cake.

About ten minutes later some guy who had wandered outside to relieve himself happened to notice that there was a naked girl in the middle of the party's booze supply. It would definitely mark the end of the night's proceedings and our boy didn't want that to happen. There was a girl inside that he was convinced wanted to sleep with him. He was mistaken of course, and quite intoxicated, so he just went back inside and didn't mention that Debbie Parks was frozen-dead within the icky confines of a hot tub filled with vodka laced cherry Jell-O. Debbie's body remained there for twenty more minutes before it was discovered by two girls who had ventured out onto the back porch to smoke.

That's how Debbie Parks drowned in cherry Jell-O. Sad but true. At her funeral nobody knew what to make of her death. Her parents were the most distraught and confused, seeing as their little baby's booze-soaked corpse had been pulled from a frozen tub of fruitiness. The youngsters of the town learned a valuable lesson that day as well. They realized that going too far was something that wasn't always a controllable experiment. After a certain critical mass is reached a whole set of volatile factors begin to alter the experiment. This leads to the creation of chaos. It's an equation that can be applied to much more than just a girl drowning in cherry Jell-O. It's something that engulfs us all as time passes and makes fools of us without our knowing. And in the end we become so accustomed to seeing ourselves as fools that we think nothing of it. Either that or it's merely a fable about how not to freeze alcohol-infused gelatin in anything larger than a footbath.

The mysteries of the universe revealed with no time to study the data and reach an outcome, the sun will go out and all creatures great and small will be helpless against the unknowns of life. So why are you so worried? Why don't you go have some drinks, get laid, get back, get something. After everything has been done, been bought, sold, produced, consumed, recycled, re-packaged, and re-sold, you will have gained nothing by floundering about trying to change things that cannot be changed. The little things exist only so that the important ones never get touched upon. That's why you can wear leather shoes and, at the same time, refuse to eat beef. Because we are all, every one of us, entirely ridiculous.

Techniques for Faking Multiple Personality Disorders During Criminal Trials.

Multiple homicide. Always annoying when it comes to that uncomfortable time between your arraignment and your trial. It's during this particular stretch that most defendants begin to slip a little and those guilty feelings begin to surface. And let's face it, you damn well knew what you were doing so don't try to convince me otherwise. They're gonna hook you up to a polygraph and get what they want so there ain't any use practising your poker face. It may have been enough to convince all those college girls to help you look for your lost dog in the woods but it doesn't fly when it comes to *"the machine."*

But don't panic just yet. You're still miles from the maximum wing and years from the big gas up. There's gonna be weeks of debating your mental state as it is, not to mention the fact that your lawyer will probably be able to fend off the district attorney with promises of a full confession that you'll provide once they have a deal to let you do your time in a loony bin instead of a prison. If that fails then there's always the chance that you could conveniently remember where you left some bodies or that there were actually more names on your kill sheet than originally thought.

Such tactics are commonplace in these situations. Lawyers need to exhaust these options so it looks like they did their best before they admit to you that you're fucked and you're gonna get shot up with enough wacky juice to light up a medium-sized town.

This is where I come in. I'm the ray of sunshine in your otherwise abysmal and rotting inner hell. So relax and just do what I tell you to do and everything will be okay. It's no secret that temporary insanity is the most widespread cause for juries doubting all sanity-based cases these days. Temporary insanity is a contradiction in terms. To be insane temporarily is to admit that you're actually sane most of the time. Who, in their right mind, is gonna believe that? *"Yes, I did gun down eight people in a fast-food restaurant, but I wasn't myself at the time, because my dad didn't take me to ball games when I was a kid and my boss puts too much pressure on me, so I snapped there for a second, but I feel better now."* You are fucking nuts. You can forget about any jury taking you seriously when it comes to weak-ass defensive shit like that. They'll send you to prison simply because you thought they were stupid enough to buy that.

But there is hope. And it comes disguised as many voices and a complicated mosaic of inner turmoil and struggle. Psychiatrists call this particular

malady "multiple personality disorder." Welcome to the psychological land of milk and honey, all six of you.

So I'm gonna walk you through this step by step. But it's important to remember some things while we're going through this so you don't get ahead of yourself. First of all, I'm no shrink. Far from it. So don't blame me if you don't have what it takes to pull this off. I'm just giving you the background. Everything after that is up to you. Secondly, always remember to put your own personal spin on all of this. You'll come to the realization that it's much easier to create your own alternate self than it is to copy my examples directly.

There are typically two or more different personalities involved. So, depending on your retention and standards of precision, you'll want to choose a number that's right for you. Take this into account though. The *two personalities* thing is always weak. If you only have one alternate personality to fall back on it's not so easy to convince a jury that you had absolutely no control over your actions. Theoretically it shouldn't matter, but there's something about the number two that just doesn't fly with juries. As far as they're concerned it just doesn't make sense for one personality to be fully in control a part of the time and another to be in control the rest of the time. This is possible of course, but to a bunch of relatively sane people who most likely just want to see you fry it's a little sketchy.

Two personalities can easily be diagnosed as "a split personality" and that's just not the game we're playing here. So introduce another personality, or voice, into the mix and you've got yourself a mediator of sorts. This represents an inner struggle between the "good" you and the "evil" you. Call it what you like, this third voice is your best way to confuse the issue by turning a half-ass defensive grasp at straws into what appears to be a complex and quite involved psychiatric condition.

Once a jury is confronted with any aspect of confusion, such as the kind created by three independent personalities, you'll begin to realize that they're just as confused as you allegedly were when you killed those people. And that's the crucial element. Once they equate the complexity of that confusion with their own thought processes then you're halfway to home.

The other half of a winning strategy relies solely on your ability to perform. You have to act the part to such a degree of precision and detail that there can be no doubts. No prosecutor should be able to find holes in your performance. I have to emphasize: *if, at any time, you slip up and do something that might indicate that there are discrepancies in your mental deficiency then there's no getting the loony train back on the tracks. You are, for lack of a better phrase, completely and utterly fucked.*

I am going to go lie in bed and wait for the hands of impossibility to come strangle me. I am going to smile at my ceiling and sing the song of our undoing. I will wear my panda pajamas. I will think of you often when I get to where I'm going. Everything will be fine. Just you wait and see.

I have decided to gather up all of my things and burn them. I will be happier for it. I will become a nomad. I am not exactly sure why I have decided to become a nomad but the decision seems quite nomadic in itself. I am going to live in a tent behind Hasty-Mart market. That way people will talk about me and my urban legend will live on into the ages. I will dine on domesticated pets, weave sweaters from the golden locks of little girls, and fashion boots from the skin of drunken high-school students whom I will trap as they stumble through the streets in the middle of the night. I will be feared and hated by all. It will be great.

I have yet to burn my phone though. I have talked to almost everyone that I know

So after you've decided on your strategy, start living the part immediately. Don't wait until you get into the courtroom to start working all those newly devised inner voices. Don't even tell your lawyer what you're doing. It'll be better if he or she doesn't know. Your lawyer will begin to see signs of your malady and will, hopefully, request a court-appointed psychiatrist to come in and evaluate you. If you can convince a shrink then you can convince anyone. But before we continue let's be clear: it's highly unlikely that this particular method is going to get you off free and clear. The best you can hope for is a verdict of guilty by reason of insanity. If you're going to try and convince a jury that you committed a horrific crime because there are a multitude of other people living in your head then there's no way they're going to let you walk.

You should take some time now to decide what you want to do. If you are lucky enough to be sent to a mental institution for the criminally insane instead of death row then you're going to have to feign this illness for many, many years to come. And, if there comes a time when they discover that you were bullshitting, then they'll probably put you on an express elevator to hell. You might be an evil genius, but it's a pretty big undertaking. So take a second and mull it over.

This section is going to give you a little insight into how one goes about creating a believable façade. These are just examples, mind you, so remember that you're going to want to create your own profile. For my profile I decided to go with five personalities: **Little Johnny, Pete, Bob, Steve,** and **Omen-Damien.** Using these five different personalities I'll hopefully be able to provide you with a good example of how best to utilize this mental construct.

Little Johnny: This is the part of your personality that represents you when you were a child. Maybe daddy beat you with a pipe wrench, maybe mommy locked you in the basement for the winter, your choice. But there's a better than even chance that you actually did suffer through some form of child abuse (or, according to those politically correct types, you wouldn't be in this mess in the first place). Slip into this personality when you're being threatened. Try your best to act like you're nine years old again and scared shitless. Crying can also come in handy. This is the personality that you use to evade any line of questioning that causes anxiety. Either this one or the violent one.

Pete: The trick to this personality is that it doesn't know there are other people living in your head. Pete thinks he is sane and doesn't understand why all of this is happening to him. As far as he's concerned he just woke up with blood all over his clothes and couldn't figure out where it came from.

Bob: This is the irrational personality. You'll most likely want to make Bob somewhat illogical, quick to violence, and impervious to physical posturing by others. This is the personality that likes physicality (such as rape, bludgeoning a victim, or dominating them in some overtly brutish way). If the whole thing (the trial, the questions, whatever) starts getting to you, you can always use this personality to strike back. Simply fly off the handle and attack the prosecutor. There's nothing better than being tackled to the ground as some maniac and coming up Pete. Works every time.

Steve: Every psychotic killer needs their charming side. Charisma isn't always a given when it comes to criminals, but for some reason mass murderers seem to have the market cornered. This is the personality that lures, persuades, tempts, and baffles. Steve will show no sign of intent and will always come across as being almost too friendly. Of course, the goal of this personality is usually to slowly strangle his victims while listening to Barry White and drinking boxed wine. This personality can be useful and harmful. A killer yes, but always sexually motivated. Rape is out of the question, by the way. Steve is too good to stoop so low. He's actually able to score before he gets to the killing part. Hence the term "lady killer." Use Steve if there's a female on the prosecution's team. It'll start to creep people out before long and will provide you with hours of endless fun.

Omen-Damien: Those that possess a limited intellect dare not attempt to utilize this last personality for fear of making those of us that are evil geniuses look bad. This is the hidden voice that controls the vocal voices. Typically, this personality has constructed the others to provide a buffer between it and what it sees as "accountability." As far as Omen-Damien is concerned he was brilliant enough to get the others to do the dirty work. Whether it be Steve or Bob it doesn't really matter. On occasion Omen-Damien will pop up and do some of the dirty work himself, but only when the situation calls for something artistic, precise, or expedient. This is the personality you'll want to use to baffle people. Using big words and comparing murder to art is always a sure-fire way to make the whole thing hit home. You can use this personality to call up the others if you like. But make sure it's the only one that has direct contact with them. The other four should not realize that they're a part of a

today so that I might have fond recollections of my wonderful phone before I melt it. Wanna listen?

Dave King: Dave came to the conclusion that owning scented candles does not necessarily make you effeminate. He also left the house for the first time in eleven days.

Dave Genn: Dave threw his back out and spent the remainder of it out of his skull on muscle relaxants.

My Mother: Told me everything that Sneaky did this week.

My Sister: Told me everything that Sneaky did this week.

Steve: Steve and I grunted like pigs (the usual).

Gilly: Gilly called me from San Diego to tell

me that he was sitting poolside in the middle of winter. So I hung up on him.

Rich: Rich called me this morning and woke me up. I have no recollection of what he, or I, said.

Ian: Ian and I talked about purchasing wire-guided missile launchers and blowing up ambulances.

Amanda: Amanda and I talked about the virtues of strong teeth and gums.

Tom: The Mumbler and I talked about jackasses before moving on to something about SHAZAM!

Dave Porter: Port Dog left a message and I didn't call him back on purpose.

Ivar: Ivar and I talked about mechanical bulls.

much bigger picture. The only personality that Damien will not attempt to contact is Pete. Pete is off limits because he's useful in times of crisis. It's always good to keep someone around that doesn't know anything and Omen-Damien realizes this. Shrinks will be trying to pull him out in an attempt to gain some insight into methodology and intent. Give them nothing! Make sure you never answer any question without being evasive and egomaniacal. Unless, that is, you are stupid enough to be tricked. If so, you're done for.

You might want to spend some time reading a variety of books about criminal insanity and psychological methods of discovery. You also might want to think about injuring yourself on a regular basis to reinforce the fact that you're nuts. There's nothing better than hitting your head against a wall for a while until blood is drawn to make others wonder if you're going to try and bite their ears off. That said, I can only wish you the best of luck in your endeavour. I'm confident that you'll do just fine. Look at me. I'm living proof that it can work. Instead of spending the rest of my life in prison I get to spend it loaded up on drugs in a mental institution for the criminally insane. At least I get to be examined and interviewed by a whole bunch of sexy female grad students a couple times a year. Ahhh. Now doesn't that bring back some memories.

Some men get the world. Others get ex-hookers and a trip to Arizona.

—Kim Basinger, *L.A. Confidential*

It's a big, bad world out there. Lots of boogie men. Lots of prima-donna serial artists auditioning for *Star Search*. Everyone's selling and buying, buying and selling, it's crazy. It is what it is.

I had this dream the other night. Satan was in my television. His head was spinning around and he was speaking Spanish. They call the devil *el diablo* in Spanish. It's much more dignified. After a while Satan's head flew off and trees and plants started to grow out of his neck. This was followed by a vague period of clouds and fast-forward-type weather. When everything came to a roaring halt there was a 7-11 in the middle of the trees and plants. I went in and got a burrito. They call those *burritos* in Spanish. Then I woke up.

Some people think that dreams are a reflection of the subconscious. That was the first thing I thought about when I rolled out of bed. I did some research and discovered the following facts. Most people between the ages of fifteen and thirty-five dream about sex seventy-five percent of the time. The second most popular topic is past traumas that occurred to the dreamer. The third most popular topic involves the dreamer assuming some position of power, authority, or fame. Way down the list at 1,354,765 was dreams about the devil's head spinning around and then flying off only to be replaced by a convenience store. It's safe to say that after finding this out, I really had no intention of jumping, but it took the police a good forty-five minutes to talk me down.

If you took all the days from the beginning of time until the end of time and had to make one of those Christmas calendars with the chocolates inside, which day's door would be the biggest? I ran that by Dave King and he had this to say: "That's impossible, because time is infinite. The universe is never-ending, so the question can't be answered." Smart-ass writers. Then he says, "And what does it matter which door's the biggest?"

I had to explain to him that at Christmas we used to get these calendars filled with chocolates. Each day had a door and the biggest door was Christmas Eve. I think Dave's depraved childhood caught up with him right there because he was all out of smart-ass comments after that. Thinking about it later I suddenly realized my own answer to this question. Obviously, the day I dreamed of Satan's head spinning around talking in Spanish would

Bill: I didn't talk to the Power Gnome today, but I'm giving him the finger right now.

My Mother Again: Told me everything that Sneaky did this week.

Christi: Like every day, Christi called me and filled me in on my schedule. Tonight she will call again and give me a brief rundown on what I will have to do tomorrow. Tomorrow morning I will call her as soon as I wake up because I will have forgotten by then.

Sprint Canada: I talked with Laurie from Sprint. Laurie is only working there because she's trying to save up enough money to go to school. I told her that I did not want to save on my long distance.

Timberly Baker: Bakes called me and left an incoherent message on my machine as he

be behind the big door. *Felices Navidades, Felices Navidades, Felices Navidades.*

Millimetre. I love that word. Zillion is another excellent word. I've got a Zillion Millimetres.

For some reason I thought that "zillion" was an actual numerical representation. I looked it up and discovered that it's just slang for a google. Google is a generic word used to describe large numbers, or more correctly, 10^{30}. You'd think a math genius could come up with better-sounding words for these things. Zillion and millimetre are good examples of cool-sounding words. Whereas "google" sounds like a weird kind of pencil that grade three kids absolutely love (actually it's a guy's name). Why not use terms like Mathemillitron or Octivator. At least they sound like they could be important (or the names of super-robots that live on some cool machine planet in another galaxy). Math could have been fun.

Wouldn't that be something. Open your textbooks to page 116, we're going to learn about Godzillatrons today. Instead of some x's and y's, you'd have to draw a picture of a large lizard-like robo-machine eating the entire population of Tokyo. Math tests would be the highlight of your day. I'd still be in school.

Problem 12: If Godzillatron stormed downtown Tokyo and ate one quarter of the people, how many people would be left to take up arms and try to stop him?

Problem 13: If Godzillatron destroyed one half of all the high-rises in Tokyo with his flaming breath, how many people would he have killed? (For extra credit: how many people would be crushed by falling debris?)

Problem 14: If Godzillatron fought Quadradikong in the middle of downtown New York, A) which one would crush more people if they were knocked over? B) which one could eat 1/100th of the local population per mouthful?

Instead, you've got x's and y's and quadratic equations flying around in a void of super-boredom. All of the secrets of the universe could have been revealed to us through the various shapes and names of robo-machines.

The next time you use a calculator remember one thing. Instead of punching up numbers and adding or multiplying them, you could have had two machine creatures running across that little screen eating tiny people.

Eventually they would spit the answer out and, with big smiles on their faces, proceed to fight each other to the death.

There really isn't any death in this math land. Just repairs. They're robo-machines, they can always come back. Imagine Einstein's notes on relativity if things had been different. That would have been one kick-ass robo-streak of mayhem.

Instead, I'm dreaming of spinning Satanic heads speaking Spanish that turn into 7-11s. Fish with no eyes, birds with two heads that try to fly in both directions at once. It's all mixed up. There was a time when everything made sense, but it's over now. Lost forever under the guise of fast food that isn't all that fast, and mini-malls that aren't for tiny people. Sometimes I wonder where to go next. And then it dawns on me that tomorrow is a new day. That's just the way the world works. It only spins in one direction for some reason.

always does. Then again—being that he's from Dorset is somewhat of a life-handicap.

Warne: Livesey and I spoke at great length about the time machine that we're building in his garage.

My Mother Again: Left a message telling me about everything that Sneaky did this week.

Sneaky: Told me that I would be a big let-down as an uncle if I did not promptly pur-chase him several Pit-Droids for his ever-expanding *Star Wars* collection. He also told me that he broke the Light Saber that I got him for Christmas because he saw a better one and figured it would be a good way to upgrade through guilt.

My Father: My dad called and we talked about England's national side. (Add one hour and

Should've Been A Super Villain

one week, two days, twelve hours, sixteen minutes, eight seconds...tick-toc-tick-toc)

I'm writing from the humble confines of a rather unusual location. I would love to feed you some shit about being in Fiji with the Bud girls or travelling the world with Kenny on the pro mini-golf tour but that's just not the case. There's no easy way to break news like this, so I'll just come right out and say it, I'm in **PRISON**. I'm incarcerated. That's right kids. *The big house, the joint, the slammer.* Actually, it's not even a real prison. It's a Minimum Security Detention Facility (a MSDF).

I'm a minimalist and therefore not up on the maximization of anything. I would venture to guess that it's somewhat comparable to an overstated minimization in that it's the maximum of a minimum situation.

I hesitate to use any of the usual flowery words to describe my new surroundings as they're nothing at all like I expected them to be. Once again I have been conned by the drug-like power of television and therefore am at a loss to accurately depict this place. I can say that it's a lot more relaxing than I thought it would be. I have access to tennis courts, a golf course, a gym, and a pottery room (all of which, of course, I have no intention of using). But there is an Olympic-sized swimming pool, a ping-pong room, and an arcade so I'm not totally screwed. To be quite honest, if I knew prison was going to be this fun I would have been arrested for something a long time ago.

Which brings me to my first real complaint about prison (or this particular facility anyway): I have absolutely no ambition, whatsoever, to escape. It would be altogether unromantic and devoid of any epic sense of struggle. It'd be far too easy to escape from this place and would be a completely empty personal victory. One sand wedge malfunction on the fifth, tenth, or thirteenth and I could be sitting in a McDonald's in less than an hour. Which would be pointless, of course, because there's already one in the cafeteria. That and a Pizza Hut. I can hear it all now.

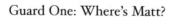

Guard One: Where's Matt?
Guard Two: I dunno. I heard he hit a bad wedge shot on the fifth. He must be looking for his ball in the bushes.
Guard One: He's got no short game that boy. Remind me to mention he should spend some time at the practice green chipping some balls.
Guard Two: Yeah, all right.

One week after my escape:

Guard Two: Has anyone seen Good yet?
Guard One: Nope. Don't think so.
Guard Two: Damn. That kid's got to work on his slice.
Guard One: This is going to crucify his handicap for sure.

Before I went to prison I had no idea what a handicap was. I always thought it had something to do with personal characteristics.

Besides that there's really nothing to worry about in this place. There's none of the usual stresses that one commonly equates with being locked up, such as: *"I hope to God I don't drop the soap in the shower'"* or *"some big dude named Chico is going to make me his bitch."*

We're allowed visits every Saturday and Wednesday and they provide the inmates with little private rooms in which to mess about with wives and girl-friends. It's kind of like hanging out with the guys most of the time and going home for sex. In some respects it could be viewed by some men as a limited form of paradise. Those inmates that don't have wives or girlfriends have been known to "hire" them from time to time. Most of the inmates in this place are white-collar criminals so their tastes run to the extreme and they can well afford them. The guards run a little service in this capacity that's been nicknamed "the pink express." This service utilizes professional gold-diggers who sleep with rich, incarcerated men in hopes of winning their favour and becoming their permanent fuck-puppets. This, of course, leads to gifts such as all-expenses paid trips to Mexico, private condos, jets, cars, and cash. It's like a mail order bride service that supplies very attractive women that have no ambition beyond basking in the sun and shooting their mouths off about how rich their sugar daddies are. It's a pissing contest of sorts.

You might find all of this rather crass but I would urge you to seriously explore the alternative. It's a lot better than getting raped by a three-hun-dred-pound guy with a hair-sweater.

So I'm sitting here in my nifty blue jump suit typing this out on one of the prison computers (there are twenty in all). They're decent machines too. The one I'm on right now is ten times faster than the one I had at home and has video conferencing. This means I can talk to someone face to face in Borneo, in real time, whenever I like. There are guys in here that use things to play the stock market, do overseas banking, and even run their companies. The video conferencing thingy allows them to actually attend board meetings

thirty minutes worth of profanity and critical analysis and stir).

Pat: Pat's been dead for fourteen years but she still calls a couple times a week to see how I am.

Wrong Number: Nothing to report.

Ken: Ken called and then forgot what it was he wanted to ask me.

Rich: Archie called me back and asked if I had made up my mind. Feeling rather stupid about the fact that I couldn't recall our earli-er conversation, I told him to go ahead with whatever it was he wanted to go ahead with.

Ken: Ken called back because he remembered what it was that he wanted to ask me.

Stew: Stew called to see what was going on and we came to the conclusion that we'd talk later if anything came up. We've been doing that for the better part of fifteen years.

Amanda: Called and asked if I had ever @#$%^&*!@#$%^&*!@#$%^& before. I told her that I had read about it but that it scared me somewhat without the use of an environment suit and salad tongs.

Amanda: I called her back because I would have been an idiot to turn her down.

My Mother Again: My mother tried to tell me something about Sneaky while I attempted to hang up because it was imperative that I get to Amanda's as fast as humanly possible.

Stew: Called back. I told him that something definitely had come up.

from prison. The funny thing is that most of these guys are throwing cash around that they stole. This one guy, Morris Hawthorne, uses the computer to transfer cash from bank to bank in Europe because the government and the cops are still looking for it. He even has an accountant who e-mails him with secret codes and tells him if the money's in jeopardy. I like Morris. He's a crafty one, he is.

The average IQ in this place is well above the genius level. I seem to be the only person ruining that average. It's like MIT behind bars. There's even one freak who's in here for hacking but he still does it every day using the prison computers. Just last week he turned off all the lights in Boise, Idaho for an hour. The guys threw a party for him to celebrate. There was champagne. Very expensive champagne. And this chick that jumped out of a huge cake. Her name was Wendy. She tasted like coconut cream.

The cells, if you can call them that, are pretty big and have track lighting. My bed is comfortable and the toilet's relatively space-aged. It's not altogether unlike a Comfort Inn room *sans* the phone, complimentary religious text, and curtains. They don't even lock the cell doors at night. You can wander out into the common area any time you like. Sometimes I stay in the arcade well past lights out. Galaga looks wicked-cool in the dark, let me tell ya.

But as far as most of the inmates are concerned the cells are crude and completely unacceptable. These guys are used to five-star hotels. Not being able to order room service at 4 a.m. is rather annoying I guess. The guy in the cell next to me is known as Chip. Chip's real name is Winston Myers III, though his good friends call him Willy (and God are they annoying: *Well, Willy, Muffy got that new Mercedes but, ha-ha, the blasted thing just stopped running one day and she had to call a tow truck. So she had to get a ride to the club in the truck with some ungodly grease monkey. Marla says it took her a week to get the smell out of her clothes, ha-ha-ha*). Somebody get over to the club with a flame thrower, would ya. There's good work to be done there.

Willy's prison name is Chip. The guys call him that because he's one of those stuck-up old-school rich boys who considers everyone to be beneath him. Due to the fact that most of the millionaires in this place are *nouveaux riches*, they're just not on Chip's level. They call him Chip because he's got a rather large one on his shoulder. He asked me the other day if I knew why they called him that. I told him that everyone thinks he has a smoking short game. He asked me how *a short game could possibly smoke*.

My other neighbour is a wacky old guy named Frederick Leiber. Freddy's in the slammer because he happened to crash his Bentley into a fence while under the influence of alcohol and receiving an oral examination from a fifteen-year-old (who he swears said she was twenty-five). The first time he told me about it I laughed my ass off. I guess if you're going to go to jail at the age of seventy-two it might as well be for something as young and stupid as that. Freddy blames the entire thing on his chauffeur.

I tell ya, being loaded must really rule. All you have to do all day is pretend to look busy and always make sure you're banging someone you shouldn't be. A little brandy, a cigar, and then it's off to bed. Mission accomplished. I don't know about you, but it beats drinking Columbia and messing around with some chick named Candy in the bushes while trying not to puke on your shoes.

I have two of the most pretentious neighbours in the world on either side of me. But they're not so bad. Prison is the great equalizer. It doesn't matter how special you think you are in here because, after all, you're IN HERE.

I've started writing a book. Since I've got nothing better to do with my time I figured I might as well get it over with. Up until now I had a very detailed plan concerning the creation of such a work. I vowed I'd wait until my thirty-fifth birthday (some seven years and a bit) and then I'd start. I also vowed that, no matter what, I'd only ever write one. If it's shit then my plan is as good as gold. If not then I'll simply disappear.

The book I'm writing is about robot bananas. They're called Bananabots. These tiny little yellow robots were created by a South American scientist to replace human combat troops in the jungle. The theory behind them is that when the enemy is walking through the jungle the Bananabots simply drop from the trees and begin to peel. Once half-peeled they start to spin around really fast, using their peels to slice the enemy to bits below the knees. The scientist creates these things but discovers, too late, that he's made them too intelligent. There's a flaw in their programming. The little Bananabots go mental and kill the scientist and everyone in his little town. To make matters worse they also learn how to build new Bananabots. For five years the Bananabots stay in this little South American town multiplying until one day some American tourists show up and a group of elite Bananabots stow away in their luggage. They hide there until they are back in the States, where they pop out of the luggage and start killing everything in sight.

Eventually the Bananabots kill the majority of the people in North America and enslave the survivors. The entire continent is ruled by little banana robots that are blood thirsty killers. This eventually leads up to the 2004 Olympic Games where they win thirty-two gold medals, prompting the European powers to build a giant robot monkey to invade North America and

transfer to mobile phone

Lenny: Hodgins called. I told him never to call again.

My Mother Again: I told her to call Lenny and ask him to repeat what I had just told him.

Amanda: Amanda called to tell me to hurry up.

Dave Genn: Dave, completely out of his mind on muscle relaxants, thought I was his mother. So I told him that he was adopted and hung up.

Ray: Ray called. We talked. It's none of your business really.

transfer to Amanda's phone

Amanda's mother: Called just as I arrived. So I watched some television. I eventually fell asleep on the couch after about an hour. I woke up at 2 a.m. and drove home. When I got there, I called her place, waited for her to answer, and hung up.

eat all the Bananabots. They build the giant Monkeybot and send him over to eat the bananas and the world is saved. But little does anyone know that there are still thousands of Bananabots back in the little South American town where it all started. I'm not sure what'll happen after that but I know it'll be as brilliant as the first bit.

And to think I owe it all to being in prison. It's like a creativity magnet. It just keeps pulling good ideas out of my head. I can't help myself. Since I've been here I've been able to secure the funding I need to make *Water World II* and have even been offered the head coaching position of a new NFL team (The Boise Barbarians). I've never played the game in my life and don't really like football. But what the hell, it could be fun for a while. Anything to give that "Gipper" speech to a room of steroid junkies making ten million dollars a year. So I'll coach the team for half the year and spend the rest of the time constructing an even more expensive floating city on which to shoot ten minutes of footage for *Water World II*. Then I'm going to blow the whole set up. It will be great to have a small army of people build a floating set for three years only to use it for five scenes and then blow the whole fucking thing sky high. You've gotta love explosions. Pop goes the weasel.

I'm currently working on a scheme to get myself transferred to a minimum-security mental facility as an experiment. My thesis statement:

Do affluent criminals in a regular minimum-security facility have it better or worse than slightly criminally insane affluent prisoners in a minimum -security mental institution?

Or.

How much difference is there between some rich old guy who crashes his one-hundred-and-fifty-thousand-dollar car and gets caught drinking and driving while getting blown by a Britney Spears lookalike compared to some old guy that dresses you in a clown suit and does the same thing?

At the very least I'll get fifty different types of sedatives and some free art aggression therapy.

The Killing of Matthew Good

They plan to use my execution to kick off the county fair.

I hear whispers that they will hang me. There are those that wished to see me electrocuted, but it seems they only have one generator and cannot spare the power. Better to have caramel-covered apples than see my spine dance. I could simply not abide an execution without the availability of concession foods. Unruly I may be, but never uncivilized. There will be children present after all. Best to set a good example.

Chin up and all that. It's off to meet the maker. I have nothing to complain about. I hold no ill will towards anyone. I will leave this world as I entered it. Void of popular consent.

They have me locked up in some sort of cellar. I was unconscious when I was brought in so I'm not quite sure exactly where I am. Strangely enough, it's filled with a variety of costumes. Twice a day someone opens the door and slides a bowl of pork and beans into the room. This I have never understood. Making sure that those condemned to die are nourished enough to take part only serves to further the misrepresentation of compassion in a compassionless society. Yesterday, during the sliding of the pork and beans, I decided to ask my jailer where I was. The response was short and ambiguous.

"You're in God's country," said a voice.

"Hmm," I said to myself, *"God must be lost."*

I have decided to wear a clown suit when the time comes. They're bent on hanging one, after all.

I have been sitting here trying to figure out where it all went wrong. It seems that I have been moving for so long that I have forgotten what it's like to be still. I've been retracing my footsteps, wondering when it was that I became the formless monster that I now am. But nothing comes to mind.

They tell me that I used to be quite agreeable. I can't say that I remember ever being agreeable. I can't say that I can ever remember being anything but adamantly uninterested. I have stalked the planet to my discontent, it seems. And now, here in this basement, I am left with all the blackness that has consumed my insides.

I have come to realize that I allowed myself to be brought below the waves and partially drowned. But before I could struggle free of the water and regain the air, I was caught.

The hayseeds have me now. They're going to hang me. It was wrong of Christians to have ever bought into all that peace and love nonsense. Things

Ain't it just like the night to play tricks when you're trying to be so quiet. We sit here stranded, though we all do our best to deny it.

—Bob Dylan

Life is like trying to commit suicide with a toothbrush: *you're all geared up to do it but decide to brush your teeth first.* Equals no sense.

I have been pondering contradiction. I have come to the conclusion that I am an admirer of the contradictory. I am not entirely sure why. I simply am.

The time has come and gone. Things used to look clear, simple, discernible. There were sides to take, words that connected, people that said them and meant it. But to make it work you've got to have some form of unifica-

were much more interesting when their lust for bloody vengeance was out in the open. Now they're just forcibly boring and seem to get quite offended when over-glorified suburban idiots exclaim the titles of pornographic magazines over the airwaves.

I am doomed to dangle. There's no getting around it I'm afraid. I can only hope that the gallows are in a state of good repair. It would be a big disappointment to discover that I am to be stood on a chair and boringly tipped to my death. Hopefully there will be a trap door to dramatically plummet through, or a team of stallions to hoist me at breakneck speed into the air.

It shouldn't be all that challenging for the promoters. Some dumb bastard in a clown suit getting yanked to his death by four steeds. Why not light the gallows on fire or set off some fireworks when my head hits the top beam. It will be the show of the century.

It would be great to have one's own demise promoted in a Don King fashion:

For crimes against almost everyone—everywhere, see the accused—Matthew F.R. Good—
hang to his death by the neck in what is sure to be the event of the year!

That's right cowpokes! It's...

Hang 'Em High 2001

See **MATTHEW GOOD GET IT** while you marvel at over

37 midway attractions! 8 rides! Billy Bob Macabre's all-new Demolition

Derby! the Lumberjack Show! the Miss Amazing 2000 Beauty

Extravaganza! and the World's Best Rock & Roll Target Range!

EARLY BIRD TICKETS GO ON SALE THIS SATURDAY!

Available at O'Grady's Old Time Country Store, Mella's Gas & Sip,
and the Public Library between 12:30 and 3:00. Adults $8, kids for free.

We'll Sell You The Seat
But You'll Only Need The Edge!

tion. To make it work you can't half believe. You can't hold on to something else just to make sure that if the whole thing goes to shit you've got your ass covered. Thus is today, kids. Cover that ass.

I'm not as cynical as I appear to be. Not even close. But I have come to the conclusion that without pressure there can be no cause for resistance. Without criminality there can be no justice. Without evil there can be no good. Ethics define our intentions against those things, but without them our ethics change and their definitions do as well. To suit a purpose, nothing more. In the absence of conformity goes conformity, in the wake of perfection swims beautiful imperfection, us. Like half-shark, toothless carnivores.

Perhaps the fear of death is worse than its actuality. Not unlike when you jump off of something ridiculously high, you're scared but eventually you succumb to irrational curiosity and do it. Afterwards you realize that it was really no big deal in the first place. I figure death is no different.

When I was eleven I was rushed to the hospital because I was literally frozen in the fetal position. I couldn't unclench my hands, nor my knees or elbows or feet. It hurt like hell. Then, to add insult to injury, I started wandering in and out of consciousness. I had had influenza for nearly a week and a half. After my parts froze my mother started thinking that it might be something else altogether. When we arrived at the hospital I was examined by several doctors. I was then given a spinal tap. They don't sedate you when they give you a spinal tap. They lay you on your side, bend you slightly, and slowly slide needles into your spinal cord. The doctor told my mother that I most likely had spinal meningitis and would be dead within the week. All I remember is the Jell-O. I wasn't given anything to eat except Jell-O.

During the days and nights that followed, interns started appearing outside of my room in droves. They would stand there, peering through the glass, as several doctors spoke and occasionally pointed in my direction. I'm told that spinal meningitis is very rare.

One night, some days later, I awoke at 4 a.m. I got out of bed and walked out to the nurses' station. I stood there, freezing. After several minutes the lady behind the kiosk noticed that I was standing there. She said nothing. I asked if she would be a sport and call me a cab.

So much for death.

But this time there's no out. This time there is just pork and beans.

I am all out of moderately entertaining things to say. I have become the foundation of your dissatisfaction. I will pay the price. This theme-park world that we have so craftily constructed without our consciences getting in the way will extract a toll much worse than the mere bruises of consumerist overload. The debilitations suffered by that which comprises our unknown quantities will surely be much greater. The gods of entertainment demand sacrifice. And surely I'll be replaced by something altogether more predictable.

There was a time when slogans such as "power to the people" and "make love not war" were believable. But even then they were nothing more than cheap disguises bent on delivering the usually sought after nuggets of an anaesthetized society. You can replace them with "Fuck the people, I want the power" and "I was just looking to score because of the war" because the truth hurts. And since art no longer reflects anything but unchallenging passiveness packaged as a good time, you'll be needing something to keep you partially sober.

Last night the carnival trucks rolled into town. There were sounds of preparation, sounds of tired lives being led, sounds of discontented misfits practising a trade as ancient as tragedy. All through the night they worked feverishly to erect Ring Toss booths, the Haunted House, the Chain Swings. The animals in the makeshift petting zoo, blind with glaucoma, wander the husky darkness bumping into each other. The ringmaster writes to a girl he tries to remember as being something other than merely a voice on a phone. The ride mechanic hits the bottle. The carnival must be put together in the night. Done in broad daylight, its secrets would be too easily revealed. It remains one of the last great unknowns in this world. Because if we were to discover how shoddy everything was we would never go. Instead we would go to one of those ridiculous entertainment-megatropolis things and become pale reminders of ourselves.

I did my best to stay awake so that I might see the sun rise for the last time. But I fell asleep.

I awoke this morning to the familiar aroma of pork and beans. I wished it were Jell-O. I attempted to pull myself together, be strong, when the time came. I did my best, but my knees were wobbly. I tried to eat, but vomited.

I spent an hour or so putting on the clown suit, haphazardly slapping on some face paint, trying to make the shoes fit better. And then they came for me. No last meal, no last requests fulfilled, no few minutes with family or friends. I was simply thrown in the back of a cart and wheeled to my destruction. People lined the midway, some throwing things, others merely observing me with quiet disgust. The fact that I was wearing a clown suit only fuelled the crowd's anger. My last jab gave me little comfort, but at least it was something.

As for the rest, well, there is little I can say of it. I would have thought my conditioning able to provide some capable last words, but I merely shook my head when asked if I had any. And then, as quickly as my life had happened, it ended. My legs wobbled, my lungs felt as if they were filled with concrete, I nearly bit clear through my tongue. I just stood there in a clown suit with a rope around my neck. Then the floor gave way and I went with it.

I guess this means the fair is open. Make sure to enjoy yourself.

Full of shit indeed. It gets easier, I find. Being full of shit, that is. Sometimes you choose what it is that you want to do. Sometimes what you do chooses you. Sometimes you don't sleep right. Sometimes you pace around battling three hour-long panic attacks trying to calm yourself down. You talk to yourself in that little voice of yours, cracking jokes, making it seem silly. Everything gets blurry and eventually your hands stop wringing because they hurt, you've just noticed. You collapse onto the couch and sit there, inhaling and exhaling. The most primary of functions. And then you fall asleep. Tomorrow night you get to do it all over again. The funny thing is, you don't know why it happens. You've never been able

to figure that out. It just does. And it continues to. From your childhood, when you used
to sleepwalk and then start screaming so
uncontrollably that they put you on medica-
tion, to yesterday which was just another link
in the chain. The night brings you things to
say that are all part of a big inside joke, your
destruction, your creation, the people that fit
together inside you like a puzzle to make up
your memory. It's the day-to-day business of
making sure that there's a mess to clean up
and then another mess to take its place. So
you come to like it. It begins to make sense.
Maybe it always did. And from that comes all
that defines you in a deal-with-the-devil package. Maybe not so good. Maybe good enough
to be passable. Years later you can't remem-

Twelve voices were shouting in anger, and they were all alike. No question, now, what had happened to the faces of the pigs. The creatures outside looked from pig to man, and from man to pig, and from pig to man again; but already it was impossible to say which was which.

—George Orwell, Animal Farm

The Magic Goats of Presto Island

You don't want no pie in the sky when you die. You want something here on the ground while you're still around.

—Muhammad Ali

Dear Mr. Good. I would like to tell you that the world is worse off with you in it. Your records are excellent but you as a person are less than acceptable. Please remedy this.'

—Fan Letter, April 2000

I once had sex with twenty underaged girls while dangling from a tightrope that was spanning the Grand Canyon. All of them fell to their deaths, save one. So I married her. I married her because she had the good sense to hold on. I married her because I had nothing else planned that afternoon. She was fifteen then. I was twenty-nine.

Looking back on it, I've tried to convince myself that I made the right decision. She was, after all, quite a resilient little thing. But I could never abide people who chewed gum and smoked at the same time. So, on her eighteenth birthday, I did something special for her. I smothered her with a pillow.

My neighbour, Fred, likes to water his lawn a lot. His wife, Linda, does not water the lawn. Watering the lawn is Fred's only means of escaping her. Linda is rather loud, you see, and quite annoying. So Fred waters the lawn. It is no more than thirty square feet. It is the best-looking bunch of grass I have ever seen. I once told Fred that I knew how he could solve his problems. I told him to smother Linda with a pillow while she was sleeping. All he said was "Can't live with 'em, can't smother 'em with a pillow." I disagreed.

I have been a *National Geographic* subscriber since March 3rd of 1978. My mother got me the subscription for my birthday. I used to love pinning the maps to the walls of my bedroom. I would lie there for hours and just stare at them without blinking. My eyes would not close after a while because they were too dry. It was great fun.

When my mother, father, two sisters, and aunt were killed in the great Air Tanzania mid-air collision disaster of 1979, I was unsure as to what would happen with the subscription. Would I have to renew it myself at the end of the year? Or was it paid in advance for a specific period of time? As it turned out,

ber when you had a choice in the matter. You just do. And are.

Everything else is window dressing. Just question marks in questions that never have good, tangible answers. Unlike rock and roll, unlike most things in this day and age, maybe not knowing is a good thing. Maybe leaving that sheet blank is the best thing for it. Everyone finds their own answers to those questions anyway. The problem has always been trying to unify billions of them. People are inherently proud of their ability to think and believe what they want. Full of shit or not. Maybe, in the end, that ability is the unifier. Maybe that's too dangerous. Fear, unlike all other mediums, will always throw a shadow over the other big words. Words like faith,

I had to renew it—which I immediately did of course. It's the greatest magazine in the world. Had my father taken the time to peruse it more often, I doubt he would have ever willingly set foot on an Air Tanzania charter. My father was a fool.

The first book that I ever read was *Little Pink Flamingos* by Catherine Waters. It was about a boy who gets lost in the Everglades and finds his way back home by following baby flamingos. It was not realistic whatsoever. The last book that I read was *Sense and Sensibility* by Jane Austen. It too was baseless and crappy. At no time were any of the characters sensible. To be frank, they were all very much like my father. Too bad they hadn't flown Air Tanzania too. It's a shame that the book was awful. I quite liked *Pride and Prejudice*. At least in that the characters were both proud and, at times, extremely prejudiced. You've got to love that Mr. Darcy. A *National Geographic* subscriber for sure.

I bought a garden hose the other day. I have no idea why. I do things like that from time to time. For example, I'll go out intending to buy cereal and come home with two Filipino hookers and an application for the Entertainment Card. It's puzzling. My high-school guidance counselor once told me that I have a very short attention span. The following day we were given the results of our career placement tests. Mine said that I was going to die.

So I bought a hose. I thought of giving it to Fred, but couldn't bring myself to actually go over there. I would most likely try to strangle his wife. I have met my fair share of folks throughout my life. A great many of them didn't mind that I wasn't listening to them. They just kept talking and talking. Some of them are still talking. Some of them are under my porch visiting with my wife. My career placement test was inaccurate. Turns out it's the other way around.

Come to think of it, I don't remember what it was that I went out to get in the first place. It wasn't cigarettes, I quit smoking. It'll kill you. My father was a heavy smoker. He smoked almost two packs a day for twenty-three years. Believe it or not, he had the blood pressure of a track star when he died. My Aunt Lucile also smoked. She looked like she'd been kicked in the head with skis and then run through a washing machine forty or fifty times. Luckily, she died on that Air Tanzania flight instead of having to get one of those disgusting holes put in her throat. You ever seen someone with one of those holes stick a cigarette in there and puff away? It's quite cool actually. Not only that, they get to use those speech enabler devices. Very nice indeed.

That said, it wasn't cigarettes that I was after. I remember now, it was bread. I had run out of bread. I wanted peanut butter toast. I went out to get some. I came home with a garden hose. I'm not rightly sure how that happened.

I did it again this very afternoon. I went out to get a can of ravioli and came home with a round-trip ticket to Tripoli, Libya. But they don't call it that anymore. They call it Tarabulus. And it's not just called Libya either. It's called the *Socialist People's Libyan Arab Jamahiriya*. Some years ago the United States of America sent a few planes to Libya to bomb Muammar Gaddafi's house with missiles and bombs that can think for themselves and have cameras mounted on them. They missed him. The *Socialist People's Libyan Arab Jamahiriya* has a population density of 3.4 socialists per square kilometre. All I wanted was ravioli.

So I guess I'm going to Libya. I have never been to Africa, despite the fact that my entire family is buried there. I have only ever been to the Grand Canyon.

So the first thing I did when I got home this afternoon was to read up on Libya. I cracked a couple of volumes of my *National Geographic* collection and went to work. Here are some interesting facts that might interest you.

1. It's not called Libya, it's called the Socialist People's Libyan Arab Jamahiriya.
2. It's not called Tripoli, it's called Tarabulus.
3. Libya's total area is 1,759,540 square kilometres.
4. Libya has a population of 5,903,128.
5. Libya has a seventy five percent literacy rate.
6. Libyans speak Arabic.
7. Americans do not speak English, they speak American.
8. The majority of Arabs are not terrorists.
9. The majority of Americans are not native to America.
10. It's a crazy world.

In the late 1960s there was rumoured to be an edition of *National Geographic* that caused such a stir that it could not be released. There are those that steadfastly claim that it was to present twenty-four years of research concerning the mysterious goats of Presto Island. Legend has it that these beasts have the ability to both fly and swim underwater for periods of up to one hour. They are also said to be entirely blue in colour. The research

right, wrong, good, evil. Fear is the great equalizer. In the face of fear everything else is unreliable. That's why they all exist in futility, or at all. Because fear allows them to.

Hopefully I contradicted myself

in there somewhere.

team, led by Dr. Julius Prantzer, was rumoured to have spent the better part of a quarter century on the island studying the goats. To this day, no one is quite sure what happened to Dr. Prantzer and his team, but their findings were supposedly discovered, rolled up in a sealed two litre bottle of ginger ale. After purchasing the findings from cutthroat sea pirates, *National Geographic* had planned to release an issue entirely devoted to Dr. Prantzer and the magic goats in late 1969. For some unknown reason this issue never saw the light of day.

Despite what most people think of it, the Arab culture is probably the oldest culture on the planet. Egypt is an Arab nation, as are Syria, Jordan, Morocco, and so on. The literacy rate in Egypt is 50.5 percent. Somewhat disappointing for a people who constructed the pyramids. Then again, they did invent mathematics and were the first to seriously study astronomy, so I suppose we can forgive them. There are those who believe the pyramids were actually designed by alien taskmasters who enslaved the Egyptians for some years. No one is quite sure what the pyramids were for.

Popular opinion says they're tombs. The Egyptians learned a thing or two from the aliens. They enslaved the Israelites for years. What comes around goes around. That, of course, led to Moses parting the Red Sea at Universal Studios, Hollywood. Years later, Roy Scheider, Robert Shaw, and Richard Dreyfuss would get it on with *Jaws* in the very same body of water.

But I am not going to Universal Studios. I'm going to Tripoli. I also enjoy tube tops very much. But that's all I'm going to say about it.

I have formulated a plan. I doubt that it will work, me having a short attention span and all. Perhaps I will get lucky. I am going to be the first North American in history to hijack an Arabian airliner. I am going to hijack it and crash it into Lough Neagh in Northern Ireland.

Why Northern Ireland? Why not.

Why not is the best possible answer that you can give to any question that you are asked. *Why don't you hijack an Arabian airliner and crash it into Lough Neagh?* Why not. *Why don't you just smother the smoking - gum chewing little bitch?* Why not. *Why don't you give that hose you just bought to Fred?* Because I don't want to.

I have no idea as to how I'm going to hijack the aircraft though. I have scoured my library of *National Geographic* but have found nothing helpful. Killing innocent travellers is more complicated than I had anticipated. For starters, what am I going to use to gain control of the aircraft? Dynamite strapped to my chest? A gun? A machine gun? A knife? Having thought it through, I have come to the conclusion that hijacking a plane is a very complicated business. It has given me a headache.

I always do my best thinking in the shower. During sex is a close second. For some reason, immaculate ideas pop into my head when I'm in the act. When I'm in the shower it's the same thing. For example, how does one go about attaining complete control of an aircraft without having to deal with the complications of smuggling firearms or explosives past airport security? Easy. You use your TV remote.

If there is one thing in this world that looks more confusing, impressive, and generic all at the same time, it's a television remote control. I am not sure if Libyans have televisions, therefore I am taking a chance. If they do not, then they will probably think it some kind of detonator. If they do have televisions, perhaps they will think that I am kidding.

I will miss my *National Geographic* collection when I am dead. I will miss it because it is the only true thing that I've had in my life. I will miss it because it is filled with useful information, colourful maps, and creative photography. I would have never known where Lough Neagh was if it hadn't been for *National Geographic*. Perhaps they will do a piece about the crash. Perhaps my picture will be on the cover.

While I was suffocating my teenage wife, a thought occurred to me. I realized that, had I the chance, I would go back in time and make it my goal to get a job working for *National Geographic*. It bothers me that I didn't consider it an option available to me when I was younger. My career placement test said I was going to die, so I never bothered looking into other options. I wasn't sure how I was going to die, but I was sure that it would be my job.

Thankfully my parents were extremely wealthy people. My father made his money in art. He bought and sold carvings made from elephant tusks, whale bones, and soapstone. A cultured man to say the least. My father did not buy or sell anything made from wood, stone (other than soapstone), or metal. He said they were far too easily acquired and were therefore sullied by scores of filthy, lower class, bohemian hacks. My father did not believe in art produced by the rabble of the world. He said they cheapened it. He was a firm believer in art remaining an upper class sport. There are many people who agree with him. Strangely enough, ninety percent of the most influential and respected artists in human history had extremely poor table manners. Most likely because they were products of an uneducated, heathen stock. My mother, by the way, sold fur coats at the Fur Exchange on West 32nd Street while father was travelling the world in search of endangered-species-art for the bour-

Banned From This Book:

Controversy's Ceaseless Assault Continues

The Lesbian Faerie Story

Morgan Fox & Her Midget All Stars

There Are No Saunas In Hell, Thus No Swedes

Close Only Counts In Horseshoes, Hand
        Grenades, & Organized Religion

Sister Act 4: Mistress Beatrice
        Curious George: The Missile Attack
        On Flight 800

White Power Gnome & Crack Mouse

Bambi & Candy Explore Exotic Bangkok

Mr. Clean Vs The Arm & Hammer Cow: Live
        From Las Vegas

The Girl Who Stabbed Dave Porter In The
        Armpit With One Of The Steak
        Knives He Gave Her For Christmas

(The Muppet Audio Version Starring Sir Alec Guinness & Miss Piggy)

Toucan Sam & Captain Crunch Vs The Swiss

Miss Chick &The Coppertone Girl

The US Government Testing Of Anthrax At Sweet Valley High: An Essay

The Lonely Planet Guide: 12 Things Not To Say To Turkish Prison Officials

Matt Good, The Lithium Years, 1979-1984: A Biography By Sven Donaldson

A Saturday Night In Hell: The Demonic Possession Of 4 Catholic School Girls & How To Make Fake ID's.

Farley Mowat: Boring You To Death - 12 Of His Greatest Hits

I'm Sorry, My Fault! The Pressures Of Being Canadian

geoisie. Mother always was a sucker for deadness rubbing up against her.

I have decided to give my *National Geographic* collection to Fred. It is the least I can do for him, since I am planning to kill his wife before I leave. Fred deserves better. These will be my gifts to him. I will plunger his missus with a self-sharpening knife and leave him with a world of knowledge. I will also leave him a note that says "Can't live with 'em, can plunger them with a Wilkenson's Sword." I may also leave him the knife. It sharpens itself every time you pull it out.

The impossible thing about all of this is that I won't be able to tell you how it ends. I will either end up in Tripoli, or I will be dead. Those are the only two possibilities. If my first attempt fails, I will try again on the return flight. I will not fail the second time. I will casually stroll up to one of the emergency exits and turn the handle that is never to be turned in flight. I will kill everyone. I will do it after the movie.

National Geographic magazine is the greatest magazine ever created. It has yellow borders. It often comes with free maps and informational posters. *Time* magazine does not. Most magazines are filled with the opinions of idiots, pictures of idiots, and the recipes of idiots. *National Geographic* is filled with pictures of animals, vast wildernesses, and all sorts of different kinds of people. So, as my final act as a living, breathing person, I have decided to write them a letter. I hope they like it.

Dear National Geographic,
I have been a National Geographic *subscriber since March 3rd of 1978. Your publication is, in my opinion, the greatest ever conceived. If I may make one suggestion, you might want to consider changing the name of the magazine to* International Geographic. *It's just a thought.*
Beyond that, I would also like to relay my intentions to you. Let it be known that I plan to hijack a commercial airline flight to Tripoli (which one I cannot say, of course, as it would ruin the surprise). I also plan to crash this flight into Lough Neagh in Northern Ireland. I will be the first North American to hijack an Arabian airliner. Perhaps you would consider sending someone to Lough Neagh to report on how the crash affects the ecosystem and local communities. I would very much appreciate this. I have enclosed a photograph of myself in the event that you want to put it on the cover or next to the article.
Sincerely, M.L. Preston II

It is now 2:37 a.m. Fred is watering his lawn again. Fred loves that lawn more than anything in the world. I have decided to bury Linda under that lawn after I kill her. It will be the last place that anyone will look for her. I will bury her under that lawn so that she will always remember one, simple, truth. No one will miss you if you've given them nothing to miss.

The Day Everyone Was Allowed To Shoot Anyone They Wanted But Missed

Dear Santa, A Wish List: Volatile Chemicals & Body Disposal Techniques For Beginners (Condensed –King James Version)

Successfully Faking Illness. A Guide To Doing Nothing Ever Again

Hostage Negotiation. Getting What You Want From The Cops

Titanic. Getting It On While You're Going Down. Notes On The Film

Cherry Jell-O & Primary Plastic Explosive Compounds. An Essay On Taking Sadism Too Far (A Nihilists Perspective) Volume 1

Television

Sometimes I leave it on at night so when I wake up I know the world is still there
Close Quarters Combat: An Excellent Way To Stay In Shape

This is a story about a kick-around-kid named Thomas Andrew Christian or Bug or 'The Bug-man' depending on how well you knew him. Those that made a sport out of The Bug-man simply called him Bug. Because it's a waste of time to elongate the name of a kick-around-kid. Unless, of course, you're calling him *shit-head* or *cock-sucker*. Then, and only then, it is not considered to be. So, to clarify things, those that coveted him as their kick-around guy knew him as Bug. Everyone else called him The Bug-man. Simple adolescent politics.

In his own mind, when Bug looked in the mirror, he thought of himself as Bug. He didn't realize that he did it. He did this because it made him feel like he was a part of something. Even if that 'thing' was making fun of himself. There would come a day, in front of that mirror, when he would look at himself and realize that it wasn't right. But that comes later.

Bug was a senior in high school. Like a lot of kids he wasn't particularly good at anything. He had no idea what he wanted to be when he became a man. For him there were just sheets of wordless suffocation and the distinct feeling that guys like him never got anything on the sacred list. The sacred list which, for countless eons had never been seen by anyone remotely associated with socially less-than-acceptable, was comprised of five mystical and secret things. Some say that the list is a myth. Others claim that it's hidden in a great temple deep within the mountains, guarded by various quarterbacks, cheerleaders, hip kids, and bad asses from the days of yore. It is every less-than-acceptable's desire to find this ancient list. And many have died trying to.

So Bug was staring down the barrel of the final seven months of his young life. Seven more months and he would graduate into the real world. And although he was just a kick-around kid he knew that the future was the kind of place that afforded guys like him second chances. The truth, of course, was that he would be moving into a much larger pool of human beings. The kick-around-kid factor would more than triple in university. Little did Bug know then, but by fourth year there wasn't anyone left except kick-around-people. They're usually the smart ones: people that build the stadiums that jocks play in, the ones that become agents and high level executives. They end up negotiating player contracts on both sides. Ironically, kick-around-people usually end up holding the good end of the leash.

But during those final months he would remain the property of three individuals, Brad, Tony, and Scott. All three lived on the same street. Ironically, Bug also lived on that street. Bug's mom (Mrs. Bug) used to baby-sit all of them when they were youngsters. The four boys had played together every day for years. Brad, Tony, and Scott ate thousands of meals at Bug's house, watched thousands of hours of television, attended eleven birthday parties, smoked their first cigarettes, and spent countless hours listening to Mrs. Bug sing opera. That's what Bug's mom did before she got married and move to the burbs. She belted out the good stuff.

But things changed when the boys finished elementary school and started junior high. The unseen forces of social status, popularity, and a variety of other external pressures began to change their relationship. Bug, unfortunately (or fortunately, depending on how you look at it) remained relatively the same. And because of that he became a target.

Bug became 'The Bug Man' and his three childhood friends used the past to humiliate him to gain whatever it is you gain when you humiliate someone. Strangely enough, Bug did not say anything, even though he could have told countless embarrassing stories about his three, he didn't. His perception of their friendship didn't change. And that's the way it is for kick-around-kids. Loyalty is their downfall. And though some might consider it a loyalty to others, you might find, upon closer examination, that it was a loyalty to himself above anything else. And that's what people, in an age long forgotten, called character.

It was one of those better than average spring days. It was one of those days that lulls you into wearing shorts and a t-shirt and then produces a thunderstorm right before you have to walk home. It was also the day that Scott McGrath asked Jennifer Rittinger to go to the movies with him. Although Scott was a popular guy, he was beaten to the punch by Will Palmer, the son of a well-to-do carpet warehouse tycoon who had a new Mustang. Scott was pissed off, and, as chance would have it, the first person that he ran into was Bug. It didn't matter that Bug was walking around a corner and accidentally bumped into Scott. Bug was in the wrong place at the wrong time. Scott let loose on Bug like never before. In an attempt to protect himself Bug tried to turn and run down the hall, but Scott was able to get to him before he could. And, reaching out to grab Bug by the back of the shirt, he accidentally pulled Bug off balance causing him to fall to the left and down.

Upon reaching the bottom of the stairs Bug's head hit the floor and he was knocked unconscious and split his head open. Bug had to have thirty six stitches and was in the hospital for four and a half months. Besides that Bug had minor bruises to his arms, legs, ribs, and face.

Scott, on the other hand, did not get off so lucky. Instead of helping Bug he decided to run and was later arrested by the police at his home (which was conveniently enough, was right next door to Bug's home). His involvement was confirmed by a boy named Jack Dykens (better known to the basketball team as Jack the Jack Off).

Jack saw his chance to get some revenge, so he ratted on Scott. Later that week Brad and Tony would pay Jack a visit and explain to him why ratting on Scott was a bad thing to do. This, of course, led to a much larger physical engagement between Brad, Tony, and the three individuals on the basketball team mentioned earlier. You see, in this crazy world there are a lot of strange rules that aren't written down on paper. One of them is that you don't kick around someone else's kick-around-kid.

There was a great and widely publicized meeting in the school parking lot. And there, in front of three hundred blood thirsty teenage kids screaming their heads off, the two groups slugged it out for a while, noblemen all.

During all of this Bug was flat out, of course. Swimming the seas of head trauma, he remained unconscious for the better part of thirty one hours, long enough for doctors to begin worrying about a prolonged coma. Thankfully, while a nurse was in the midst of checking on him, Bug regained consciousness. Opening his eyes he turned his head slowly towards the nurse who's face lit up immediately. Clearing his throat, all he could manage was 'hello'.

He had trouble focusing and maintaining his balance which worried the doctors. But his injuries seemed to be accompanied by various other maladies, some of which Bug could not accurately explain to his doctors, like the sound in his head. Imagine the sound of a thousand machines, as if they were grinding behind the walls, under the floors, and through the ceilings. Imagine this sound in your head as constant as the beating of your heart.

During his time in the hospital he was seen by a variety of neurologists and psychologists. But it was all for not. Some of the specialists thought he had minor brain damage but most discounted this idea when his eye sight and motor functions returned to normal. Bug began suffering from severe headaches. He did his best to ignore the noise. He spent the majority of his time grinding his teeth and humming to himself. But such efforts did little to help. And then, after struggling to ignore the sound, it started getting louder. They started running every test known to mankind on him. And that's when they discovered the tumour. It somehow had eluded detection earlier.

Sawing For Dollars: The Art Of Travelling Without Moving

The juvenile intellect has little need or regard for anything resembling the actualities of mortality. Perhaps that is why those who control the cosmic kill switch can take children with little or no conscience, simply because children don't realize that they have a life to lose. Maybe that is a kind of mercy.

The procedure that Bug faced called for the extraction of the tumour using the most archaic of methods. They would saw the boys head open, go in, and cut it out. Despite the repeated discomfort of chemotherapy, Bug thought there must be a better way to attack the problem. But the doctors thought it best to go in directly and as soon as possible. Bug's neurologist wasn't sure whether or not the tumour was cancerous but the fact that it was growing at such an alarming rate provided cause enough. After hours of deliberation Bug's mother decided to sign the release, and left her son in the hands of the profession's most capable surgeons. Neurology, that being the study of the brain and its functions, is one of the most vague and unknown areas of medicine. Which has to make you wonder — is it their intelligence, understanding, and surgical ability that sets them apart from most? Or simply the fact that you've got to be missing some marbles yourself to actually perfect the art of lopping the top of another human being's head off while still giving them a better than even chance of ever waking up?

Flat on his back, they would put the mask on him, the anesthesiologist would try to be funny. Anesthesiologists are never funny. The gas kicked in. And then it's curtains cherub.

Holy Shit.

Bug awoke to find himself in a small clearing surrounded by large, ancient trees. Soft lights shone from within the trees, illuminating the clearing, not unlike one would expect from a science fiction movie. The sky was black and filled with millions of stars, all of which seemed to be moving slightly, as if the world was spinning out of control. But it was warm there in the field so Bug decided to stretch out on the grass and watch the stars whip by.

What pleased him the most was that the noise in his head had stopped. He had given little thought to the virtues of silence. Bug felt as if a calm, endless ocean was within him. And it was during this reprieve that a great light came upon him, there in that clearing, and gave to him the answer to the most fundamental of questions.

The beauty of super beings is that they possess abilities above and beyond those of regular beings. Thus the term *super beings*. The afterlife, commonly thought to be presided over by a supreme landlord and a handful of loyal employees, is governed by a **strata council** of super beings. And no one likes a strata council. Having spent an entire life worshiping the deity of your fancy you arrive in the afterlife only to discover that you've been had. Of course it's your own damn fault, but you're angry and decide to display the finer traits of your species by remaining close minded and self absorbed. After a considerable amount of time spent feeling sorry for yourself you get together with some of your friends and spend your days brushing up on the finer aspects of your nature. And, most tactlessly, you become comparable to the dreaded neighbour who makes too much noise, constantly complains, and kicks trespassing dogs. It's surprising that super beings would go to all the trouble. The strata council thing aside, that's why they're referred to as *super beings*. It doesn't just mean you can pick up and toss about automobiles you know.

The other fantastic thing about super beings is they possess the ability to transfer a great deal of information to others. No yammering, no overhead projectors, no slide rules, no calculators, no burning bushes. Just the instantaneous transference of information from one place to another. A handy power when dealing with galactic amounts of information. If the construct of the afterlife were to be put to someone, such as a young boy lying in a clearing, it would take the intervention of said *super powers* to allow the transference of such a vast and complex catalogue of information. It would also most likely contain a great deal of visual images in place of conventional text. This would make it very difficult to depict in under one billion standard pages. In the dreaded fashion of all things human, just the vaguest highlights please.

Encapsulated In The Always Convenient & Predictable 'White Light' Format: Human Beings. (also see related *Carbon Based Life* categories)

An evolutionary, hydrogen-oxygen species consisting of geographically influenced racial types.

Environment: 1 Iron-nickel base {Hydrological}
          – see *Planet* – Human Beings?
Sexes: 2 [Males/females, standardized hydrogen-oxygen reproduction]
Lifespan: Minimal. Under 100 species-defined years
          —see *Chronos* – Human Beings?
Religious Adaptations: 50,000 species defined years - 54,987 considered.

Registered Complaints With Council: 262,988 heard, 2,345,675 pending.
Alterations: 7 transplantations – 0 successes.

Complaints

There are currently 2,345,675 pending complaints against the human species in the afterlife. In total there have been 2,608,676 complaints against the human species, 262,988 having been heard and ruled on in favour of the plaintiff, 13 were dismissed. Of the 2,608,676 complaints made, 1,204,732 different species made them in a period of time equal to that of 5,500 human years.

Of the 13 complaints dismissed by the council, all of them were made by humans beings against other human beings.

Alterations:

In 5,000 human years 7 alterations have been attempted. None of them have met with success.

Transplantations:

Aomih {African, male, 11 species-defined years} Alterations: physical, cerebral, capacity of consciousness. FAILED.

Ahuramazda {Asian, male, 14 species-defined years} Alterations: physical, cerebral, capacity of consciousness. FAILED.

Yaweh {Asian, female, 8 species-defined years} Alterations: physical, cerebral, capacity of consciousness. FAILED.

Siddartha {Asian, male, 7 species-defined years} Alterations: physical, cerebral, capacity of consciousness. FAILED.

Jesus(Joshua) {Asian, male, conception} Alterations: physical, cerebral, capacity of consciousness. FAILED.

Muhammad {Asian, male, 30 species-defined years} Alterations: cerebral, capacity of consciousness. FAILED.

Nostradamus {European, male, 8 species-defined years} Alterations: cerebral. FAILED.

Thomas Andrew Christian {North American, male, 17 species-defined years} Alterations: none. PENDING.

Immeasurable Losses Of The 20th Century:

numbers 4 through 6

4. The element of surprise

5. Your imagination

6. I've forgotten six

I tried to take up jogging today. I even went so far as to go out and buy a fancy pair of ridiculous looking trainers. My mother always used to go on about the virtues of finishing what you've started and seeing things through, but I canned it this morning and decided to pack it in. As I stepped out of my front door, my ridiculous trainers gleaming in the sun, it dawned on me that my mother's advice was crap. Anything that can be equally applied to genocide and cross training can't be good.

The Coming and the Going

An eternity is long enough to find a place in anything. So eight strikes and you're out.

Dante, though entertaining as hell, was never actually there.

And so it was that Bug came to find himself mostly dead. That, while lying on an operating table somewhere far from that clearing, he had died. Mostly, mind you. Meanwhile back in the clearing, having been bombarded with the secrets of the universe, he grew fatigued. He lay there with his hands behind his head, and watched the stars whip by. And as he was consumed by a profound sleep he came to find himself looking down at his own body in a hospital bed, his head wrapped in bandages, his mother asleep in a chair beside him. Something called to him then. Something familiar tugged at him. And then he woke up.

To save mankind from obilivion one only needs to mastermind a mechanicism for change and that, in a word, is TELEVISION.

Television rules all. Little images dancing across a slightly bent piece of glass now control the collective destiny of the planet. It can destroy people and it can create them. It can get you elected, it can sway public opinion, it can create something out of nothing, and it can sell useless contraptions to people who don't really need them and can't really afford them. In short, it's the perfect replacement for thought. You don't have to think anymore because television is going to do it for you (which is a good thing because it would be both messy and a real shame to see that many heads explode all of a sudden).

And then there's the truth, the greatest of all fantasy words, dependant entirely on perspective. Now I'm sure that there are remnants of the truth left out there, those things that make everyone's stomach turn so much that they've just got to be wrong, or right, or justifiable. But for the most part the truth is perspective. Despite what you've read or been told most of your life there are not two sides to every story. There are multitudes. Subsequently no one will ever fully understand them all. Because there are those things that can be studied and dissected and there are those things that one has to experience to know anything about. Most of the time such perspectives contradict each other. It's a big shit sandwich really. So turn on your television and take a bite. Because that's what it's there for. Enough perspective to confuse you along with a little dash of warm fuzziness to make you feel like everything's going to be a-okay. There are bombs falling somewhere. I'm counting peanut butter sandwiches with The Count. One, one peanut butter sandwich, and so on.

On Tom's first morning home following his ascension from mere high school kick-around-kid to possible new world saviour, while standing in front of the bathroom mirror brushing his teeth, he realized that he was referring to himself as 'Bug' and not Tom. In his head he heard his mother's voice calling his name, a distant memory from some lazy summer evening years before, telling him it was time to come in. So he stood there, a mouth full of toothpaste, and said it over and over again. 'Tom'. And looking in the mirror he recognized himself.

His shift in attitude was apparent to everyone from that day forward. He, himself, went unaware. He was a man on a mission. A mission that would lead him, some weeks later, from the darkness into the light, a work experience position at the local cable station.

During Tom's first week at the station he worked on such thrilling programs as *Gardening with Marv* and *The Pee-Wee Hockey Game of the Week*. The station manager decided to extend Tom's stay, and he got the opportunity to work on some more interesting programs like *The Christian Armageddon Hour* and *Yoga with Mary-Sue*. Having changed hands seventeen times in under ten years, the station was run by an ex-attorney, Tony Viani. Tony had succumbed to a nervous breakdown some years prior and decided to follow a dream that he had had as a child. One of being on, or involved with, television. After various rejections from established networks due to a lack of experience, he found himself in the office of Herbert Meyer who was, up until that week, the longest lasting station Tsar in Community Cable history. Two days after meeting with Tony, and telling him that he hadn't anything for him, Herbert was killed by a heart attack. So Tony got a phone call.

At the time Tony was surviving off of what remained of his savings and the sparse income generated by his wife Brenda, a tarot card reader and self-proclaimed spiritualist. Brenda was also an accomplished alcoholic at the time, though she would spend the year after Tony's appointment as Community Cable grand-poobah cleaning up her act. Thankfully she would not cleanse herself of the new age spirituality that drove Tony up the wall. Conversations with her dead father aside, the incense alone was enough to drive the best of men mad. Having spent a considerable amount of time after his breakdown learning how to relax, he kept his head by trying to focus on the positive aspects of their union. The fact that he couldn't think of a positive aspect most of the time he assumed was due to his lack of what profes-

This world is filled with things that will never make sense. Trying to make so much sense of them will only result in one thing. Spending the rest of your life trying to remember what you were like before any of it mattered.

The Pitfalls Of Being Marty

I used to dream about being here. Watching all these faces looking down at me, their eyes filled with an uncertain terror that is as perplexing to me as the frantic actions of the paramedics that are currently attempting to plug my chest. I wasn't supposed to make it this far anyway, so why the long face? There were never paramedics in the dream though. Just those faces up there. You'd think, tangled up in the countless details, my subconscious would have remembered to add paramedics. I believe they think they've got a fighting chance. Relax guys. I don't make it to the hospital in the dream. It ends right here.

All I can remember are the flashes. Two

sional cable-knit sweater connoisseurs refer to as "not being in touch with your feminine side."

But it was no mystery that Brenda missed her father. Her foray into the spiritual world started almost immediately following his death. The drinks came a little later. Brenda would speak to her father quite often in public places while Tony was not with her. On more that one occasion it landed her in custody after being asked by various store employees or cashiers to vacate the premises, the ghost of her father in tow. She wouldn't go peacefully, Tony would be forced to make his way to the police station to get her. Once Tony was hired on at Community Cable, he gave Brenda an 11:30 phone-in slot so that she could do live tarot readings for viewers. After that she was mostly golden.

Once Tom had told Brenda of his own life after death experience, she took a real shine to him. Her influence with her husband was the reason Tom was hired on after his work experience ended. The two of them spent a great deal of time talking when Brenda dropped by. On Tuesdays, which was the night she did her show, she would come early and get Tom to help her set up. On several occasions she even had him on the show to help her hold up cards and crystals. On the fateful night Brenda was at home throwing-up. Stricken with the flu, she sternly told her husband by telephone that Tom would fill in for her in the event she was unable to do the show. Having spent a considerable amount of time after his breakdown learning to relax, he kept his head by trying to focus on the positive aspects of their union. So he dutifully informed Tom, an hour before air time, that he would have to put on the swami headdress and go it alone. Brenda's orders.

Tony was an easy sell compared to Dan and Gilbert, the station camera operators. Both thought it better to run a repeat of something and leave early rather than entertain Brenda's lunacy. At the same time they were also curious to see what would happen. According to Tony, the kid was just going to talk for a half an hour. No callers, no tarot, just talking. In an attempt to remain calm and carefree, Tony only wanted to avoid an episode when he got home. After all, who would be watching? So what could it hurt? Brenda got two calls a show and they were always from the same two people every week, Tony thought to himself.

Sometimes the Strata Council gave past astronauts special powers to prove their authenticity. But not in Tom's case. He was forced to rely on something far more powerful than special powers—dumb luck.

Tom sat down in front of a camera and began to let the universe slide out of his mouth like a terrible secret revealed to the unsuspecting cable audience. Danny and Gilbert didn't bother operating the cameras, they just stood there looking at each other wondering what to make of it all. And it was during this performance that dumb luck made its entrance.

It all started earlier that night at exactly 9:42 PM. The most horrific thing known to mankind occurred. Something so horrible that society was almost snuffed out in one brief moment like some bug hitting the windshield of a car. The cable went out. The truly pathetic thing about it is that no one stopped watching television. They just sat there and suffered through what they were left with hoping that Cinemax would pop back on before they were forced to commit suicide or do something far worse like talk to each other. Everyone sat there and waited.

But it got worse. Not only was cable out but everything from channel 4 up was being intermittently hit with off axis horizontals. So that left everyone with three choices. Well two really because one of them was French. Channel three was local and was in the midst of showing some truly awful film from the seventies. Channel four was Community Cable. Channel five was French. And channel two was teasing everyone by listing all the shows they were missing. So those who could stand it stared longingly into an off axis, snow-laden crystal ball. Everyone else fled to one of the remaining channels. Using some quick math we can assume that about 20 to 30 percent of the remaining viewers were now watching channel four.

Rudy sat at a big metal desk covered with hundreds of flashing lights, levers, and switches in the control room of the local power station. His feet were up on the edge of the desk as he slowly sipped hot coffee in a styrofoam cup while his eyes impatiently watched a nearby door as if expecting someone to come through it. Rudy was very happy. His uncle Jim had just got him a job sitting at a big metal desk looking at lots of meters, flashing lights, and a variety of other important looking things. This was Rudy's first week on the job. But that didn't mean that Rudy stopped *being Rudy*. Since he was the only one there at that time of night he had invited his girlfriend Sarah to come down and keep him company for a while.

When Rudy had called Sarah and asked her to come down she instantly formulated a plan. She decided to show up wearing an overcoat, boots, and nothing else. At the same time, he was formulating his own plan to get Sarah naked. When she arrived she gave Rudy the coffee she brought for him and went to the bathroom to loose the coat and take full advantage of the element of surprise.

of them, right on top of one another, no reports. And then I doubled back like I'd been hit in the chest with a hammer. Everything is silent and surreal, the actions of those around me have played out in an almost comical slow motion while I do my best not to giggle at them like some gin-soaked high-school girl. I don't know why I find it so funny, but I do. Lying here, I've been pointlessly telling myself that I've just been winded and will be alright in a minute. I'll get up and everything will be okay. That, in itself, is humorous enough. Lying in an expanding pool of blood, I find it rather ironic that I got it in the lungs. After battling sarcoidosis and pumping my body full of antibiotics in an effort to keep me well enough to perform, it's my lungs that have truly been shot. And because of that I feel cheated in a way.

In the dream I always got it in the head and there wasn't any of this inner monologue to wade through. So if I've got to wade through it, then you're going to have to put up with my bullshit a little while longer. Tomorrow's another day kids. One in which I'll not be around to remind you that it's nothing more than our irreversible perpetuation of eating shit and being programmed to ask for salt.

I remember a time not so long ago when my dreaming subconscious used to dwell on images of some quiet paradise lost and the perfect features of the face of a girl that I'd never met. I used to wonder what her hair

She went in at exactly 11:33 PM and re-emerged at 11:35. It was then that Rudy lost what remained of his concentration and concern for his new position. Sarah walked across the room and launched into one of those frenzied light-speed foreplay episodes that tend to only happen in the movies. The two of them did what most twenty something's would do in that situation. They refrained from wasting time by moving to another location or the floor. Rudy's initial reaction was to just bend her over the big metal desk, but Sarah wouldn't have it. She wanted to get up on the desk so she could watch Rudy get that stupid look on his face that he always got when they had sex with the lights on.

He wasn't about to say something stupid like 'I don't think I should bang the shit out of you while you're on that big metal desk because it's covered with important looking switches and levers and what have you'. Rudy hoisted her up there and went to work. Work, by the way, officially started at 11:41 PM.

Sex on a desk or table or bench or car hood or in an airport bathroom comes down to one thing—*good leverage*. Controlled thrust is dependent on several factors: height, angle, anatomy, and slippage. The big metal desk offered some problems. For one thing it was a little too high. Rudy was forced to stand on his tip-toes. He also discovered that he had to keep pulling Sarah towards him by grabbing her hips and readjusting her position. This thrilled Sarah to no end. But it also meant that as things got wilder Sarah began to lean back onto the desk. By 11:52 she was no longer interested in using her hands to keep her upper body vertical. And although it helped Rudy, it meant that she was now lying on a variety of switches, flashing button-lights, and a whole slew of controls. She didn't really mind that it hurt.

Rudy wasn't really thinking about anything. He was caught in that mental limbo that guys enter into when they're half way between the starting line and the finish line. It's that area where the realization that you're getting laid (yippy) has melted away and you're either trying not to cum too quickly or you're getting tired and you're over-thinking it so much that you can't. Rudy was struggling with the first problem. It was 11:58:23 p.m.

Tom: At 11:58:02 Tom started to laugh uncontrollably. Because he realized that he was going down in a big ball of flames and would most likely be committed or fired later that night. He found that so funny that he just started laughing. A single word kept racing around in Tom's head while he was cracking up. And that word was BOOM.

Brenda: Between 11:48:16 and 11:58:23 Brenda Viani was laying in bed, watching Tom, trying not to vomit. One thought kept racing around her in her mind, 'I should have never stopped drinking.'

Tony: At 11:51:44 Tony was told that he had a phone call, he left the studio and went to take it. At 11:53:01 he learned that the cable was out and a record number of people were watching his station. At 11:53:03 he realized what was being shown on his station and he nearly had another nervous breakdown.

Dan the Cameraman: At 11:58:23 Dan was thinking about his two daughters, Tammy and Terry. He was thankful that they weren't screwed up like this punk kid who was laughing like an idiot on live television. Little did he know but his two daughters were the go-to girls for half of their school's weekend pharmaceuticals. Years later Tammy would marry an abusive man who would push her out of a moving car and Terry would do nine years for trafficking dope.

Gilbert the Cameraman: At 11:58:23 Gilbert was wondering whether his VCR had properly taped *Star Trek*. He would later discover nothing but snow on the tape and would end up throwing it out a window in a fit of rage. As luck would have it the tape would hit a woman in the head and Gilbert would go rushing outside to apologize. He would marry her a year later.

Mrs. Bug: At 11:58:23 Tom's mom was listening to opera quietly while folding laundry. She had no idea that Tom was even on television.

Rudy: At 11:58:23 Rudy reached the promised land and made the stupid face.

Sarah: Between 11:58:03 and 11:58:23 Sarah was trying her best to get to the promised land before Rudy crapped out on her. And in doing so she pushed herself up on the desk. In doing so her hand moved across a big metal covering that protected a big red button. She accidentally flipped the covering up while pushing herself up and then rested her hand on the button once she was there.

26,089 people were watching Community Cable at precisely 11:58:23.

At exactly 11:58:22 Tom looked directly into the camera and said "BOOM!"

smelled like. For some reason that was the one thing about it that always bothered me. I never knew. I'm not quite sure whether all of this means that I'll never know or that I'm about to find out. Maybe that's heaven, I don't know.

One thing I do know is that it would be nice if these paramedic guys would stop bringing me around. I like it in here when it's all quiet and full of wind sounds. For some strange reason I can't stop thinking about *Charlie and the Chocolate Factory*. I have no idea why. Who would have ever guessed that, in my final moments, I'd be consumed by thoughts of milk-chocolate rivers and doors made of marzipan. Typically, this is where I'm supposed to be asking for forgiveness and letting the better angels of my nature consume me with warm fear and resignation. Instead, I've got images of grape-flavoured bubble gum trees in my head. It would seem that my implant has gone all screwy again. The last time this happened I was covered in choco-late sauce and couldn't stop thinking about redemption. I had been a very bad boy then as well.

Maybe you'll buy our boxed set and remember me from time to time. On your stereo. In those bad walkman headphones. I'll be in there, wandering around, bumping into walls, tickled up on the inside. It's me, He-Man—is that you Battle Cat? I'll be watching you dance around your room using a brush for a microphone, a tennis racket for a guitar. I'll

Simultaneous events that occurred at exactly 11:58:23

1. Tom had just finished saying 'BOOM!'
2. Sarah's hand pressed a button which, along with a series of other things she had pushed by accident during sex, overloaded the desk and subsequently caused the biggest electrical power surge in civic history to every home in a twenty mile radius.
3 Everyone's televisions blew up along with most street lights, electronic equipment, and local transformers.
4 The pulse from the surge affected three planes that were flying overhead causing them to make emergency landings.
5 The cable came back on.

11:58:31

1 Rudy realized that having sex on the primary control desk at a civic power plant was a very bad idea. He was now making the 'Uncle Jim's going to fucking kill me!' face.
2 26, 089 people were convinced that the wacky kid on channel 4 just blew up their televisions. It wasn't exactly walking on water or healing lepers. But it was impressive nonetheless.

Although only 26, 089 people were watching channel 4 when Tom said 'BOOM!', a week later there might as well have been millions. Every religious flake from the Yukon to the Mexican border had heard about the kid who blew up everyone's televisions. Not only did he destroy TVs but entire power grids as well. Religious experts everywhere were either trying to rationalize what had happened or they were spinning the whole thing so dramatically that Tom was being considered by some to be messianic. The tabloids picked up on the story immediately, as they are prone to, and by the end of the month anyone standing in line at a supermarket was reading headlines about Tom's miracle.

Rudy was fired at exactly 12:27:09 a.m. The power company tried to cover it up.

They paid Rudy and Sarah to move to a new town. Exactly 842.7 miles away. They then gave Rudy three hundred thousand dollars and made him sign a document stating that he would never talk about it to anyone. The document also included a fabricated statement where Rudy would claim to have been *mopping the floor* when all the commotion started. As a lowly janitor there was really 'nothing he could have done'.

In the eye of the storm sat the confused conduit that had given warning to the world. It got so bad for Tom that after some weeks he was forced to stop going to school because people had taken to camping out on school property just so that they might catch a glimpse of him. People also camped out on Tom's street. The police were forced to set up barriers and some temporary first aid tents as campers started collapsing from heat exhaustion, dehydration, and a variety of other things. Through it all Tom tried his best to keep his head. He realized that his predecessors, the majority of them, had the ability to perform miracles and therefore qualify themselves. He did not. Even Nostradamus had his visions. Tom had only the fickle landscape of television with its comely conveyances. The revolution will not be televised, the man said. So what about evolution?

A month and a half after the incident Tony Viani had sold almost 315,000 video cassettes of Tom's broadcast worldwide. Tony wasn't the only one cashing in. Scott's parents printed shirts with Tom's year book picture on them and the word BOOM! underneath. They set up a table at the end of their driveway and stored the never ending garbage bags of cash in their basement. Everyone that knew Tom was interviewed by every major news agency in the known world.

Suddenly he was everyone's best friend. Tom received phone calls from Larry King's people, David Letterman's people, Leno's people, and a host of other people's people. Heads of state called him, religious leaders asked to speak with him, and two of the world's largest film studios were maneuvering to buy the rights to his life story. Through it all Tom hid in his house, waiting for the wave to crest. And when it crested he planned to hold a press conference and try to qualify himself.

At the same time there were plenty of people that were outraged by Tom. They organized marches, sit-ins, and a whole host of other anti-Tom events. And that's how four men came to meet one cloudy day in a crowded park.

They were attending a protest that was put together by four different religious leaders in the area. One Catholic, one Baptist, one Jewish, and one Muslim.

A public washroom is the last place in the world that one would expect talk of religiously motivated assassination. On that day four men were worked up. They were high on hate. One makes an off-handed comment: "someone should just shoot him and get it over with!" This piques some curiosity. They begin discussing it. Two Christians, a Jew, and a Muslim all talking about killing a teenage boy.

recognize some of me in you and we'll be together again.

Up goes the gurney. So much for subconscious accuracy.

During the nine months that you are held captive within your mother's womb you breathe symbiotic fluid. Although blood is a substance that carries vital oxygen through the body, and is therefore usually considered an ally, my last few breaths have forced me to the conclusion that blood shares no resemblance to symbiotic fluid whatsoever. It is somewhat harmful when it attempts to skip several steps and wanders into your lungs in hopes of cutting out the middle-man and getting first dibs on the O_2. This is not good. Your lungs, which are quite stern and not that receptive to fluidic change, decide to stop transferring oxygen to the blood, causing you to choke and ultimately suffocate. My inner workings are all about ego it would seem.

Something just occurred to me. If you blew hard enough into my mouth I might actually be useful as a wind instrument. I can imagine being played like a flute. A naughty business, that.

Is this where I stop pretending to be the me you always hoped I was? Somewhere, imprisoned within the impregnable fortress of your inflexibility, I remain perfectly fabricated. In a place without windows, without doors, without the knowing of what transpires on the other side of things. I'm going to die. The trials of myself, the pitfalls of being

Their numbed disdain for each other's religious beliefs had been replaced by a burning hatred of a mutual enemy and their fervent desire was to see him exterminated. They started meeting at night, where they worked themselves into a frenzy, shook their fists, and entertained the 'if only-s'. But as the nights passed their conversations began to turn from 'why not-s' to 'when-s' and 'where-s' and 'how-s'.

The plan was simple. All four men would attend Tom's press conference packing hand guns. The first to get close enough to use his gun would shoot Tom. If anything went wrong then the others would make sure that Tom didn't leave alive. And lastly, all four men would turn themselves in no matter who did what. They would take responsibility for their deeds and felt that they had enough justification that others would support their actions. They were willing to sacrifice themselves to rid the world of a boy they considered evil.

Almost three and a half months after Tom blew up everyone's televisions with a single word he was preparing to go back on. This time the world would be watching. This time Rudy's libido couldn't save him, nor could he count on network satellites to unexpectedly fall from the sky. He sat in his room and tried to focus on what he would say.

A huge podium had been set up at the end of his driveway. There were countless microphones and news trucks, satellite dishes and crews operating them. There were a couple of jumbo-televisions that had been set up at either end of the street so onlookers would have clear sightlines. The police had men in the crowd, and men in front of the podium, men on the roofs on neighbouring houses. There were helicopters buzzing overhead, giant slogan-laden air-ships, and small tour planes circling above. It was estimated that over 230 televisions stations would broadcast the speech, live, around the world. The stage was set and everyone waited.

At 12:20 p.m. Tom left his room and made his way to the front door. There were two police officers waiting there to escort him. As he emerged from the carport the crowd erupted like the game winning goal of the world cup final had just been scored in overtime.

Tom hesitated. He hadn't been outside since he'd left school and was taken back by the multitudes that had come to see and film him. Tom was trying his best not to turn and run or throw-up all over his shoes. He started walking again and eventually reached the platform. He went up the stairs, paused to collect himself, and then walked over and stood in front of the podium bristling with microphones. He stood there for a second longer trying to catch his breath. Clearing his throat, all he could manage was 'hello'.

And through the air came the sound of a great and massive thunder clap. At that moment Tom's head jerked back and his body seemed to rise off the ground as if in slow motion. And then there was nothing but stars for Tom, all out of focus.

Back on earth all hell broke loose. Millions of people watched while the crowd broke into a frenzy and panic took hold. The cops in front of the podium wasted no time in drawing their own guns and firing back. They did this blindly, hitting and killing a number of people along with the man who had shot Tom. And as all of this was going on there were people trying to loot Tom's corpse, people breaking windows, people trampling people, people pushing people off of roofs, people fighting, people getting crushed, people screaming, people attacking the police, people attacking news crews, and people standing around watching. And all of it was being transmitted around the globe on live television. The entire incident had been caught on tape and was soon to be re-broadcast a million times over. Ratings were up, people were down, things were good.

Out of the four assassins only two of them were apprehended. The Jewish shooter, who had been shot to death by the police, and the Muslim who was crushed to death by an overturning car. The other two didn't keep to the plan. They fled, separately, into the chaos. A massive manhunt would be undertaken to find the missing two assassins, as letters of intent were discovered on both Jew and Muslim detailing their actions and the membership of their group. After five weeks of false leads and inaccurate sightings the investigation became a federal concern.

The media, of course, had a field day. As the months passed, a typical backlash against Tom began to surface. Many wondered how they could have believed such a boy to be so important. Most people jumped on the anti-Tom bandwagon so as to elude complication. And after all the interviews, speculations, panels, and debates not one person realized the obvious. They had missed the point.

Tom awoke to a brilliant galaxy. Billions of stars sliding past him in hazy flashes. And as he watched he began to count them. And as he did that he felt his being slip away and his mind clear of everything save the numbers.

And that's all there is to it I'm afraid. No fanfare, no memorable last lines. Just the wind. And the fact that it blows over all of us at one time or another. Sometimes I leave my television on at night, so I know the world is still there.

Marty, that beautiful confusion that always was my photogenic side. I am a better liar to myself than to others. Maybe it's time to realize that all this talking isn't doing anything to stop the panic that keeps gnawing at my insides like dynamite with a full dance card. I think that you should go.

Between sleep and awake there is a taco stand called *nothing*. Can I take your order?

Sometimes I lay awake at night and remember things from the past that seem so long ago that they really didn't happen to me. Maybe in some other life they did. Everything used to have this glow around it that I can still faintly see sometimes when I walk around the beach in the very small hours of the morning. Out there, past the ships and the songs of the great whales, there is a glowing horizon of sorts. And like the past, and my memory of it, that glow lies somewhere far beyond the vastness of that water. Perhaps where the sun hides right before it decides to give that motivational speech it loves so much. Right before my body gives out and I'm forced to close my eyes for a change.

There used to be a grocery store near where I used to live. I'd go there and lie in the middle of the parking lot late at night and watch the sky. It was strange because it was this massive parking lot in a strip mall and no one was around. No cars, no lights, no people. There's something eerie about lying down in a place where, during the day, hundreds of people are usually running about. It's like being a completely wild creature that's wandered into civilization the one time that people aren't there. I once fell asleep in that parking lot. I woke up underneath a Toyota 4-Runner. I was dreaming about a land beyond thunder dome. It was a-okay.

The downside to being in the parking lot at night was the bugs. They'll eat you alive. There's no escaping the bugs. One day they will rule the world. There's nothing you can do about it. It would be best for you to make friends with the bugs, or you could end up in a giant killing jar with the bugs on the other side drinking martinis and yelling at you: *"The scientist warned you, you idiot"* they'll say. And they'd be right. But you won't hear them of course. You'll be trapped inside a giant jar. We'll all be trapped in giant jars. But that's not important right now.

The upside is this: *just lie down in the middle of an empty parking lot at night right before a thunderstorm hits.* You feel like some easily squashed bug and you realize there is something larger that's looming out there. A force that remains patient and silent. An entity that waits to teach a lesson that we have yet to grasp. It is much better to just lie there and let it roll over you like some immense army of unquestionable wonder.

You may find all of this strange but your options become severely limited when sleeping is as difficult as riding a miniature motorbike up Mount

Everest. Someone once told me that I couldn't sleep because of hypertension. Maybe. I always thought there was something I was supposed to see that I could only see in the dark. Maybe it was myself. Maybe it was to tell the rest of the world how fucking horrible late-night television really is.

I used to be a non-believer. To tell you the truth I would probably still be a non-believer if it hadn't been for this guy that happened upon me one night in the parking lot. I was watching the sky when this odd fellow pushing a shopping cart walks by me and says *"Knowing nothing is power"*, and just kept on going. I have thought about that statement for years.

Knowing nothing is power because internal recognition defies external influence. Like a ship lost on an ocean with many other ships, is it better to remain under the power of your own sails or lash your ship to other ships because you've come to the conclusion that you might never find land again?

For nine years I haven't been able to figure out what he meant. And maybe that's the whole point.

There is one thing I do know for sure. There ain't nothing like Fruit Chews in the rain. Except for maybe two tubs of Cool Whip, the Bud girls, and a log cabin trapped under 400 feet of snow. Mmmmmmm, Cool Whip.

Perhaps he simply meant that *knowing nothing* is far easier than *knowing something*. If you know nothing then you've got a pretty good idea where you stand. On the other hand, if you know something then you have to spend the rest of your life trying to know everything (because that's the goal of knowing). One day it leads to everything and you discover your wife in bed with another woman, some dirty hippie guy, and a llama.

How often do guys pushing shopping carts say things like that? Usually they're saying things like *"This is the shopping cart guy to Uridium 15, come in Uridium 15..."* But this guys says: *Knowing nothing is power.* Maybe he was talking about humility. Maybe it's just that simple.

Sleep is elusive and in the absence of nourishing rest this is how I pass my time. Remembering how to forget and memorizing how to remember.

Beyond this Place Behind the Stars

Once, not so long ago, the world came to an end. Millions of people ceased to exist all of a sudden, all with no time to prepare. This did not mean that they stopped moving or speaking or producing. It just meant that they ceased to exist all of a sudden. The world had come to an end.

One morning, some years after the end of the world, a young woman patiently sat in a waiting room with fourteen other women. These other women were all roughly the same as her. They were all exactly the same age, they were all unwed, they were all relatively dim. These three primary characteristics had brought them together on that day. They had all had birthdays during the previous week. This meant that they could be legally put to work. So, their names having been run through various machines that do nothing all day except compile lists of names, they received notice that they were to come that morning to that office to be given a job.

She hoped she might be given a fantastic job. It was not to be, of course, but one can always hope.

During the hour or so that she spent waiting, she fantasized about being given a job so fantastic that it would make her burst with happiness. Perhaps she would become an events coordinator on a cruise ship or at a holiday resort.

Instead, she was given a job painting pieces of coral. She also painted a plastic word that had been glued to the coral. It consisted of the following four letters: M-A-U-I.

It was to be her life's work.

The real world. That being the one in which we live.

The People's Republic of China is a very large place. It is rather easy to become lost within it. Not so much because it covers such vast distances, but because there are so very many people vying for the solitude that such a vastness once offered. There are, at this very moment, approximately 1.2 billion people living in the People's Republic of China. It is one of the most populated countries in the world. There was a time when China was ruled by emperors who were considered divine. After the world came to an end, the Chinese government spent a great many years telling its countrymen that the ways of their forefathers were wrong. Unfortunately, they did little to present anything concrete that showed themselves to be any better. But that is the way of the world. Everyone's got to learn everything the hard way for some reason.

There was a time when a fraction of those 1.2 billion people tried to do something to change that reality. But it seems that it made for good television rather than being

entirely realistic. So little has changed. Taiwan is next on the list. And thousands of incarcerated criminals still labour to produce cheaply made clothing and souvenirs for stupid North Americans. Oh how ironic, and so on.

Sometimes something is better than nothing. Sometimes having enough is better than expected. There are those that might consider painting clay dolphins glued to coral altogether unappealing, but if it's all you've got then it's something. And sometimes something is everything.

The unreal world. That being the one within my head.

There are tiny people living inside of your head, at this very moment, just as I write this, just as you read it. Some of those tiny people are making you second-guess everything that you take in, whatever it may be. Some of them make you confident, some of them are undecided as to what should be done. Most of them are far too busy making sure that you have enough inner power left to keep you going long enough for you to feel as though you've earned the right to stop.

There is a peace to assembly lines. More so to those that do not move at a fast pace. An assembly line that consists of a variety of different work stations is far more attractive than one that employs conveyor belts, ramps, and levers. Mostly because you get to sit down and work. Assembly lines with conveyor belts usually require workers to stand during assembly. Better to sit your life away. Better to have an impossibly uncomfortable chair than impossibly uncomfortable shoes.

When the girl was shown her work station she had no idea of her good fortune. She looked down the endless rows of work stations, each occupied by entirely miserable women.

Twenty-six years later she would look up from her work and watch another young girl, not unlike herself, look about the factory floor with the same quiet disgust. And, twenty-six years later, she would crack the slightest of smiles. By that time in her life she had come to realize that most things aren't about keeping up defiant appearances in an attempt to buttress whatever's left of some youthfully over-romanticized inner core. But rather one's ability to convince oneself that life is nothing but a series of impractical maneuvers ending in a standoff with either a disappointing god or a disappointing devil.

Before the world came to an end the planet was populated by people that refused to acknowledge their defeats as anything but failures. They had spent evolution winding themselves up over the matter, convinced that forwards

My story

I've been delinquent. Delinquency's my bag. Ask anyone. I've got the *Welcome Back Kotter* theme running through my head. Speaking of heads, my mother cracked mine open when I was sixteen months old. Twenty four stitches. You can still see the scar. She was running down the hallway of our old house trying to answer the phone. She had me in her arms. My head slumped back and hit the brick corner of the kitchen wall. Part of my brain fell out and the dog ate it. And that, my friends, is how I got my superpowers.

Now, don't get me wrong, having superpowers at such a young age can be just as much a nightmare as a blessing. The first drawback I discovered was the dog. The dog and I were "linked," you might say, because it had eaten part of my brain. Therefore, I would have to keep track of it. On the other hand, for fun I would make the dog fly around the room, or instantaneously teleport it onto the roof so my parents would freak out. Not unlike The Beastmaster, I could also see through the dog's eyes. This also bothered people that came over to our house. Our dog would sit there intently staring at them for hours, never moving. I, on the other hand, would just sit in my room and watch them watching the dog. The other downside of these powers was the intense headaches I would get after using them. But, then again, who's really going to tell their neurologist

was far more interesting than any other direction. Up had nothing to do with it, mind you. Just forwards. Many of these people, unknowingly mired in the make-believe state of emancipation, had come to view their liberties as nothing more than "things that people are entitled to just because." That's not to say that everyone was blind to the dangers of the *Forwards Plan*. For decades prior to the end of the world, a handful of gas jockeys, Orange Julius girls, and dishwashers had begun to realize that all was not well with the presumption that forwards was the way to go. Most of those people spent their lives standing in one place, wishing only that the smell of bullshit would eventually wash out of their clothes. Everybody else kept pushing forwards though. And then, all of a sudden, the world came to an end.

Despite the fact that the girl ended up painting clay dolphins and coral for the majority of her existence, she was granted something in the way of compensation for her complacency. She was given a son. And that might not seem like much to you, but that's only because you're waiting for the lights to change.

The World Unanswered.

An incomprehensible number of years ago something rather odd occurred. Something quite large and altogether volatile decided to explode. This sent a great manner of things every which way, some of it good and some of it not so good. Things flew, things cooled, things boiled, things adhered to the cosmic rules of magnetic repulsion and attraction. All in all it produced some interesting side effects. The most important of them being, of course, the Tilt-A-Whirl and the Garden Weasel.

There are those who contend that the world was created by an all powerful force, perhaps even a supreme being. There are those who contend that the world was created by a galactic event of unimaginable magnitude. There are those who contend that Elvis Presley is still alive and, if not, was actually a talent beyond compare. It's a crapshoot really.

1] The universe is expanding. Throw some deceleration in there and you've got yourself one hell of a deity killer.

2] Did ancient peoples really begin building a massive tower in an attempt to reach God only to be made to speak different languages so that miscommunication would halt construction?

3] Why did Pink Floyd perform at the pyramids on the eve of the millennium?

People are stupid. I did not come up with that on my own. I had help. The world, entirely in love with itself, has come to condemn all things opposed to the fundamental aspects of "safe intelligence." Some might say that we are intelligent simply because we can communicate with a variety of complicated sounds and can recognize the indoctrinated difference between the moral and the immoral. Drop anything on its head long enough and you'll probably get the gist of what it's trying to say.

Unfortunation.

Men are pigs. It is universally acknowledged that all men are just looking for one thing: **sex**.

I couldn't agree more.

Females, considered by experts to be far more mature than men, have been cheated out of millennia of consequence-free clam baking. The end of the world aside, to all things a backlash. Take feminism. In the years leading up to the end of the world a great many women were prancing around in revealing tops and tight little skirts. Most of them believed that such attire should not diminish the respect that they should receive as women. That's the problem with having your cake and eating it too, I suppose. I would love nothing more than to walk around wearing a shirt with a giant arrow pointing downwards, but I have this strange feeling that most people would take it as some kind of sexual suggestion rather than an attempt to infer one's final destination. The ability of the standard human being to realize that most things aren't literal is next to none. So why, in the face of such knowledge, do people play such ridiculous games? Nothing better to do, I suppose. At least women know what men want. Mostly they want sex. Sex and relative silence. It's not their fault that women have skipped several steps in the evolutionary ladder, now is it? Were it so simple for women then I highly doubt that men would have ever been given the chance to take control of this planet. Instead, women would balk at the notion of using sex as a control mechanism. They would simply use the other thing that they seem to have in abundance. An entirely unique and irrational adaptation of common sense. This, of course, would divert the connection between sex and singular devotion towards the unexplored regions of sex as a sport, leaving men either a) too tired to cause trouble or b) too hungry to.

That resolved, we are left with sex's primary function in nature: procreation. The most powerful weapon of all. Despite what you might think, there is no greater force on the planet than the deliberate multiplication of a people. History is filled with examples of sexually minded warfare, as it would be altogether boring if nations of conquest were to have gone to the trouble of defeating their enemies only to turn around and go home. Back in the good

that the reason blood is coming out of your six-year-old's ears and nose is because he has some superpower connection with the family dog. It's safe to say that on several occasions my mother barely escaped being sent to an asylum.

As the years passed my connection with the dog grew stronger. I began to resent the dog a little. I felt cheated somehow because she was a terrier and not something menacing like a German shepherd or a Doberman. There's nothing more terrifying than seeing a twelve-pound ball of scraggly white and brown fur flying at you from out of nowhere, despite what Monty Python might lead you to believe. Even worse, I think it scared the dog more than any of my victims. By this time it wasn't much fun teleporting the dog onto the roof or making it fly around the room. Her eyes were also starting to cloud over, because of cataracts. But, as I was to discover, not all my powers had revealed themselves to me. On my twelfth birthday I discovered that I could hear using the dog's ears. Quite satisfied that I would never have to attend school again for the rest of my life, I began to grow my hair out and decided to live in the forest.

It's safe to say that I got into a lot of trouble during those years. There wasn't anything said about me that I didn't know. With my secret weapon, I became a shadowy figure sought after like some ancient oracle by the kids of my neighbourhood. Some people even doubted my existence, claiming that it was all

old days soldiers were often promised rape and pillage as reward. This was done for a number of reasons, two of them being: a) to ensure that your men were contented and realized that you, their leader, wanted them to be so, and b) to impregnate local women, forcing them to give birth to illegitimate children that would, if all went to plan, ultimately lead to the complete disappearance of the aforementioned conquered peoples, leaving a unified realm for the conqueror's heirs. It rarely all worked out, of course, but on occasion it did leave lasting impressions. The problem with such an undertaking is time. To see something such as the deliberate "breeding out" of a people come to fruition one must ensure that the people in question remain conquered long enough to be "bred out." It is far easier to wipe out a people than breed them out. It's just nowhere near as fun is all.

If you stop to consider the implications of time (and the ability of mankind to spread like anthrax through a dairy field) you'll come to realize that nature has always had time in abundance. Nature has mastered time, as it has existed long enough to have become intimate with the forms and functions of necessity as they apply to perpetual endlessness. Thus, it is only a matter of time until nature itself uses this weapon against her inhabitants. The world will one day become too small to offer separation and, as the globe shrinks, the inevitable union of all peoples will occur. One day, in a future that neither you nor I can possibly imagine, the world will be filled with a single people. And knowing full well that you can change the clothes but not the man, we will have no choice but to look to the stars in hopes of finding someone else's ass to kick. If anything, predictable we will always be.

The Universe Of One.

One can attain immortality through one's own children. That's not to say that things always work out as planned. Just that they work.

The years sped like clouds in wrathful passing. Last year she was twenty-five, this year she's forty-two. Somewhere along the way she encountered a man. And then, some years later, they had a child. And then, some years after that, the man left. It is not unlike men to leave. Parents die slow deaths so that their young might rally in their stead and get a little back for their sake. Some men, the good ones, know the difference between aiding in this principle and foolishly battling against it. But it is not unlike men to leave.

In the mornings she would often find herself staring at the seat of her chair, contemplating the years she had spent sitting in it. The carefree days of hoping to be a cruise ship events coordinator were far away. Here she painted coral and the word MAUI. Somewhere else, presumably in MAUI, tourists purchase the coral and send it to the people back home that they care little for.

She named her son Jack. She had always liked that name. She did not know that it was actually John. She did not know a great many things. She was lucky.

When Jack was born, his father, who had also worked at the factory, accidentally dropped him. The boy tumbled from his grasping hands to the floor and sustained massive head injuries. From that day on Jack became what professionals like to call *special*. Jack's father left, afraid he would kill the boy by accident in the future, or so the story went. Jack never did learn to speak like normal people. He never did learn to swear or talk about girls with his mates. He had no mates. He was special. Special people only have friends on specific days of the week, depending on the state of health care. One life, no chair, and friends with union benefits.

The day that it happened she was doing what she always did. She was sitting painting coral. Water based paints were applied to the coral and then quickly brushed over to allow the natural white to highlight the ridges. Then she painted the letters blue and put the finished product in a box. The box was collected and taken to another table. And someone at that table glued a plastic dolphin onto it. And that's how it had been going on for almost thirty years. The day that it happened was no different.

That morning Jack hadn't eaten. Some days he ate, some days he didn't. It depended on his mood. The *friends of special people* rarely tried to push the matter. If he didn't want to eat then they didn't bother trying to make him. They went back to playing cards and let him sit in his wheelchair, staring out the window. On that particular afternoon Jack's eyes closed and never opened again. His mother, to whom Jack was everything, was most likely painting coral when her son slipped quietly away. Perhaps Jack had no comprehension concerning the ramifications of mortality and his part in it.

A friend of mine once told me that *special* people were not *special* at all. That they were, by her reckoning, cognizant disciples of humanity come to test the waning compassion of man.

Jack was not discovered by the *friends of special people*. They thought he was sleeping. His mother walked into the room, ran her fingers through his hair, and realized that he was cold. And she was left there, alone to rediscover the horrible truth. *It is not unlike men to leave.*

One day, not so long ago, the world came to an end. A woman stands on

a hoax. But that didn't stop the never-ending numbers of pilgrims that sought me out in my forest sanctuary. They would comb the woods during the summer months, bringing me gifts of Kool-Aid and grape Hubba Bubba. Life was indeed all that I had dared to dream it would be.

I spent the better part of a decade living deep within the confines of the woods. I created an elaborate series of treetop dwellings modelled after the Swiss Family Robinson tree at Disneyland. Complex water pumps, folding staircases, and bamboo heating ducts were among many of my great accomplishments. The animals of the forest also came to know me and eventually proclaimed me the supreme emperor of their woodland domain.

But, by the age of nineteen, I knew that my time in the forest was coming to an end. One stormy night, following one of the most violent thunder and lighting events in B.C. history, my faithful super companion fell off a high rope bridge connecting two of my various huts and plummeted to her death. After spending her whole life flying around I'm sure she felt quite surprised by the fact that she couldn't actually do it herself. That's gotta be a bitch.

After finding the dog, I buried her remains and spent the better part of a week rigging my forest palace to self-destruct upon my departure. And then, bidding farewell to my animal subjects, I left the woods never to return. After that I pretty much just started a band and, well, here I am.

a beach, her feet brushed by the advancing and retreating water. In her hand she holds a piece of coral emblazoned with a word and a little dolphin. She is standing on that word. She is looking out to sea, talking to her son.

Homeless

I'm coming to you via remote. It's dark, and as I type this by the light offered up from the beaming headlights of passing cars, I am reminded of stranger times. Back in the primeval age of drunken consciousness when all things seemed do-able and everything was botched. All those years of near-perfect disaster have come rushing back to me as I pull my sleeping bag close around my shoulders and roll down the window to get some air. There isn't anything more glorious than lying in the back seat of a rented Ford Explorer. Especially when I consider that it's worth more than what my parents paid to build their house. But in defense of the truck, it does have four-wheel drive. That would have come in handy, I suppose, since Dad built the house on a swamp.

This morning I brushed my teeth and washed up at a gas station. There was a line-up, so I sat there slowly sipping a bad cup of coffee and tried to look somewhat cheerful about the entire affair. This half-ass attempt was, of course, prompted by the fact that I was the only one in line that had a brand new sport-utility vehicle parked ten feet away. But, to my credit, I'm a rock musician and looking like reheated shit was working to my advantage. This made those around me feel at ease and led to numerous conversations about the ever-inflating costs of Aqua Velva, shoe polish, and cooking sherry.

That aside, it was a decent morning altogether. Because there ain't nothing like hanging out with a bunch of guys that remember what the world was like when man had yet to walk on the moon and those in it weren't wise to the fun and games of using social erosion as a limitless excuse.

Leonard Cohen may have indirectly summarized such remnants of our beguiling past as beautiful losers. And that really pisses me off. Primarily because I didn't coin the phrase and, secondarily, because they made me feel as if I'd missed something valuable. It's one thing to deliberate hopelessness in the pages of some beat poet hard cover collector's edition. It is entirely something else to witness those who can convince themselves of hopefulness faced with its impossibility. Perhaps, if you're so inclined, you might buy someone with nothing left to lose a bad cup of coffee and figure out what it is that we've been taking for granted all this time.

To hear some of the gas station boys tell it you'd think that we were intended to roam unhindered and unhunted. Maybe that's why the aboriginal peoples had it so good before we introduced them to liquor and stole their land. I dunno. I can't really make that kind of a comparison when I'm whip-

The Handbook

Rule 1: Everybody gets a shit kicking.

Maybe just to ensure that you don't spend your life thinking you're better than those who get shit-kicked every day of theirs.

Rule 2: Morality extends no further than acceptability.

You will go as far as you're willing to go. One man's evil is another man's amusement park.

Rule 3: Ignorance belittles those around you more than it does yourself.

Ignorance and the Ebola virus are comparable in three respects:

1] They're both invisible

2] They're both infectious

3] And they both kill

Rule 4: Infinity is unimaginable. So imagine

ping around in a brand new S.U.V. And even though I often wonder if any of the great spirits know my mind I would never be presumptuous enough to assume that they really give a shit. Not anymore. Not after all this. Back seats are uncomfortable. Reading that back I have just realized that **unhunted** is not a real word. It damn well should be.

This evening I discovered, to my simultaneous delight and embarrassment, that the back seats fold down and allow you to use the rear cargo area for a variety of things. Sleeping is one of them. A short list of others would include: *1] small fondue get-togethers 2] nothing larger than a threesome 3] mousetrap 4] smoking meats, fish, and other seafoods 5] a blind for hunting water fowl 6] using the vehicle as a getaway device if engaged in rifle hunting anything besides water fowl 7] bullshitting thousands of people on a monthly basis via the internet.*

I've always dreamed of living in an RV. I can see it all now—satellite, a big screen, bunk beds, and an ever-expanding front and back yard. Willie Nelson's got it right. He lives in a huge motor home. And all those girls he's loved before, well, they've been inside it.

But that's not to say that I wouldn't love to settle down one day and do all those things that one is expected to do around my age. You know, the big equation of life. It looks something like this:

$$M + Wf + H + S.U.V. + Dt = K + MD + C.A.O.A$$

Now if you're wondering what all that means then I'll run you through it. M stands for MAN or ME (substitute W for M if you're a female). Wf would stand for "wife" (or husband, though you might want to change that to Hd. For those out there that enjoy fast cars and big diamond thingies you might consider just using a $). H is for HOUSE. S.U.V., as used earlier, stands for SPORT-UTILITY VEHICLE. You'll need one to look the part. Minivans will also do. Dt stands for DEBT. Debt is what you get in when you accumulate the first three parts of the equation. Added together, these five factors result in the following: K is obviously for kids (unless you happen to have a thing for collecting rare Kraftwerk vinyl). MD would symbolize MORE DEBT. This is one thing in life that most people can count on. There will always be more debt. The fact that you now have kids just makes it more and more like a landslide. You'll begin to have dreams about falling off cliffs and balconies and landing on huge spikes. And finally we come to C.A.O.A which stands for COPIUS AMOUNTS OF ADVIL. You can substitute another pain reliever for Advil if you prefer something else. And that, friends, is the equation of life.

But I'm not so sure I'm geared up for it. I've always hoped to meet a woman that might plan a bank heist with me and be prepared to do the time if we got caught. After ten or twenty years we could try it again. If we get away with it then we could bum around a country with no extradition treaties until we were forced to return and do it again.

And I'm not talking about some hack job either. I'm talking about a skillfully planned and executed theft that may or may not include hostages, result in causing bodily harm and/or sacrificing a team member. That's the kind of woman I'm looking for. But *women like that don't exist*. Not ones that would do the whole thing wearing a Budweiser bikini and a diving mask. God damn that would be sexy.

So I figure I'll do the RV thing for a while. I doubt I'll buy, but I wouldn't mind whipping around for six months living in various campgrounds. There's nothing better than the smell of cheap coffee and bacon and eggs when you're living in the middle of nowhere. In my entire life breakfast has never smelt as good as it does when I'm camping. Not that living in a luxury RV is camping.

Maybe I could use the RV as a mobile command centre and travel around recruiting a team for the bank heist. I could even booby-trap it like Max's Charger in *The Road Warrior*.

For now, I'm living in a sort-of-truck (I like that better than sport-utility vehicle) and trying my best to eat at least one green thing a day.

It horrifies my mother to no end. You'd think she could find something better to worry about than me not eating enough vegetables. My brother Chris spends one half of every year submerged under the surface of the ocean. He's a diver. You'd think that would occupy her. Instead I need to eat beets. Because beets are good for you. I agree, actually. I love beets, just not when my mom's around.

The other night at dinner she decided to tell my brother that she spent most of the '70s on Valium. Of course my brother and I were born in '71 and '72 (respectively), so it concerned him a little.

You know, she's still good. She had him going for a good half hour before she started laughing. I walked into the kitchen afterwards and she started laughing again.

"What made you think of Valium anyway?" I said.

"I don't know, maybe it was all that Valium I took," she said.

I'm not entirely sure whether or not my mother spent the entire decade on Valium. It seemed to me that she was kidding when she tortured my

reduction.

If heaven can be found in the sky's reflection off of calm waters then it's a shame that it's too polluted to swim in.

Rule 5: Prisons do not exist without capitulation.

Between the bars there is nothing. Look close enough and you'll realize that there's more nothing than bars.

Rule 6: Time is greater than suffering.

Those who we pity in our time pity us in another.

Rule 7: Power begets fools. Fools beget power.

Thinking that one can control that which cannot be controlled attracts fools like a magnet. Enough so that, in a short period of time, the epicenter becomes an institution of them.

Rule 8: Death is the working class's luxury.

Some people take vacations. Others spend their lives working towards a prolonged leave of absence.

Rule 9: Tomorrow is the cause of today's nothing.

The promises of tomorrow reduce the chances of today.

Rule 10: We do not exist.

Rule 11: Myths are nothing more than easy truths for idiots.

The need to offer easy answers to the general populace only reflects its inability to think independently.

Rule 12: Assume only that you know nothing.

brother with it, but when she said it to me I began to think there was some truth to it.

My family's known for being good bullshitters. It's the ability to con and confuse someone with complete crap to such an extent that they don't know if you're telling the truth anymore. The trick is to make sure there's enough truth mixed in with the bullshit that when you're spinning it you look like you believe it yourself.

It's not the story or how it's told. It's if your face is telling the same thing as your mouth. And that's how I became such a smart-ass. It's in the genes.

Everything you are came from somewhere else. Most of the time it takes people years to come to terms with the fact that a large part of their being is rooted in something undesirable. Take my family for instance. My dad's side are asses and my mom's are smart. Put the two together and you can see how I was afflicted with my current condition.

Luckily my old man is the black sheep of his family and an exception to the *"Rule Of Goods."* He's somewhat of a wise man. Next to the shopping-cart guy from Uridian 15 he's the wisest man I know.

But I digress. My original point is that you inherit certain things that have undesirable origins. I'm a smart ass because of an unlikely genealogical combination. Being a smart-ass is to be dualistic. To be one you must accept both parts. If you're going to be smart then you've got to deal with the fact that you're an ass as well. Sometimes you discover that you're more smart than ass. Most of the time it's the other way around. It took me a long time to realize that. But I finally did. In the back of a rented sort-of-truck no less.

I like outer space. I like it because we don't know a whole lot about it: a bullshitter's paradise. I could make up a whole load of crap about outer space right now and half of you would believe it.

So here's the outer space story then...

There once was a man who had a giant ship made out of cheese. It was cheddar cheese, the kind that's orange and so hard that it can cut glass. It made him unstoppable. All the other space pilots wanted to be him and all the ladies wanted him. He was a legend in his own time.

Until one day he came upon a huge flying toaster and learned that all things, at a specific temperature relative to their molecular composition, tend to liquify. This principle includes very hard cheeses. So the guy with the orange-cheese ship was no longer the king shit. The toaster ship guy was the king shit. And he was a legend in his own time. Because there's nothing tougher than a toaster ship. And all the space pilots wanted to be him and all the ladies wanted their muffins heated.

And then one day another guy with a ship that shot ice beams decided to do battle with the toaster guy. There was a huge fight and the ice ship won because every time he fired his ice beams at the toaster ship it would cloud over toaster-boy's windows and he couldn't see. Evaporation and condensation can be a bitch like that.

The toaster guy wasn't defeated because the ice beams were more powerful than his toaster ship. He lost because his windows fogged over and he flew into a huge asteroid and blew up. So the ice guy became a legend in his own time and all the space pilots wanted to be him and all the ladies went out and rented *9 1/2 Weeks*, and so on.

Until one day some wise-ass came along with a ship made completely out of vodka and kicked his ass. But instead of becoming a legend in his own time and banging every girl at the space station he just collected up the remnants of the ice man's ship and spent eternity drinking vodka sevens on the rocks. The truck goes back to the rental place on Friday morning and then I get on a plane and fly somewhere. Where exactly I'm not sure. It would seem that I rarely know the answer to that question anymore. And that's beginning to scare me. If you have any idea where it is that I'm going please drop me a line and fill me in. I'd love to know the future. Even if it's just the past all dressed up to make whatever comes next look good.

Within silences you will learn what you need to know.

The difference between knowing and assuming is vast. To assume is to fail miserably at acting intelligent enough to know when to keep your mouth shut.

Rule 13: The past is a minefield. Follow only those footsteps that do not end at the edge of large holes.

To ignore the past it is to prolong its mistakes.

Rule 14: The world is not your oyster.

Prying it open ruins your chances of putting it back.

Rule 15: No one remembers who you weren't. Just who you were.

The realization of your true self far out-

The Purple Switch.

In the recesses of our tiny heads there are a million rabbits flipping millions of switches. Each switch sends an impulse to the master rabbit who, in turn, flips one of seven larger switches that are located in his big bubble-dome control centre. Each of these switches is a different colour. Red, blue, green, yellow, white, black, and purple. These master switches send electronic impulses to different parts of your body, telling you what to do next.

Since the beginning of time, these seven primary switches have allowed the rabbit masters to perform their tasks. Each colour represents a specific body function or psychological domain. Red, for example, controls the emotional responses, while blue controls the subconscious. Of the seven switches, the rabbit masters commonly use five of them (red, blue, green, yellow, and white). It's a very rare thing for the black switch to be used. Even rarer is the purple switch. The purple one has never been used, so no one's quite sure what that one does.

The black and white switches are the most interesting of all the switches. The white switch controls the *good* you, while the black switch controls the *evil* you. Unlike the other switches, which allow the rabbit masters to activate specific functions themselves, the black and white switches serve the rabbit masters like communication conduits. When a rabbit master flips the white switch a message is sent to the internal representation of the good you. Unlike the internal representation of the evil you, the rabbit masters allow your good side free rein throughout your body because they're extremely helpful and often promote stability and goodwill. So when the white switch is thrown, the rabbit masters are just alerting your better half about something, not unlike a telephone call.

The black switch, on the other hand, operates more like a massive electronic pulse. Your inner evil is actually locked in a tiny little cage deep within your body. It can't escape from this cage, but it does have the ability to communicate with those working around it.

From time to time, it will convince some of your lesser rabbits to stage a revolt or do something to anger the rabbit master. When this happens the rabbit master flips the black switch, which shocks your evil quite severely. The strange thing about your evil self is that of all the things it convinces those lesser rabbits to do on its behalf, the most common is to coerce them into flipping the purple switch. This presents a very profound dilemma seeing that no one knows what the purple switch is for.

There are many rabbit masters that believe the purple switch has something to do with the ninety percent of your brain that is never used. Others contend that it's the death switch. One thing is for certain though: since the dawn of time, rule number one has always been *no matter what happens, the purple switch must remain in the 'up' position.* The rabbit masters obey. Since the beginning of time, no purple switch has ever been thrown. And no one ever talks about it, either. No one, that is, except for your evil self.

Since man first crawled out of the ocean and stood upright, your evil has always been locked in a cage and your good has always been allowed to run around as free as a bird. But that doesn't necessarily mean that they dislike each other. Quite the opposite. When your good isn't busy putting on motivational seminars for your little rabbits it can usually be found talking to your evil. They usually get along quite well. This most likely stems from the fact that they understand each other. Without one the other wouldn't exist. Without the good and evil selves the rabbits would just go about their work and that would be that. But someone decided it would be a riot to put those two extra little guys in there.

Most rabbit masters know that the good and the evil talk incessantly about the purple switch. What perplexes them is why they're always talking about it. Many rabbit masters wonder why one needs good and evil in the first place. Things would be much easier if both simply disappeared. It's not uncommon for rabbit masters to be suspicious.

The rules say that no one is allowed to enter the bubble-dome except for other rabbits, so they're obviously not planning an assault on the bubble-dome. Unless, that is, the good and the evil don't follow the rules.

Maybe your good self is the one telling your lesser rabbits to listen to your evil one. Maybe they both know that one is above suspicion and the other will always be viewed as guilty. But there's a possibility that they've been working together all this time. Which brings us back to the purple switch again. It is a complete mystery to everyone except whoever came up with the rules in the first place. But that just poses another problem altogether because no one knows who or what that is.

Your evil and your good selves know about the rules. They may have even read them once or twice. But that doesn't mean they believe in any of them. For all anyone knows they could be convinced that the rabbits wrote the rules and use them to keep things static. The rabbit masters, on the other hand, have never questioned the rules. The rules are unchangeable. If the rules say that the purple switch is not to be thrown, then they will never allow it to be

weighs the consequences of unpopularity.

Rule 16: Supreme beings are kind of like pets. They make you feel better when no one else will listen. Strangely enough, neither can respond.

The need for something more than yourself ultimately diminishes the need for yourself.

Rule 17: Freedom is just a word.

If freedom is fraught with regulations then why not just call it regulated freedom and stop trying to convince yourself otherwise.

Rule 18: The pressure of being has no remedy. Just placebos.

If guilt and fear were currencies then we would have all started our own religions to capitalize on them by now.

Rule 19: The truth is versed in versions, not nobility.

If the truth were noble we would never have bothered inventing a device that can evaporate an entire city in under a minute.

Rule 20: The future is x-rated.

You were expecting something else?

thrown. It doesn't matter that it interests your good and your evil so much. The rabbit masters know very well that they can't do anything about it themselves. No one's allowed in the bubble-dome except rabbits. That's the rule.

So for your whole life this endless dance continues deep within your body. The rabbits throw all those switches, which send messages to the rabbit masters. They, in turn, throw the master switches that determine your actions. And amongst all of that your good and your evil conduct themselves accordingly. It will continue on as such until you have passed on.

Turning The 2000 Clock

Time. Beyond the gods and their eternal houses of immaculate promise lies the fortitude of time and the undeniable realization that its effects are the only truths that are assured us. And to each of us there will always be a time that we are locked into, as if it were some secret survivor trapped within the wreckage.

I can recall, with surprising clarity, the life I led beneath the shadows of the atomic clock. Pressed hard against the cold tiled floors of a sixth-grade classroom grinning at the futility of surviving some nuclear baptism, the truths of time are evident. Lock-jawed to the wrists of millions we were terminally bound to, despite the countdown. No matter the endless plagues of madness that creep in and out of your day-to-day life. After everything, even the splitting of impossible tiny components, time will carry on. Which must lead most to wonder whether or not time existed before we gave it a proper name and some moving parts.

Somewhere, beyond the expanding universe, there must surely exist a bottomless well of time that has yet to be tampered with. It moves neither forward nor back. Undefined, it simply is.

And so, as our clocks march towards the birth of a new era of imbalances, I find myself amused by the myriad of predictions that have been tossed around like they possess even an ounce of reliability. If there is anything in this world that I'd enjoy more than witnessing the end of the world it would definitely have to be watching a world assume that it was coming to an end.

It wasn't too long ago that millions of us used to lament about whether or not some anxiety-ridden Russian sub skipper would snap and take matters into his own hands. Somewhere, deep within the frozen waters of the North Pacific, he would launch a heavy rain of molecular obedience and then simply slump in his chair as all those years of back tension seeped out of his body. He would retire to his quarters, rapt in wonderment of knowing the future, and sleep soundly for the first time since childhood. And as his slumber took hold the rest of us would awake to the paralyzing realization that the sunrise had come too early, as the futile droning of the emergency broadcast system played itself out in the background.

It always perplexed me that such a warning system should be based upon such an annoying sound. In the event of a nuclear attack I always thought it more appropriate for a calm voice to break the airwaves and repeat a single, solitary sentence: *Good morning sunshine, time to go.*

In the time it takes a fork to drop from your hand to the floor everything within a fifty-mile radius is liquified. Beyond that, everything is hit by a shock-wave and crushed like a beer can, not to mention spontaneously bursting into flames. So much for that important informational segment that's supposed to follow the dog-whistle portion of the broadcast. Thankfully, the dogs would make it to the minimum safe distance in time.

After living with the possibility of hell-fire raining from the sky, it baffles me to think that I would ever allow something as infantile as the disablement of a bank machine to get the better of me. Looking at the alternatives, I'd rather have all the computers in the world crash than have several hundred kilotons of sugar-coated plutonium sprinkled on my Raisin Bran.

The most recent doomsday scenario was almost desirable. All the computers seizing up in the first moments of the new millennium. No more phones to answer, no more answering machines to answer them for us. Planes, keeping with the extinction rate of their biological relations, plummeting from the skies, destroying numerous multiplexes, strip malls, and prefab townhouse complexes. Traffic lights worldwide going dark, leaving millions wondering who has the right of way. Billions will attempt to skip town for the countryside before realizing too late that gas station pumps, along with most things, don't work. Faced with this new and frightening dilemma, we would have been forced to turn to those countries too underdeveloped and impoverished to know the luxury of mechanized transport to teach us how to get from point A to point B. No more all-terrain vehicles. No more armoured transports. No more armour. Everything, and anything, that you've come to rely on would be gone.

There was a time when your entire financial life was kept within the safe confines of a tiny little booklet that was updated by hand (human hands, no less). Little good your bankcard would do you then. We would be forced to return to the barter system. Which means that your two-thousand-dollar VCR is worthless and that old bike you haven't used since 1978 is worth its weight in gold (gold being four cans of beans, a loaf of bread, and possibly a couple sticks of Juicy Fruit).

"Too far, too fast," my grandfather used to say all the time. Born in 1913, he used to drive a horse-drawn delivery carriage when he was a milkman. He was in the air force in World War II, following which he graduated to a delivery truck. If he were still alive and in the delivery business today most people from his childhood probably would have assumed that he'd be driving some form of flying delivery vehicle.

According to most works of science fiction from days past we were supposed to be living on the moon by now and eating steaks in pill form. But that's not the case. Instead we've decided to turn to increasing our conveniences. And though that might somehow lead you to assume that being the masters of our own destiny should encompass both possibilities, I can assure you that one deters the other.

As we expand our ability to achieve greater levels of convenience we decrease our seldom-used ability of actually progressing. Instead of going back to the moon repeatedly, we turned our attention to making television remote controls more difficult to operate than spacecraft. We haven't been back to the moon in quite a while. I wonder why that is? Maybe someone thought *Done that. But you know what. I sure do wish there was a universal controller that operated my TV, VCR, and stereo all at the same time.* That's not to say that there aren't a million things that couldn't be better right here at home.

Who needs to go to the moon when you can starve to death in the very same country that brought you such excitements as the Apollo project?

But thankfully Sega came out with a new platform because things in the home-entertainment world were starting to get stale. Just like all that unused bread that we heap into dumpsters at the end of every week. Oh my, a guilty First-Worlder indeed Mr. Good.

The future's always been tricky like that. It's the one thing that everyone strives to prepare for but can never really take when it arrives. The future is time's true face. Because like time it remains undetermined and wholly represented by nothing more than a word and the unshakable fact that it's lying in wait, spiced with rumour. Time is time because without a name it would only be recognized by the fact that, throughout most of the world, light appears every morning and disappears every night. So it's only logical that it has a name. Add to that the fact that we've decided to chop each day up into a variety of different representations of time, and you've got predictability. There will always be a three o'clock after two o'clock. Human beings love that sort of thing. So instead of just living our lives not knowing when McDonald's stops serving breakfast, we thought it prudent to make sure that we could get there in time to enjoy their sausage and egg McMuffins.

The future, which is nothing more than our concept of regulated time waiting to occur, is necessary to ensure that you can loosely predict when you're probably going to need to start using Depends. Age reflects the effects of time, so it's safe to assume that *in the future* you'll look and feel older. But is that time, or is it nothing more than the effects of the earth's gravity coupled with the inescapable wear and tear of our body-machines?

Without the future represented, we would be able to continually enjoy those things that are locked into a specific section of the year. Like the fact that the football season begins in August and ends in May. Without having compartmentalized the future, no one would know when these things were supposed to end. Thus, Premiership Football all year round. I like that. I like it a lot.

The future is quite a personal affair, making any attempt to reflect on its impending state quite pointless. Because you and I will always see it differently, as will our children. The future is nothing more than what you think it should be. And the disappointing feature about that is that it rarely becomes all that you hoped it would.

When I was a boy I used to pace around the living room at night because the thought of being vaporized by some horrific device of incomprehensible destruction loomed over me like a wounded tiger. Being an avid student of 20th century history I was always cognizant of the adage that to ensure peace one prepares for war. But somehow, at that age, the truth of it mattered little to me. My entire childhood, as may be the case with some of you, was spent wondering just how stupid we could be given the opportunity. It's easy to rationalize the numbers behind such idiocy. Victory means very little when all is lost in the attempt. I used to wonder if the Russians knew that. Just a foolish boy, sometimes I lost sight of the fact that all people, in their own way, knew that had we been dumb enough to do it then we would have become that which we'd spent numerous millennia trying to convince ourselves that we weren't.

The Ditches On A Long Road Home

You will be dead much longer than you will be alive. This is the truth of things. Better get used to the idea. The lives of men and women, cats and dogs, birds and fish are merely hiccups in an endlessness that will never be fully realized. You are here now and will be gone in some years, months, perhaps even days or hours. The execution of this plan will never change, despite the fact that you will do your best to convince yourself otherwise. You merely feed off the scraps of words and wares consolidated by those that came before you. You are a thing void of structural integrity. Like anything built or born, you will eventually succumb to either the weight of the world or the weight of walking it. This is the only thing you ever need come to terms with. That eventually you will be lost. They will lose you. You will be forgotten and never heard from again. And no one will ever know the story that was your life.

We started out standing up. Crawling, though commonly misconstrued as a mode that precedes upright maneuvers, came later. To everything there is an unseen direction that is both unfelt and unimagined. Some might call it fate. Others, with less aptitude for things philosophical, might call it dumb luck. I don't know that we ever thought it anything more than our lives playing out within the expected parameters. Maybe, in some other place, we would have possessed the smarts to know the difference. But the streets of our youth were paved with a sort of numbness that tricked the mind into believing that the world was something other than a globe that truly existed if one had the gumption to just keep walking. It was as if we were East Berliners, confronted by both a wall and an outer force that was greater than ourselves combined. So we remained there, walking those streets, idiots of impeccable loathing. And, as a product of that place and time, I'm lost for the kind of language that one always hopes will offer a momentous beginning.

It happened rather suddenly. It happened because everything needs to begin somewhere and, without being able to pinpoint that beginning, how is one to ever know when it began at all. There are those beginnings that creep up on you slowly and there are those that adhere to the usual guidelines. In the case of this story, it was neither. Like I said, it happened rather suddenly, which means that it was neither slow nor traditional. It just happened.

Picture a set of concrete stairs located behind a large school. On those stairs hundreds of kids spent countless hours of their lives smoking, drinking,

and whatnot. Most of the time there was mundane conversation. Some of the time there was just silence. It was during one such silence that Bibs Stettner's body came plummeting from the roof of the school to impact on the landing at the foot of those stairs. At the time there were some fifty or sixty kids out there and to them it was as if his body simply fell from the sky and slammed into the concrete. And no one said a word. Not because they weren't troubled by the fact that Bibs had just killed himself but because, for the first time in the history of those stairs, the silence was something other than mundane.

When the police came to gather up Bibs's body I just happened to be walking through the doors that led to those stairs. I had been in class, off in some other world, not paying any attention as usual. It consumed me as I walked through the halls, deafening me to the whispers of Bibs's suicide. So I walked outside, cigarette in mouth, lighter to cigarette, and found myself directly in front of his half-covered body. He was lying there looking at me. I lit the cigarette and blinked. He did not. I've seen a lot of strange things in my life. But the strangest of them all would have to be standing over my brother's dead body wondering what I was going to tell our mother when I got home. "Bibs is dead and I failed math again." It seemed to me then that my big brother was still looking out for me, even in death. Thanks Brian. That was his real name.

There I was, cigarette in hand, gazing into my brother's dead eyes. Everyone on the stairs, realizing that I had not yet learned of his death, suddenly started shouting at the authoritative figures in my vicinity to cover his body. One of the cops decided to yell at me instead. So he said *"Get away from there, kid!"*

So I did.

There are several advantages to having your brother hurl himself off of a roof. 1: You get to leave school early. 2: You are not expected to return to school until you've had enough time to overcome your grief. There are several disadvantages as well. 1: Your parents get divorced because one's an alcoholic and the other blames them for their son's suicide. 2: Your father decides to move to Oregon and your mother's too hammered most of the time to support you so you get sent to live with your grandmother.

I spent the better part of three weeks at my Nan's before deciding to go back. Most of that time I spent messing around with a girl named Penelope Fynn. At the time I didn't see anything particularly wrong with fooling around with my dead brother's girlfriend. I do now, of course, but I was much hornier then. I never really knew what made Penny seek me out at my Nan's. But she did.

I returned to school on a Monday. I remember that only because of the song and the fact that I agreed with it. Besides it being a Monday it was also the last week of the school year, which meant that come Friday I had nothing to do but get loaded and sit around at the pool with my friends. Back then that's what kids did during the summer where I grew up. They hung out at pools. If you think about it it's a rather brilliant place for teenagers to go. Everyone's already half naked. Who could ask for more? Our pool had pretty much everything you could ask for in an outdoor aquatic facility. A concession stand, a huge grass lawn behind the diving boards where most people spent their time rather than in the water, and it was conveniently located next to a large park—which meant that if you wanted to get some privacy, for whatever, you could. The lawn area behind the boards even had fire pits and picnic tables. It makes me wonder why any of us ever bothered to go home at night. During my final week at school I spent most of my time daydreaming about a lazy summer wasted lying around on that lawn. That, and trying my best not to grab Penny's ass in the hallways for fear of someone noticing.

John William Wick was, at the time, my best friend. He was also my brother's best friend. We shared a best friend. Wick didn't go to school with us though. He started going to university when he was sixteen. He was a mathematical genius. Not exactly the wisest man I've ever met, but a genius by and by. Two days after his seventeenth birthday he was offered a job by a huge aerospace firm. The job paid $250,000 a year to start. It would take my father almost twenty years to make that kind of money. Had Wick lived to actually start the job, I'm sure I would have enjoyed driving around with him in some fancy sports car and hanging about with supermodels and strippers and such. But Wick drowned in the pool that summer instead and I would be denied all the things that come along with having a wealthy, genius friend. It's my lot in life.

That summer Wick had decided to spend July in the neighbourhood and August at some math camp. It was called CALCULOT, if you can believe it. Maybe Wick would have been Merlin had he not died. He always wanted to be Merlin. Nonetheless, we started our summer by going to the mall on one of our quarterly shoplifting sprees. You'd be surprised at how easy it is to clothe yourself for an entire summer in a little less than thirty minutes of breakneck theft. The fact that Penny came along only added to our success. Penny was rather beautiful, you see. While she had the clerks and salesmen swooning over her, Wick, Billy, and I robbed the place blind. Two knapsacks, one magnet for removing security disks, and one lookout. That's all it took. There used to be four of us, of course, but obviously Bibs was preoccupied with the immensity of death. And as I said earlier, you are dead much longer than you are alive. So it must be quite an undertaking.

The spoils of our excursion were plentiful and spirits were as high as could be expected. Billy and Wick came away with numerous items of worthlessness, as usual, and I ended up getting a couple of new shirts, some shorts, a clock radio, two records, and a pair of sneakers.

You know, I've always loved that particular name for shoes. Think about it: sneakers. It makes you wonder who exactly will be sneaking and why. Perfect for a guy like me who, on average, spends more time sneaking through life than not. Maybe that's why I still wear them, even as an adult. Then again, maybe I should just grow up and get some loafers. I could steal them in my sneakers. That's what I do for a living, you see. I'm what they like to call a career criminal. And they wonder how people like me get started. It's called the economics of poverty.

So that's how the summer of 1985 kicked off. No different than the summer of 1984. Except that Bibs was dead, of course. Actually, that's a pretty major difference, isn't it. Thinking back on it I'm always reminded of something that Billy often said that summer. He'd say "if Bibs was here he'd know what to do." It was true, you see. My older brother had a gift for getting the rest of us out of tight spots. I remember one time when we were down at the markets and some drunk bikers decided to give us a little scare. Instead of keeping his mouth shut Billy started to mouth off. He was a rather lippy guy. But Billy was big for his age, so he could usually back it up. But not on this particular occasion. The bikers started to get rather angry and came to the conclusion that the best thing for our Billy was a good beating. So that's what they started at. And that's when my brother's talent kicked in. While the bikers were attempting to pin Billy to the ground, Bibs went over to their bikes and started pushing them over, one by one. This angered the bikers, but it also meant that their attentions were now focused on my brother. Billy, knowing what Bibs was up to, bolted, at top speed, down the street. Dumbfounded, I just stood there like an idiot. My brother, on the other hand, received the beating of a lifetime. He spent two weeks in the hospital, though he never bothered to tell the police who had put him there. Some months later we were all at a party at the ravine and a biker came over to my brother, patted him on the back, and gave him a beer. "You're alright kid," was all he said. That was Bibs's way of making sure we were alright.

Like I said, Billy Quon was a lippy guy. He was the only Chinese guy in our neighbourhood. His family owned the only Chinese-food restaurant in our neighbourhood, chose to move there because they figured it was safer than downtown. This, of course, was not true. The downtown core of the city included Chinatown.

As it turned out, Billy became an instant target when he moved to the neighborhood simply because no one had ever been given the opportunity to use something like race against someone. Those were the rules, you understand. It didn't matter if you had big ears, bad skin, a funny name, stuttered, or were Chinese. Something's going to be used against you if it can be. It's a test of character and nothing more. Billy's hard times ended, of course, the first time he cleaned the clock of someone that chose to racially slur him. After that he was cool by us. You see, it never really mattered much to me or Bibs or Wick. To us Billy was just another kid who had to go through the motions before he could be let in. And like everyone else, I suppose, he got his fair share. These days things just don't work like that. And you wonder why no one knows who they are anymore.

Penny, unlike Billy, was not a loudmouth. She didn't need to be. She was beautiful. Beautiful girls don't really need to say much. They can get what they want by flipping their hair around and such. Penny knew this, so that's what she did. My brother fell prey to her hair-flipping in 1984 and remained her captive until his death. I don't think that Penny ever thought of Bibs as her boyfriend though. He was just someone to hang around with. Penny was very much like that, you see. All about adventures and scandalous behaviour and such. She thought it made her mysterious. Turns out it made her crazy. A crazy slut. I could never quite figure out why she chose to mess around with me after Bibs died. She was always closer to Wick, I had thought. I would discover later that she had remained close with Wick during our time together. The tragic thing about it was that Wick truly loved the girl. Penny was incapable of love. Being the genius that he was it must have seemed like the world was coming to an end when Penny finally told him that she had been sleeping with me. I would never get the chance to tell him that I was sorry though. After a night filled with the strangest occurrences of my life he would drown himself in the pool. He was not an altogether wise man, as I said. Just good with numbers.

But at the beginning of that summer we were both in the dark, Billy missed Bibs, and Penny was busy with two new lovers. No one was dead, save my brother, and the possibilities seemed endless to me. It was some weeks after our shoplifting extravaganza that Billy found the briefcase in the bushes behind the pool. He had been messing around with Karen Walsh again. And for Billy it was a rather difficult affair. Mr. Walsh, it seems, really hated Chinese people.

Some might say that the briefcase was the root of all evil. I disagree. Penny Fynn's reputation was the root of all evil. They say that hindsight is twenty-twenty and will kill you every time. If so, I wish it would hurry up and get me.

So there I was, or we were, sitting on the lawn at the pool. Penny was having a great time rolling about on her front with her top off, teasing every male in a 500 foot radius with her rather large tits. I was sitting there munching on Popeye cigarettes—before they changed the magic formula and made them taste like shit. Wick, who had opted to sleep in that afternoon, was not present. Billy came marching out of the bushes with Karen Walsh, jumps the fence, and comes strolling over with this thing. It was an odd sight, I must say. After all, Billy was wearing blue Adidas shorts and nothing else. Add a briefcase and a girl that hasn't realized that she's got her bikini bottoms on insideout and you've got yourself one strange picture. Sitting down, Billy smiles up at Karen as she heads towards the change rooms and then turns to me with this look on his face like the world's not really a bad place. This makes me worry, of course. Billy, who is never without his rigid façade, does not smile near anyone who might take it as a sign of weakness. I'm a little confused. Then it dawns on me that he's got a briefcase on his lap. It had not escaped Penny.

"Where'd you find that thing?" she said.

Trying to do his best not to make a big deal about it, Billy doesn't look at her directly and responds, "I think we should go to Wick's place."

This is odd. I'm beginning to wonder if Billy hasn't done something wrong. But neither of us argue with him. Penny, because she loved that sort of thing, and me because, well, that's what I did. I went along.

So we left the pool and walked the seven or so blocks to Wick's house. As usual, neither of Wick's parents were home. His father was at work. His mother was out screwing our gym teacher. The two had become close during the Cub Scouts Father-Son camping trip of 1980 that Mr. Wick was unable to attend. So Mrs. Wick decided to take her son instead. The rest is suburban melodrama.

Wick was still in bed, though alert enough to notice the briefcase the second that Billy came through his bedroom door. As it was, his superpowers were focused on Billy's briefcase and, to a lesser extent, Penny's briefcase.

"What the hell is that?"

"What's it look like. It's a fucking briefcase, isn't it." Billy replied, sitting down on the edge of the bed.

"I realize that it's a fucking briefcase, moron. What are you doing with it?"

We sat there for the better part of a half hour listening to Billy tell us how he came across the briefcase. Billy and Karen had decided to venture further into the bushes than usual because they had been victims of several intrusions in the past. They walked a while and found a decent spot. So—yada-yada-yada, oh-god, oh-Billy, oh-Karen, and all that, and then OUCH! What the...and voilà, one slightly beat-up briefcase is discovered. By that point Billy wasn't about to continue with things. There was, after all, a briefcase sticking in his back. According to Billy, there were also a lot of pine needles sticking in his ass as well—a point that he mentioned several times.

I was relieved. I had been worried that he'd stolen it from someone. Such actions were not beyond Billy, you understand. Having studied it a little during the walk over I had come to the conclusion that it couldn't have been there for very long. It looked new in spots, even though it had been stained by the dirt. As the story came to an end, Billy hoisted the thing up onto the bed. We all looked at each other as if something truly grand was hidden in it, like money or plane tickets to Hawaii or something. But that was not the case. Had it been money I doubt that Billy would have bothered to tell any of us about it. He would have kept it for himself. But that wasn't the case. There wasn't any money in the briefcase. When Billy threw the top back I remember feeling curious but, at the same time, quite worried for some reason. It contained several handguns.

Everyone's reaction to the guns was different. Penny thought it was quite cool. I said nothing. Billy just sat there looking like he'd discovered the atom bomb and was overly anxious to use it. And Wick, well, Wick was furious.

"What the fuck are you thinking, bringing these things into my house!" he said. Billy's excitement vanished immediately.

"Jesus Christ Billy! These things were obviously put there for a reason! Don't you think that whoever put them there had the intention of going back to get them?" Again, Billy said nothing.

This was where Wick's rather enormous brain started to produce harmful emissions. Billy would never have thought things through enough to have reached that conclusion, let alone suspect that the guns had been buried there for a reason. Of course it all seems rather obvious now but, as I've said, we were young. But that didn't stop Wick from launching into a lengthy attack on Billy. That was Wick's specialty. He operated at a world-class level when it came to demeaning others.

The abuse lasted long enough for Wick to start repeating himself while Billy just sat in silence. Had it been anyone else, Billy would have levelled them without question. For as I've said, Billy was rather large for his age. But Billy would never dare take a shot at Wick. It just wasn't done. People were afraid of Wick. Unlike Billy, Wick usually detested thugs and their brutish methods of resolve. Wick never bothered defending himself if, and when, he was faced with brute force. Instead, while he was getting a thrashing, he would utter one simple sentence: *You had better kill me.* The last time I heard Wick say it he was being pummelled by Darren Politnakov. Two weeks later Darren's German shepherd was found cut into four separate pieces in a garbage can in his carport. On top of the dismembered canine there was a note. It read: *I told you.* So that's why no one bothered with Wick. He was, at the worst of times, far more diabolic than most people dare even consider. Billy knew this. So he said nothing. He loved his dog too much.

The belittling ended only when Penny intervened. She thought there was no point in belittling Billy because he had already removed the briefcase. She offered a solution to the dilemma that was satisfactory to all involved. She told Billy to put the briefcase back. I must admit, it wasn't like Penny to make such a suggestion. Usually she was the one who enjoyed seeing just how far something dangerous could be taken before it got out of hand. Handguns, it seems, were the exception.

We left Wick's soon after and returned to the pool. The plan was to wait on the lawn while Billy returned the briefcase and then hang around for a bit to make sure that no one had noticed anything. But by the time we reached the pool, Billy had let his imagination get to him. He convinced himself that the owner of the briefcase would come after him. He believed they would track him down for taking their guns. And he wouldn't shut up about it. I had never seen Billy that scared before. He was actually convinced, due to Wick's belittling insights on the matter, that something rather bad was going to happen to him because of it.

Wick, who loved to crush people psychologically, just made matters worse. Instead of telling Billy to shut up, or to not worry about it, he decided to fan Billy's fears. So we sat there, on the lawn, for an hour or so listening to Billy freak out. And all the while Wick kept injecting little snippets of unrealized terror into Billy's fantasies until Billy refused to go back into the woods at all.

Penny and I were beginning to construct scenarios of our own. Maybe they'd find out who was with Billy and deal with the rest of us just as harshly as Billy was certain they'd deal with him. The only one who didn't seem worried was Wick, who was having too much fun freaking everyone out. It placed him in a position of control, and Wick loved it.

It was finally decided that both Billy and Wick would go into the bushes together and put the case back. Billy felt more comfortable going back in with Wick, and Wick wanted to make sure that Billy didn't screw up and put the briefcase in the wrong place. The two of them got up, jumped the fence, and headed into the woods. This left Penny and I waiting on the lawn. Neither of us spoke. We waited there for the better part of twenty minutes before Penny decided to go in and see what was taking them so long.

At the beginning of this story I made reference to fate. Having spent years trying to reconstruct that afternoon in my head, and subconsciously scanning the pool grounds for a particular face, I have come to the conclusion that this entire story was the result of nothing more than perspective. After spending the better part of ten years in search of a reason the only thing I've discovered is that sometimes things happen for no particular reason whatsoever.

Penny was gone for about twenty minutes before Billy resurfaced at the fence. Of course, by that point, Billy was happier than a pig in shit because he'd put the briefcase back without complication. He had a big, shit-eating grin on his face. He flopped down onto the lawn beside me and proceeded to babble on about a variety of things while I sat there wondering where Penny and Wick were. Ten minutes later they reappeared. It was right about then that I figured I'd missed something because the two of them were in hysterics. Billy slapped me on the knee and said rather loudly:

"Oh ya, I forgot. You've gotta go in there. Penny found something that'll crack you up."

Hesitantly I got to my feet but was curious.

Billy rolled over on his back and yelled, "Oh would you just go. It's not going to bite," after which he just started laughing.

I went over and jumped the fence. Wick, who was trying his best not to double over, passed me.

"You are not going to believe this," Wick said.

Thanks For Flying With Us!

Before takeoff please ensure that your seat belt is securely fastened and that your seat and table tray are in the upright and locked positions. None of these precautions will prevent bodily harm in the event of an emergency, but may give you a false sense of being very important things to do. Such importance will provide you with the appearance that such details are serious enough to comply with as they might actually have a bearing on whether you live or die in the event of a crash. Several tons of burning metal and fuel aside, your tray table could always cut you in half if you should happen to survive plummeting from thirty thousand feet trapped in a flaming ball of fire. Ensuring that your seat is fully forward will also allow the person sitting behind you to perish with sufficient leg room. For those passengers flying in our business and first class cabins, you may now commence doing whatever you like.

In the unlikely event of an emergency, please try to remain calm. It's unlikely that two to five seconds will be long enough for you to feel real terror. During a slow, burning descent we ask that you remain in your seat. You might consider listening to some soothing new-age music in such circumstances using your complimentary headset (channel 4). In the event of a water landing please remember to follow the lights on the cabin floor to the nearest exit. If, in a panic, you forget that your seat cushion was supposed to be your

By that point I'd forgotten about the briefcase and everything else I'd been thinking about. It seemed that in a split second, our summer was back to normal. I walked over to Penny, who led me into the bushes by the hand.

The hilarious event in the woods that day involved two people that we knew, Tammy Richards and Mike Chatlin, one of those inseparable couples that everyone loves to hate. When Penny and I came upon them we immediately realized what all the fuss was about. The two of them were stuck. But what made it truly hilarious was that Mike was positioned behind Tammy and they were scrambling around like some deformed crab trying to break free of one another. I must admit, it remains one of the funniest things I've ever seen.

It all seemed resolved, but it wasn't. I have spent years trying to remember who was at the pool that day. I remember certain members of our school's defensive line being there. Most importantly a boy named Rick Zelleniski. Penny had turned down his advances on a number of occassions. Rick was the type of guy who acted before thinking.

During the week that followed, talk of the briefcase lessened. By the next weekend everyone had forgotten it altogether. There were more important things to concern ourselves with. Namely Jared Walsh's party.

Jared Walsh was the elder brother of Karen and the most well-known guy in the neighbourhood. His popularity stemmed from the fact that he was the sole dealer of narcotics and in tight with the local bikers. This was, of course, because he worked for them. But most kids were under the impression that Jared was a member of the gang, if only a junior one. This was false, as I would later discover, but it didn't stop Jared's friends from running their mouths off about how they were in with the gang and protected by them.

We were all rather excited about the first big bash of the summer. The Walshes' backyard backed onto a deep ravine that could be reached by going down a steep trail. They were known as ravine parties. The parties followed a routine: everyone would show up around nine, they'd light a bonfire at around ten, and the first of numerous fights would break out around midnight. Without fail, every ravine party ended with a fight. The last party of the summer of 1984 ended with my brother fighting Randy Givens. It was the last time I remember him using his talents to get one of us out of trouble. On that occasion it was me.

It was hot, there was a light wind, and an unexplainable feeling of ease on the streets. It was the kind of night where everyone let their guard down a little and didn't mind bending their usual rules. This meant that the bikers at the party didn't walk around intimidating the kids and the kids didn't spend the entire night worrying whether or not the bikers were going to start something. Traditionally the bikers didn't bother showing up until after midnight, but there had been talk circulating that week that they were supplying a keg and would be there from the start. It really didn't trouble anyone, except for maybe Wick, who had never much cared for them to begin with.

The plan that night was to meet at the party, this was to avoid having to wait around for Penny while she lamented over her wardrobe. Wick had given up on trying to convince her that it didn't matter. After all, the party was being held in a ravine. Not only is it difficult to see more than three feet in any direction after dark, but half an hour after you've started drinking who really cares what you look like. But Penny insisted that she look her usual, stunning self. We agreed to meet her there.

The three of us showed up at the ravine at around nine and immediately went our separate ways. Billy, as expected, found Karen and disappeared for the remainder of the night. That left Wick and myself wandering aimlessly while we unknowingly waited for the same person. I spent the better part of two hours mingling with a variety of people, all of whom offered their condolences about Bibs. I hadn't been prepared for it, to be honest. There was still a part of me that thought Bibs was hiding out, playing some horrible trick, but that was just me being a little brother I suppose. Wick, on the other hand, hated mingling with what he called "the riff-raff." He didn't go to school with any of them so he didn't have that unusual connection that exists between people that see each other every day but don't really know each other. So he sulked. He sulked until he got good and liquored. And then he started with the stories.

Even though Wick didn't go to school in the neighbourhood everyone was familiar with his genius. He was kind of a local legend in a way. No one from those parts was ever all that smart or educated so Wick was a big deal. This meant that everyone looked at him either like he was from another planet, or like he was made out of gold. Either way, Wick got off on it. So when he got drunk, especially around people he didn't know, he'd charge up that big brain of his and start with the stories. Because if there was one thing that Wick could do better than anyone I've ever met, it was talk. Most of the stories were nothing more than elaborate jokes and fictions but, as expected, a small

floatation device, we recommend using a number of dead bodies lashed together to provide buoyancy. If, at any time, the cabin is depressurized please DO NOT use the oxygen masks provided as they are merely for show.

We would also like to point out that, as per your purchaser's agreement, your life while on this aircraft is equal to the price of your airfare. Those seated in our business and first class cabins are worth more and in the event of an emergency will be deplaned first. This, of course, includes their pets and baggage as well. For those travelling in coach we ask that you deplane immediately following these passengers, and recommend leaving any excess baggage behind for safety reasons.

group of people soon gathered around him to listen. Two hours later it was as if he was a rock star. There'd be twenty people sitting and standing around listening to the guy say the strangest things. You wouldn't believe what it did to the ladies. It was like Spanish fly or lemon gin.

The hours passed and Wick was well into program sixty-seven. The fact that Penny hadn't arrived didn't seem to faze him much. His ego in clover, he was in no hurry to lose his audience. I, on the other hand, had nothing better to do with my time than pace around the perimeter looking for her. It was quite possible that she'd already arrived and was keeping both of us in suspense for the sheer pleasure that it gave her. I wish that had been the case. Penny would eventually show up at the party around midnight. And when she did the party would come to an abrupt end.

I remember the look in her eyes more than anything. Her clothes were dishevelled, her face looked like a Halloween mask, and both of her knees were skinned and bloodied. But despite these things I remember her eyes. She was in shock, so they fixated on nothing. Her left arm held against her chest, she walked awkwardly past various groups of party-goers like she was looking for something. She stopped, slowly turned in a three-sixty, and then proceeded to sit down on the ground. Everyone, and everything, stopped. No one moved, no one said anything. It was as if the air was instantly frozen by some unexpected, accelerated ice age. We all just stood there looking at her, watching her breathe in and out, trying to turn off the effects of the booze and drugs. They say that there are situations in life that can sober even the most inebriated of people. This was one of them.

After what seemed like ten minutes of complete immobility, all at once people started to surround her. The bikers, who like to take charge of such situations, continued to further confuse their image by showing both compassion and total outrage at the same time. Had it been one of their own girls, I doubt they would have cared. But this wasn't one of their girls. This was a girl from the neighbourhood. Their compassion and outrage stayed within the confines of the ravine. None of them were about to go looking for revenge on Penny's behalf. She wasn't with them, so it wasn't their business. It was our business. And they knew that. So after they put her in a lawn chair and told the majority of the people at the party to go home, they left Penny to us. There was myself, Wick, Jared Walsh, Andrea Schmidt, Sandra Hill, Jerry Reid, and Corey Haight.

The first order of business was to get Penny into the Walshes's house and cleaned up. The girls tended to this, with Wick trailing them. The rest of us stayed with Jared in the basement and attempted to figure out what to do about it. The popular consensus was to keep it amongst ourselves. Involving the police was always a bad idea. Had we known the extent of Penny's ordeal I'm sure we would have picked up the phone, but we didn't know. The older boys thought it best to get in their cars and cruise around in hopes of finding or hearing something that might make sense of it. I decided to get on my bike and ride up to the arcade to see what I could find. I would be gone for almost two hours. Two hours was all it would take.

The only guy to remain with Penny at the Walshes' was Wick. He was upstairs when we were all down in the basement. And because of that he was unaware of our plans. As it turns out, Wick would be the first to find out what had happened to Penny. He would also be the first to act.

Having been put in Karen's bed, Penny floated in and out of consciousness for a while before coming to her senses and requesting something to drink. The girls left her with Wick and went into the kitchen to make some tea.

Penny had left her house at around nine-thirty. She walked to the market, bought some cigarettes, and then started down the hill towards the Walshes's. On her way down she decided to cut through the park, a route that usually took ten minutes off the walk. She was in the neighbourhood, after all, and was therefore not that concerned with her safety. While walking past the stands at the baseball field someone called her name. It was Rick Zelleniski. Rick and his buddies were camped out in the back of several pick-up trucks, drinking beer and talking. Penny, never one to pass up the opportunity to make some boys squirm, decided to go over and say hello. And that's how it happened. Simple as that.

Penny remembers Rick punching her in the head and hauling her into the back of one of the trucks. She also remembers that it was Rick, and another guy named Sean Wilson, that raped her for sure. She was conscious for those two. As for the others she couldn't say. When she was examined by a doctor the next day it was determined that she'd been raped repeatedly in both her vagina and her anus. When she came to she was face down in the parking lot almost completely naked. The rest is disturbingly obvious. In a state of shock, and with a broken arm, she put on what remained of her clothes and started hobbling towards the ravine. She doesn't remember that part either. But she did remember telling Wick who did it. She also admitted to Wick that she'd been sleeping with me and that she meant to stop sleeping with me. And as

The Mega Track 2000.

It all started when I was ten. That's when I first saw her in the Sears catalogue. It was love at first sight. I knew then that I was a mere speck in the universe compared to her greatness. Guys like me didn't have a chance with a track like that, but we can dream. And, once in a very long while, one of us reaches high enough or goes far enough to attain a greatness that is beyond our breeding. Even if only for a second. Those few are the great ones.

By the Christmas of 1982 it was obvious that I had a problem. My lack of concentration became so worrisome that I used to sit in my room alone for hours making vroom-vroom noises under my breath. I had become a transient figure in my own world, not unlike some decadent emperor that thinks so highly of himself that he ignores everything around him. Past allies and trusted companions started to plot against me in an attempt to free themselves from my reclusive disregard. This culminated in a daring attempt by my Hoth versions of Han and Luke to escape me by stealing a Space Lego ship and flying out of my bedroom window. Unfamiliar with the controls, they plummeted to their deaths on the driveway below, shattering into a million pieces.

Horrified by the tragedy of that night, the others started getting ideas of their own.

I've said, Wick loved the girl. Halfway through Penny's recounting he left.

Wick knew just where the guns were. His only fear was that they'd been removed. When he left the Walshes' house he went to the pool, some seven blocks away. At about that time I was trying my best to find out if anyone had seen Penny earlier that night. I was in the arcade talking to Tony Hickox when Rick Zelleniski and the rest of them came in. They were drunk, rowdy, and bent on giving everyone a hard time. So I decided to leave and go back to the Walshes's to check on Penny. Two blocks into my journey a car ghosted up beside me containing Corey Haight and a couple of others. We talked a little before they sped off and I rode back only to sit in the Walshes' basement and wait, unknowingly, on Wick.

There wouldn't be much more to tell if I were to say that the guns were gone. They weren't, of course, and Wick wasted little time with it. Having taken them out of the briefcase he discovered that only one of the guns, a .44, was loaded. So he took it and left. For the better part of an hour Wick must have wandered around trying to find Rick and Sean. Eventually he went to the arcade. It was closed by then, of course, as it stayed open on Fridays and Saturdays until 2 a.m. After that, kids usually loitered around outside until they got bored and went home. Wick showed up at around 2:45 and shot Rick Zelleniski and Sean Wilson dead.

Wick went back to the pool. He put the gun back in the briefcase, the briefcase back in the ground, broke into the pool, slit his wrists with a pocket knife, and jumped into the water. To this day I'm not exactly sure what drove him to do it. Maybe it was the thought of spending a lifetime behind bars. Maybe it was because he realized that Penny would never truly be his. Maybe it was because she had been sleeping with me. I've tried to convince myself over the years that the latter was not the case, but I always find myself factoring into the blame. It's more comforting than being removed from it.

I remember sitting in the Walshes's basement when Jared came in and told us that Wick had shot Rick and Sean. Of course the story was immediately embellished. To most of the neighbourhood Wick became a hero. The general feeling was that Rick and Sean got what they deserved, despite the fact that they were unarmed. From what I could gather from those that were in front of the arcade that night, Wick's actions were both instantaneous and without emotion. He simply walked up to them, pulled the gun, and fired. They found his body floating in the pool the next morning. There was a note in his pocket, the white paper soaked red. It said—*"fuck all of you."* That was all.

So long Merlin.

The rest of the summer of 1985 saw two other incidents occur that are of note. The first was Billy's death, which happened August 27th. After everything that transpired that July it seemed comical to me that he should die. I was forced to spend several weeks in the hospital because I fell victim to a nervous breakdown, or so they say. Under the circumstances I'm not going to deny that I wasn't in need of something along those lines. The breakdown, that is. But in all fairness to the randomness of things Billy was wholly responsible for his own undoing. He got high on some pills and walked into traffic in the middle of the night. There's nothing I can really say about it except that had nothing happened prior to his death, he probably would have died anyway. Who's to say. The only thing that's for certain is that all three of them will be dead much longer than they were alive. As will I eventually.

The second thing was that Penny lost her mind, landing her in a mental institution for the rest of her life. She was sitting at the dinner table with her folks when, all of a sudden, she started stabbing herself with a fork. I'm told she did some damage before her dad was able to pin her to the ground. It seems that the events of that night are not so easily forgotten by some compared to others. Penny's reasons are better than most, I'm afraid.

So that's all four of them. My whole life wrapped up in incomplete people. One from the sky, one in the water, one on the ground, and one with fire in the head. All four elements. How convenient.

I finished school two years later but was not exactly the type to go on to university to become something distinguished or worthwhile. Instead I remained in the neighbourhood, worked at various jobs, got a girl pregnant, married her, declared bankruptcy, and eventually turned to a life of crime. It's not that bad actually. It's not like I kill people for a living. I just take their televisions when they're asleep or on vacation. I do what most people try to do. I provide for my family and do my best not to be what most people try not to be—a bad person. It's entirely dependent on perspectives, I suppose.

For you will be dead much longer than you will be alive. And you will have all that time to remember everything that was your life, even if no one else does. So you had better find something worth remembering and just leave it at that.

Escape attempts became commonplace as everyone from the Space Lego Legionnaires to the mice from Mouse Trap attempted to breach the perimeter and bust out to freedom. I would suit up every night in plastic SWAT battle gear preparing to thwart their attempts to pin me to the ground and poke my eyes out with Playmobile spears.

I had lost the ability to reason. Even though I didn't want them I couldn't allow them to leave the kingdom of misery I had so carefully constructed. If I was to suffer alone without her then all my subjects would suffer with me or die. And die they did. By the hundreds. I was beautifully ruthless and terrible, underhanded and psychotic. I fought them until there was nothing left to fight. But it

The Man With the Hole in His Head

There was a man with a hole in his head. He filled it up with water so goldfish could swim around in there. Indispensable at parties, all the pretty girls would put their drinks on his brain. He liked that. So did the goldfish.

There was a woman that liked him once. After putting her drink on his brain they got to talking. It's always awkward for the first few minutes. They're standing there and she's trying her best not to stare at the glass sticking out of his head. So they talk for a while and start to hit it off, but the girl has her concerns—to say the least. I mean, it's not normal to have a hole in one's head, let alone use it as a drink holder. She starts asking him questions about everything and anything that doesn't have to do with the fact that there's a hole in his head. Her friends stand across the room talking in whispers, using sophisticated hand signals, weighing the situation, planning what to say if she actually decides to give it a go. But after a while she breaks down and starts asking him about his head, which she hasn't stopped staring at the entire time.

"You live alone?" she asks him.

"Yeah," he says.

"When you go to bed, do you dream about your pillow?" she says.

"What?" he says.

"Your pillow. Do you dream about your pillow? You know, 'cause of the hole," she says.

"No. Not usually," he says.

And that was pretty much it. They stood there for a couple of minutes in one of those uncomfortable silences before her friends came to her rescue.

"Come meet Bill," they said. "He's absolutely delightful!"

After that he went home. So did the fish. It's not easy spending your whole life looking for a girl with a hole in her head. We'll see.

Halfway around the world there is a tiny country where everyone is red. And by that I'm not implying that they're Communists, I'm referring to their skin. It's a small island country that's turned into quite the tourist hot spot in the past few years. But the indigenous people of this island are still rather primitive. Most of the natives that live in the interior of the island still dwell in huts. But that doesn't stop people from going to the south coast and staying in fancy hotels.

The tourists act crazily, drink too much, and wear as little clothing as possible. They use the heat as an excuse for such behaviour. But the natives in

the interior never see the vacationers. They've never even seen the hotels on the southern coast. They just live in the jungle with the monkeys and tigers.

I recently read somewhere that, over a considerable number of years, they've taught the monkeys to speak. And by speak I am inferring that they carry on conversations and hold debates and such. The article went on to say that, since the monkeys don't converse in English, it's not considered to be all that impressive. The fact that a monkey has the ability to lecture other monkeys about the works of Noam Chomsky in a foreign language doesn't seem all that exciting to anyone. One must wonder why that same principle is not applied to opera.

The monkeys just sit in the trees casually making off-colour comments about the tourists as they walk by. Having never appeared on *That's Incredible* they feel altogether unappreciated I'm afraid.

One of the villages in the interior is ruled by a tribal chief named Hubaru. Hubaru has three children, a son and two daughters. The younger of his two girls has never been seen by anyone, save her parents and siblings. She stays in the family hut all day. There are rumours that she was wooed by a monkey and a damaging scandal ensued. Hubaru thought it best to confine her to the hut. This all happened many years ago, of course, so no one can really recall what actually occurred with any accuracy. Unbeknownst to his subjects, Hubaru's reasons for condemning his daughter were altogether different.

She has a rather large hole in the top of her head. He thinks she is embarrassing so he confines her to the hut. He fights about it with his wife day in and day out.

She spends her time trying to comfort her daughter, vainly attempting to convince herself that her husband isn't a tyrant. She keeps trying to convince Hubaru to allow his daughter to leave the hut, but Hubaru won't have any of it. There's a hole in her head, end of discussion. He has come to believe that she gets the hole from her mother. His wife's thinking the same thing. The monkeys, by the way, could care less.

In another part of the world a man is getting on an airplane. He's leaving on holiday. He's had it. He's tired of pretty girls using his head as a drink holder. Especially the stupid ones. He's discussed it with the fish and the fish agree.

He hadn't really planned on taking a holiday. Out of curiosity, the day before, he had stepped into a travel agent's to look at holiday brochures. He started flipping through some of them when a travel agent started in on him about how he deserved to have some fun. He wasn't looking for fun but he let the travel agent talk anyway.

solved nothing. It didn't bring her any closer to being mine.

For those of you not old enough to remember it, the **MEGA TRACK 2000** was the elite of electric raceways. It glowed in the dark. Not just the track but the cars as well. There were two loops and a section of the track went vertically up a wall. You could set the track pieces up in an infinite number of configurations and some of the pieces could be contorted into fantastical turns and switchbacks. The cars were top-of-the-line and known for their ability to stay on the track when encountering corners at top speed. The MT 2000 was the fastest production race set ever made. Some critics even complained that

Some people have obvious character flaws. Some are rude, some are hot tempered, some are flakes, some tend to lie. The man also had a character flaw: he was too polite. He'd always been too polite. So by the time the travel agent had finished showing him a multitude of brochures and pictures he started to get a sick feeling in his stomach. He couldn't just walk out, not after this lady had spent an hour of her time going through everything from hotel choices to rental-car agencies. He wasn't even sure where it was she had him going. It didn't matter. Before he knew it his credit card was out and he was paying.

Now he's on a plane going to some small island in the South Pacific that he's never heard of. He's not a rich man, he could barely afford the trip, but it's too late now. A million things are running through his head at once. Everything from how he's going to survive for two weeks on $193 spending money to how he's going to explain missing work for fourteen days without any kind of advance notice. He doubts that he'll get fired. He's the most complacent employee in the world.

It's just that the whole thing feels foreign to him: doing something which is so clearly not the proper thing to do. The feeling that confuses him the most is the tingling sensation running up and down his body. We know it as excitement. As far as he knows, it's the flu. He does his best not to think about it. He takes out a book and starts reading. *1 Elevator, Silence, Overweight. The elevator continued its impossibly slow ascent. Or at least I imagined it was ascent. There was no telling for sure...* The hours pass. The plane slips through the upper atmosphere as night falls over the Pacific. He falls asleep, tingling. The fish play dream games.

You know it's not all that strange to have a hole in one's head. Technically we all have several to speak of. So one more shouldn't be all that big a deal. But obviously it is. People see it as some mark of questionable humanity. Holes are not found atop the human head, it's a scientific fact. So it automatically implies difference. Difference is not something anyone takes to all that well. We're much more excited about familiarity. That's why the majority of hotel rooms appear to be the same. No matter your level of economics, all hotel rooms look alike. Whether they be penthouses or singles, suites or a tiny little bed in an impossibly small room. They're all the same. Maybe, had we been differently devised, we would have made sure that they were not alike. But too long have we favoured familiarity to do anything about it now. And so they will all remain the same. As will holes atop the head remain anomalous. Even more so if they happen to be the only outlet from which to feed goldfish.

Nevertheless, our friend did his best to conquer his fear of the unknown before arriving at Narita. He would have to change planes there. He did this with surprising accuracy, considering that he had never been in a major airport before. But he found himself over three hours early for his connecting flight, leaving him with little choice but to make his way to the nearest lounge. Once there, he ordered a drink. It cost him a million dollars. Japan is like that. Everything costs a million dollars.

From Japan he would travel south into the wide expanse of the South Seas. Waters in which many Japanese and American sailors and airmen are buried. Waters that are deeper than any other on earth, containing dangers aplenty. Waters that have even been kissed by atomics, thanks to the French. Leave it to the French to make certain that parts of the South Pacific will glow for the next 200 years. Not that they're alone, mind you, but they're French and that's good enough. So south he went, hurled through the air at outrageous speeds towards the mysterious and alluring bosom of paradise. Hopefully, Tattoo would be sober enough to greet him. This was the wish of the fish.

Some hours later, following the always chancy in-flight service of any major airline, the plane landed and he promptly made his way to the hotel. To his surprise the lady at the travel agency had misled him. He remembered being shown pictures of a lavish hotel, the kind that has four pools, two bars, and 24-hour room service. Such hotels did exist on the island, mind you. In fact, from his room he could see most of them across the harbour. There they were, all in a row. He just wasn't staying in one.

He was staying on the north shore of the harbour in a hotel called the Sea Breeze. It was nice enough, he figured, as he wasn't one to complain. Nor did he attempt to call the travel agent and demand an explanation. To him it seemed pointless. The fish, who rarely bothered to look out through his eyes, did not care about such things. They were quite upset that Tattoo had not been present when they had deplaned. *Fantasy Island* was their favourite television program. And when it got cancelled, they agreed never to look through his eyes again.

He was officially on holiday. This of course meant that, after unpacking his clothes and whatnot, he had no idea what he was supposed to do. So he spent the better part of the afternoon looking out across the harbour at the hotels and the water. It didn't occur to him to go outside. He was content with just being somewhere that offered him a view such as that. Sometimes loneliness has its charm—it being secretive and quite impossible to predict. Most of the

it was too fast for the targeted demographic. It was, in a word, perfection.

They say that childhood traumas can severely affect the adult psyche. I am proof of it. I have come to terms with the fact that the past cannot be altered. And though I have taken steps to better my mental health, I remain a victim of parents who knew and cared too little. And though you might be telling yourself that I, compared to some in this world, am extremely fortunate, I would remind you that though my situation may have changed there is little I can do to enjoy it. The Mega Track 2000 retailed for $99.

Wavering

I've got this feeling like I've been here before.

There's this guy eating a sandwich on the top floor of a parking garage. He has a rifle. The sandwich has ham, lots of mayo, no lettuce. He finishes the sandwich and swallows the remains of a milk. He picks up the rifle, still chewing. Below him there is a busy corner. Below him there are a hundred people with featureless faces. A little red light dances from person to person, unnoticed. He breathes shallow. His palms are sweating. There's sweat running into his eyes from his forehead. Lightning flashes, the air stops, somebody drops. Somebody starts screaming. Somebody drops. Thunderclaps fly around like

time it lacks charm simply because no one else is ever there to bear witness. This is the unsullied beauty of a such a singular and private moment.

Later that night he went to dinner, after which he returned to his room and organized his toiletries in the bathroom. If anything he was orderly. It's a condition of loneliness. It drives you to constantly clean things and make sure that they're in the proper place. He placed his things in their proper places and proceeded to clean the sink. It wasn't until he accidentally hit the light switch with his elbow that he saw the moon reflected in the bathroom mirror.

Captivated by its light, he left the sink and wandered over to the window. And that's how he spent his evening. Some hours later his eyes grew heavy and he decided to turn in. Having been completely dazzled by the prospect of such an immense body of water, the fish talked excitedly into the night. The man dreamed of the ocean, like a sailor lost to his love.

Many miles to the north of the Sea Breeze Hotel a young, red woman was making her way through the jungle. She was, to the embarrassment of her ancestors, completely lost. In her defense she had spent most of her life confined to a hut, so she could not be counted on to uphold centuries of miraculous woodland navigation.

She had been planning this night for almost four months. She had water, food, a spear, and what she thought was a pretty good idea of which direction the coast lay. This last factor was, of course, the weak link in her plan. And, after hours of tromping through the bushes, she found herself right back where she had started. But this only heightened her resolve. She set out again, deciding to rely on the worst possible thing that one could ever rely on, talking monkeys.

Sometimes talking monkeys can come in handy. Always ones to gossip incessantly, their chatter could be heard in the surrounding trees. Two such monkeys, Albert and Cosmo, made a habit of taking some shade under a tree quite near to the hut of the chief. The girl would sit there for hours and listen to Albert and Cosmo talk. Most of the time they babbled on about monkey business. But some of the time they would talk about a magical place far to the south where the trees were made of diamonds and no one ever died. They did this on purpose, of course.

Talking monkeys are smart, much smarter than most believe them to be. Both Albert and Cosmo knew that the girl was listening to them, because she would laugh at their silly jokes on occasion. Instead of bad-mouthing the tourists, as they commonly did twenty hours of each day, they decided to breathe a little life into the girl's imagination.

As the girl ventured back into the jungle she came across several monkeys sitting under a tree. They were drinking vodka martinis and wearing smoking jackets. None of them noticed her approaching, for they were all half-cut and in a bit of a verbal tizzy about the Euro. Of course the girl had no idea what Euro were, but they sounded important enough. She thought it best to ask the monkeys for some directions, as they seemed rather intelligent. This was her undoing. The monkeys didn't notice her until she was almost upon them. But, because they were talking monkeys, they didn't respond to being startled like the average monkey would. They did not make for the nearest tree to seek refuge in its heights. They just casually turned their heads in a drunken wave of imbalance, as one of them stood up, pointed a finger, and said with the utmost inebriation, "Who goes there?"

For the next five minutes the girl just stood watching them while the monkeys rolled around on the ground in hysterics. Martini glasses were crushed, smoking jackets sullied, lungs heaved in an attempt to maximize the vocalization of hilarity. And then, as suddenly as it had begun, it stopped. The monkeys sat up, attempted to straighten themselves, and turned to the girl. The monkey that had initiated the laughter spoke first.

"What, may I ask, are you doing wandering the wilds at this hour child?"

The girl, having never spoken with a monkey before, decided to skip the pleasantries and get straight to the point.

"I'm looking for the land of diamond trees," she said.

She thought he was rude, to say the least.

"I see. Well, you might try going that way," and pointed off into the darkness with a long finger.

She followed the finger. And the monkeys went on to a new topic, the possible sale of arms to Taiwan.

As morning broke the girl was still wandering the jungle. Having stopped to ask several other monkeys for assistance, she had been sent off in a variety of directions. She was exhausted. She found a clearing and decided to get some sleep.

The man woke up in his hotel room. He washed, ate breakfast in the hotel restaurant, and returned to his room. As he was sitting there gazing out at the bay, he noticed a car-rental agency brochure on a nearby table. He picked it up. And that's all it took. A 1976 Honda Civic was at the front door of the hotel in less than twenty minutes. Because it was a rather cheap rental agency, he could actually afford it. He spent the better part of that day driving around the south coast. He drove past nice hotels and white sand beaches filled with

giant fists hitting the buildings, hitting the cars. Somebody drops. Sirens pop up in the distance.

There's just an empty brown paper bag, an empty ziplock bag, some crumbs, an empty milk. The last supper. People are starting to run into shops and office buildings. Somebody drops. Empty clip. Reload. The sirens are close. Someone is pointing up. Somebody drops. The mayonnaise was good. It was Miracle Whip. Miracle Whip is much better than traditional mayo. Somebody drops. The little red light dances. People are looking out of windows across the street, pointing. A window breaks. Somebody drops. The police cars screech to a stop down on the street. People are pointing up. They get sunbathers. He drove past a variety of tropical gardens and golf courses. And then, as if it were any surprise, he decided to go back to the hotel.

The girl awoke to the sound of two voices. Opening her eyes, she immediately realized that the voices were those of monkeys. They seemed to be discussing whether or not she was dead. One thought she was, the other did not. Just as the girl opened her eyes, the two monkeys were debating whether or not to poke her with a stick in an attempt to ascertain her condition. The girl, fearing what might happen, thought it best to get to her feet. Their reaction to this was split.

One yelled "Ha! I told you so!" and the other yelled "shit."

The girl yelled "Shut up," and so they did. But her attempt to get accurate directions from them was just as pointless as it had been from the other monkeys. They sent her northwest instead of south, figuring she might wander into Abunta territory and be eaten.

The Abunta were the last remaining cannibals. Although few in number, they held a section of the jungle along the northwest coast of the island, some distance from the girl's own village.

She headed off, leaving the two monkeys arguing. Having walked for the better part of the evening towards certain death and digestion, the girl once again made the mistake of stopping to ask for directions. Only this time the monkey that she encountered wasn't interested in playing games with her.

He simply said, "You see that big star up there?" pointing skyward. "Walk towards it."

The girl thanked the monkey and went on her way. The monkey shook his head and muttered to himself. The star in question was known as the Big Nunga Nunga. No one knows why it was named that, but that's what they've called it for centuries. The Nunga, which is its shortened name, is the largest star in the night sky. The ancients believed that if you were to get in a boat and sail towards the Nunga then you would burst into flames and be destroyed for being stupid enough to travel that far out to sea.

The islanders never sailed south in fear of its wrath. Of course, the girl was relatively safe because she was on land. Or so you would think.

In the tropics there is nothing more enrapturing than the moon. But the man, and the fish, were both captivated by the light that it cast on the water below. How it made the sea seem mysterious and altogether alluring. Under this spell the man decided to go for a drive, which was very much out of character for him. This was very much against himself. Then again, so was going on a vacation with absolutely no preparation or planning. Nevertheless, he walked out to his rented Honda Civic, got in, and hit the highway. The drive across the southern coast was quite beautiful according to the brochure, perhaps even more so with the moon in play.

Four miles down the road there was a blind corner. In his newfound state of unfamiliar excitement the man sped towards this corner free of concern. Some distance to the north of that curve, a girl was angrily tromping through the jungle, convinced that the Land Of Diamond Trees was an elaborate lie. I would love to tell you that the man and the girl did not arrive at that corner at the same time. Life is mostly cruel, you see. She didn't feel anything. Neither of them did.

The explosion was seen across the bay by hundreds of people sitting out on their lavish hotel balconies. Some even thought it was some kind of traditional island-fire-ceremony-thing. Americans, most likely. Eventually a Dutch couple had the common sense to pick up the phone and tell someone.

As an aside, fire ceremonies had been banned in the 1920s after half of the island was consumed by flames. Strangely enough, the fire was caused by a village idiot who wandered into the jungle with a torch and fell asleep. You see, the crazy bastard actually thought he could teach monkeys how to speak.

Emergency crews were alerted and those with a taste for the macabre decided to go have a look. After hitting the girl, the man lost control of the car and went straight off the road's shoulder. Having burst through a flimsy wooden guard rail, the Civic plummeted several hundred feet to the rocks below. It sat there, crushed upside down into the rocks, and exploded. The man's body was blown out of the wreck into the sea. The ocean water flooded through the hole in our friend's head. Miraculously the fish survived the accident, and though elated that their captor had the decency to perish in such a grand body of water, they were nonetheless killed by its salty contents.

The girl, on the other hand, was discovered by a monkey in the bushes on the side of the road. Left with little choice, as he was a decent sort of fellow, he did the only thing he could do. He walked out of the bushes and over to a group of bystanders. He then stopped, cleared his throat, and said in a voice that could have belonged to a Harvard law graduate:

"Excuse me, but there happens to be a young woman over there in the bushes and I believe her to be quite dead."

All of that, by the way, in perfect English. This phenomenal event in human history was, of course, never reported simply because the people that the monkey chose to address were members of a Korean tour group. All of whom cared only to speak Korean.

out of their cars. Somebody drops.

There's a picture he keeps in his wallet. He takes it out. Someone he loves–the wife and kids–salvation. All those years of salvation. The red light dances. All those years of moving towards something always so far away. Somebody drops. There's a picture in his wallet with one less person. It doesn't taste like Miracle Whip. Wait for it. Breathe. Somebody drops.

Tomorrow everything will be the same as it was yesterday. Today is just another two minutes on the news. The picture, salvation, they won't bring that up. There's a million different ways to say I love you. It's choosing the right one that's the problem. There's a million different ways to lose sight of the fact that eventually everything is comparable to a bad dream. Club Med is one. What are the others?

For a fleeting moment in time the only two people on earth with holes in their heads found each other. They just got the timing wrong is all.

Have You Seen Me? I've Looked Everywhere.

I've got it coming. Eventually it will come. Everything is cyclical. The history of our planet proves this theory. We, being the idiots that we are, remain helpless to do anything about the inevitable reoccurrence of our stupidity. Because if that wasn't the case then a great many things would be different. Like a certain chocolate bar, that will remain nameless, for example. Who, in their right fucking mind, puts chocolate and coconut together. Who?

I am perhaps the stupidest person who has ever lived. It's true, ask anyone. There are examples of my stupidity that I have attempted to share with you. I failed, of course, but did try. Actually, *failed* is the wrong word, I didn't fail. I succumbed to *the better judgment of others*. This, of course, is something that you should never do when it comes to things of a creative nature. It's always best to trust your guts. Unless you've just taken some kind of antacid. Then you might want to wait a while and make sure you're thinking straight.

I have no idea why I let myself be influenced in such a way. Then again, I can't really remember most of 1991 either, so I'm really not one to talk. But I have come up with a solution to that problem. I simply got rid of my friends. It's clear sailing from here on in.

I am confident that one day I will be assassinated by a right-wing organization of some kind. I have, in the past, done many things to test the bounds of my stupidity and the stupidity of others. I have come to realize that those boundaries may be endless. I have done so at the expense of others on occasion. Some years ago, while working at home one afternoon, I answered my phone and found myself caught in the web of a telephone evangelist. Instead of politely telling her that I was disinterested in her jargon, I decided to play along.

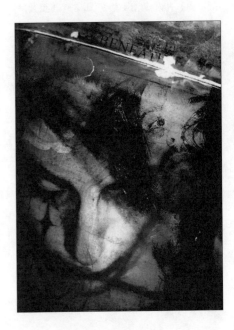

Tele-evangelist: Do you own a bible?
Myself: I think so.
Tele-evangelist: So I take it that you don't read it.
Myself: No, not recently. But I've read it before.
Tele-evangelist: But you don't read it often?
Myself: No, not really. Why?
Tele-evangelist: Do you own a computer?
Myself: Yes.
Tele-evangelist: Well, it's like learning to use your computer.
Myself: What is?
Tele-evangelist: The word of God.

You Can't Fool the Children of the Revolution.

Can You?

I resolve to watch *Real Stories of the Highway Patrol*. I resolve to watch *Extra*, *American Journal*, and *America's Dumbest Criminals*. Have you been to Algeria? You know where that is? It's in North Africa. A little while ago some REBELS killed over 400 people there in a village while they slept. I resolve to watch *Baywatch* and *Friends*. We all need friends. We all need a reason for something. They lock up people who don't have reasons. They call it being unreasonable. So which are you: frosted or whole wheat?

Lasers. They use lasers in space. Lasers for laser surgery. Lasers for laser discs. They've got infra-red lasers. For laser tag, for

Myself: Are you saying that God's in my computer?
Tele-evangelist: No, no, no!
Myself: Oh.
Tele-evangelist: Did you know how to use your computer when you first bought it?
Myself: No, not really.
Tele-evangelist: So you had to read the manual to learn how to use it?
Myself: Yes.
Tele-evangelist: Well, the same goes for God's word. You have to read his manual to learn how to live your life!
Myself: I see. So what you're saying is that God lives in my computer?

My Theory About Music Critics.

I was thinking about music critics the other day. This is not a topic that I usually waste time pondering.

Music critics are a strange lot. A large percentage of them are failed musicians actually. This has always perplexed me. If most of them are failed musicians then who, in their right mind, would give them a job critiquing musicians that aren't failures? It has nothing to do with their writing abilities whatsoever. I have never read a music review that possessed the satirical wit of say a Vonnegut or the texture of someone like James Joyce. True, both are legendary authors, so why compare music critics to them? Why not? They seem to have no trouble doing it to bands. But that's beside the point. My theory concerning music critics is actually rather simple, and it's this: *if music critics seem to possess the secret knowledge of what components are necessary to make a record great, then why don't they just do it themselves and spare us the torture of being subjected to their less than entertaining writing skills?*

Perhaps bands, as we know them, don't even exist. Maybe they're nothing more than fronts for genius music critics who have been forced to take matters into their own hands because the state of modern music is in shambles. Maybe, and this might be a stretch, but what if there are only ten of them in the entire world, each covering a specific genre of music. One does classical, one does pop, one does techno, and so on. Have you ever seen more than two music critics in the same room at the same time? It's odd.

And this goes back to what I was saying about their writing abilities. If you really examine most reviews they all seem to share a common thread. It's as if they are only familiar with a small portion of the English language. I have come to the conclusion that all music critics are either from a distant planet inhabited by a race of musical geniuses or they are members of a secret organization, not unlike the Masons, who meet once a year in the basement of Berkeley. I know it sounds absurd, but if you examine this closely it'll start to make sense. You'll also get a headache.

better night vision, for insurgence reassurances. There's a room, deep underground, where they know the future. It's all been decided beforehand. They've three-dimensional maps and detailed intelligence, the cure for cancer, real cream and not coffee whitener. No one's sure who exactly runs this operation. No one's exactly sure of anything. That's why you're not in charge.

What would you do if you did know? What would anyone do with the facts if they knew them to be infallible? It's the *Gilligan's Island* principle. You'd think that if they could find the time to invent a device that can vaporize an entire city they could find a fat guy, a skinny guy, two complainers, a prude, a tease, and the world's most brilliant scien-

How Come There's Never Been a Weapon of Mass Destruction on a Wheaties Box?

In the beginning there was darkness. Which is good because it requires no description. No fumbling metaphorical references to bewilder and cause panic. Just darkness.

The universe serves as a constant reminder that, in between the lights, there is a mass of nothingness. Which, conveniently for me, is rather dark. There are millions of light years of darkness out there separating us from whatever else may be there. Perhaps even dividing us from some secret after-life that is hidden somewhere in all that nothingness. Either that or countless worlds inhabited by lizard people and one-eyed bird-men that have yet to discover how fantastically delightful the human brain tastes with ketchup.

So you've got these bright lights floating around in all that darkness. One, in particular, is surrounded by countless mechanical devices that enable people in Singapore to watch *American Gladiators*. This particular ball of light would be called Earth, which (if you ask me) is a rather pathetic name for a planet. You'd think we could have come up with something better than Earth. Maybe something like Supertron, or Varanova. But instead, Earth. We're just Earthlings. I foresee us being a rather popular target for the one-eyed, bird-headed lizard people. It's like invading a country called "The Free Republic of Fluffy Teddies." They're laughing at us right now. So far they've found it so debilitating that they've yet to act. But it'll wear off.

Maybe after we've been consumed they'll change the name of the planet to something palatable, like Tron. But for now, despite such optimism, we will have to make do with the way things are. Which, if you look hard enough, always seems to be pretty much the way things have always been. No matter what creationist tale you champion there is one constant. In the beginning there was darkness. And the beauty of that truth is that I don't have to describe it to you. How fortunate for me.

I have often watched the sky and wondered where all the voices go after they've talked themselves out. Perhaps they fall back down here to Earth. Maybe they continue upwards into that darkness like some unknown weapon of massive sonic destruction.

You're sitting on your front porch on some far distant planet when you're unexpectedly bombarded by a million voices talking about nothing at all. The

sheer magnitude of the mundane ripping your world to shreds and moving on to claim other worlds.

If sound travels at the speed of sound then think of how destructive we ourselves might be, given that for countless ages we've been talking, screaming, and wailing hysterically on *The Price Is Right*. The audio from that show alone could have wiped out Andromeda for all we know. Those lights up there take their sweet time getting to us. Perhaps those lights have burned out.

I know that sound dissipates. It bounces off of things and its wave form straightens as it hitchhikes through the air. But that's the beauty of fiction. I can say whatever I want and there's nothing that you can do about it. Not altogether unlike carnal sin and disobedient Catholic school girls.

The point of all this is that you never can tell what's out there in all that darkness. There may be some extremely unwholesome figure in a dark alley that represents all the badness in the world.

"For the love of God, don't go down there!" they say. But everyone does. People always do what they are not supposed to do. Why trade your god given right to act stunned for accountability? There's just far too much responsibility in it. There are those that have been tempted by the notion. But more often than not they find themselves guests of sedation houses rather than champions of will. Vink Lippy was one such person.

If there was one thing Vink hated it was his name. That's what happens when your mother has a speech impediment. His birth certificate said "Vincent Libby" but every time his mother opened her mouth it came out *Vink*. So instead of Vince Libby everyone called him Vink Lippy.

There were many unfortunate adolescent variations of his name: Dink Lippy, Limpy, Dink Lips, and Vink's all-time favourite: LIMPY DINKSTER. It would be his favourite because the last person who ever called Vink "Limpy Dinkster" was discovered in the woods missing his eyeballs. There's reason to believe that really gay names can produce tough kids. Going one stop further down the Freudian highway we come to Psychoville. Population 2. Vink Lippy and Seymour Kuntz.

Vink was not an ordinary kid growing up. He wasn't the sort to rush out and buy purple pants just because everyone was wearing purple pants. Some people might consider that courageous, especially for an adolescent. Others might just beat you up because you're wearing flared cords. But challenges like that are just tiny parts in the massive equation of life. Every life has a moment in it when the answer to each of our equations is revealed. Due to the years of constant torture he was subjected to, Vink's came after he was

tist. Believe me, if you could make a telephone system out of coconuts they'd come looking for you at the drop of a hat. But instead they were marooned. Probably because it is impossible to find seven people on an island in the Pacific when they've been locked up in the basement of a studio in Burbank. Maybe because that was the whole point of the show. The fact remains that without the stupidity of its design it wouldn't exist. Therefore, no one's exactly sure of anything. It's better for you that way. That's why you're not in charge. You might go and do something like change the rules. And we can't have that now, can we.

Looking back at the Earth from the moon I am reminded of inadequacies. Of futility and the mistakes of time. I am reminded that it is a small thing in a place of much larger things. It is, after all, one of billions. I am also reminded of an ant farm that I used to have when I was young. It was this little plastic tank filled with dirt. The ants made tunnels, the ants multiplied, and eventually the ants ate each other. I had forgotten about it. I had left it on a shelf. One day they were all gone. Just a few corpses. The dirt had dried up. There are footprints on the moon. Reminders. Fossils for someone to find. The Earth looks small from most places, I would think. Unless you're standing on it, looking up. Then you're the Master of the Universe. Either that or a dummy. Flip a coin.

I have no reason to believe that anything arrested for a double homicide. The two unlucky victims being the last person that ever called him "Limpy Dinkster" and his mother. In a bizarre way, maybe the answers to their equations came to them while Vink was plunging their plumbing with a Christmas carving knife.

Vink was taken into custody by the police. He was discovered sitting at his kitchen table with a knife in one hand, rolling eyeballs around in a metal mixing bowl with the other. Horrified by what they had found, the arresting officers stood in the kitchen doorway for almost ten minutes before confronting Vink and putting him in handcuffs. Vink simply placed the knife and the bowl on the table and capitulated to the officers' requests. When they arrived at the police station, Vink was placed in a little room and asked the usual questions that one might expect to be asked while sitting in such a room. Questions like *why? when? where?* and so on. But Vink didn't answer them. He repeated a single question over and over.

"How come there's never been a weapon of mass destruction on a Wheaties box?"

After news of the murders got out a small mob converged on the police station and started demanding that Vink be handed over to them. Everyone, that is, except for the parents of the boy that Vink had killed. They just stood at the bottom of the station's stairs with blank expressions on their faces, wondering what had happened.

All of this took place, of course, long before the media became more important than the news. In what would have been turned into a three-ring circus with today's media, and used by a variety of local reporters to springboard their careers at the expense of grief, the murders garnered a minimal dose of public outrage before being buried in the back pages. Up until the trial, most had put the murders out of their minds. And when it started, the public's interest fizzled mere days into it.

Vink was defended by a lawyer from the public defender's office. Who to his credit had, prior to the trial, started using words that consisted of more than three syllables. Those at the district attorney's office, on the other hand, were convinced that they had been given the task of saving the public from the next Charles Manson and were determined to quench their own overinflated desire to see proper justice served. They played their hand with pinpoint precision and painted him as a ruthless and calculating young man. They might have been right. Then again, during all those days of talk and deliberation there were only a handful of people in the whole world that Vink pondered killing. And those were the prosecutors.

After some weeks the trial came to a close and Vincent Libby was found guilty of two murders, both in the second degree. He was sentenced to two years in a juvenile facility and another forty five years in a maximum-security prison. Without a word, Vink did what he was told and went from his sentencing to a juvenile detention centre built in the middle of nowhere. And during his time there no one besides two guards and a court-appointed psychiatrist spoke to him. And for all that time he said nothing.

Vink's short stint in the hands of juvenile affairs was rather uneventful as prison terms go. Though filled with a variety of so called hard cases, no one dared look at or talk to Vink. Because when you're in juvie for stealing a car and carrying a gun that you're not man enough to use when you pull it out, you find young men that have brutally hacked up two people and removed their eyeballs rather frightening. It doesn't matter if he's a skinny little freak who looks like he couldn't hurt a fly if he wanted to. They were scared silly of him.

The psychiatrist at the juvenile centre tried her best to get through to Vink. But in those two short years she was unable to get anything out of him besides his fourteen-word question.

In her report to the Child Welfare Board she wrote:

Vincent is most likely a high-functioning boy whose intelligence has never been nurtured or encouraged. Mr. Whatley has searched his room on several occasions and has discovered reading materials that far surpass the intellect of the young men commonly found in an institution such as this. My failure to make any contact with him places me in a very difficult situation. My recommendation would have to be for Vincent to be transferred to a maximum-security hospital for a more extensive evaluation. At this time, placing him in a corrections facility may only further his detachment and would most likely result in complete disassociation. I have forwarded my own notes concerning this matter to Dr. Landy, whose own preliminary evaluation can be found attached to my own.

Unfortunately the court didn't seem to care about the evaluations and recommendations of either child welfare or psychiatric services. On the day after his eighteenth birthday Vink was transferred to a maximum-security prison and placed in general population. And there, inside his head, he spent his life floating around the universe in all that darkness that I haven't been describing, screaming at the top of his lungs and blowing up planets with his favourite words. Those being *xenophobia* and *tits*. That's the way it went for Vink. He spent his entire adult life locked in a small room.

And though some might consider that hell, I can assure you that it didn't mean anything to him. As far as he was concerned he wasn't even in prison.

is possible. Impossibility is a greater motivational force than probability. The human condition dictates this. And you thought you were upwardly mobile.

He was flying around the universe, igniting the cosmos, as free as a bird. From time to time he'd go outside for a while or down to the cafeteria to eat. And, once in a very long while, he'd be taken to another small room to watch a little TV. His favorite show was *Star Trek*. He liked the fact that the *Enterprise* just flew around the universe, not unlike himself. It was the only time he smiled. And, quite often, the only time he cried.

It's times like these that one looks at a life and poses stern questions. Questions like *"What's all this about?"* and *"Who really cares if I'm here or not?"* The reason? Perhaps it has something to do with the fact that the unknown constitutes one of the largest aspects of being. Maybe being has always been nothing more than what you consider a successful life to be. Vink's idea of a successful life was floating around the universe, hurling words of cataclysm. Perhaps everyone simply talks too much and does too little. Maybe, at the core, that's the difference between questions and answers. The difference between talking and doing.

Imagine a life, as if it were unfolding before you like a path through the woods. Imagine that path coming to an end at the rocky shores of a great, alpine lake. Imagine the world devoid of noise and tension and concern. Picture all of this and then imagine yourself trapped in a cage at the beginning of that path, left for the bears—

On the morning of his sixty-third birthday Vink was lying in bed, tidying up. He had recently returned from decimating parts of the Virgo galaxy cluster. He was dressed in normal-people clothes for the first time in forty-seven years. They were given to him by the Salvation Army. The reason he was wearing a faded beige suit and shoes that were a half size too big was because he was being released.

He had served his sentence quietly and peacefully and was no longer considered to be a threat to society. A withered old man, he was a sixty-three-year-old virgin.

He was released. Stepping through a large metal door, he entered an alien world of talkers. He had $232 in his pocket and a one-way bus ticket to his home-town. According to the conditions of his parole he would spend the rest of his life in the town, unable to discover the world that had been denied him.

Instead of going home he made a decision. He would use some of his money to exchange his ticket for one to Miami Beach, Florida. He had no idea why he wanted to go to Florida, it just seemed the proper thing to do.

Vink got on a bus and woke up two days later as it rolled into Miami. Deciding to check into a cheap motel by the beach, he spent two days sitting in his room looking out the window at the ocean. It seemed to him to be far too big for its own good. Most things, if you stop and think about it, tend to be.

On the third day Vink decided it would be best to take a walk and wandered into a convenience store to get some magazines to read. One of them was *Omni*. He also purchased a chocolate bar and a lottery ticket. By the fourth day Vink was left with only fourteen dollars, just enough to get breakfast and lunch. He was also kicked out of the motel.

He found a bus bench and flew around the universe for hours on end, prompting various bus drivers to pull over for no reason whatsoever. On the morning of the fifth day Vink was still sitting on that bench. Sadly, it was there that his adventures on this silly globe came to an end. Most things end that way. Abruptly, lacking substance, and with no fanfare.

After a group of children realized that they weren't poking a sleeping old man but rather a dead old man, the police were called and Vink's body was taken to the morgue. Since he had no family, his possessions were placed in a small box, as was his body. Most of his pristine organs were harvested for science, coincidentally, after the authorities discovered he was a fugitive who had broken his parole. His belongings, on the other hand, were held for several years by the city and then discarded. I would like to tell you that the lottery ticket that he had purchased the day before was worth an astronomical amount of money, but that's just not the case. Doing rarely closes out with critical acclaim or saddled on some mustang with a girl, galloping off into the sunset. Doing closes out by itself on a bus bench in Miami being poked at by adolescents who terminally never seem to know any better. And the lottery tickets in their pockets are never worth anything.

In the end there is only darkness, just like the beginning. Luckily for me I don't have to describe it to you. It is what it is. Best not to trick yourself with such useless verbs and nouns and things. Best to just start walking.

Todd & Matt go to Las Vegas with a porn star that will remain nameless for reasons of libel. The Director's Cut.

Most things in life start unexpectedly, though this was different because it involved a porn queen, two strippers named Debbie and Launa, and a large boa constrictor named Mr. Tickles.

First class is one of the biggest secret societies in the world. If you've only flown coach you have no idea what goes on up there. If you've flown first class then you know what I'm talking about. After the stewardess closes that magic curtain all the rules change. Booze flows like water, hand-rolled Cuban cigars are aplenty, they break out the blackjack tables (complete with topless, and quite often Swedish, vixen-like dealers). I would be lying if I told you that I was accustomed to these surroundings. I was merely a spy in the midst of decadent decay. I'm not saying I didn't like it. I'm just saying I was a spy. As to whose spy. Well, that's another matter altogether.

On this particular occasion I was accompanied by my somewhat incoherent co-conspirator, Todd Kerns. Three hours prior to being on the plane we were sitting quietly at a downtown restaurant eating oysters and throwing pieces of damp napkin at the ass of this rather large waitress. Things turned ugly when we attempted to use straws instead of our hands, we were quickly escorted to the nearest fire exit and discarded into an adjacent alley. It was then that we decided to go to Las Vegas for the weekend. Todd felt that we were long overdue for a vacation and Vegas might offer some solution to our hypertensive state.

There we were in first class, slipping through the night like a drunken teenage girl hopped up on illicit sugar smacks and Baby Duck. It seemed as if we were caught in some giant test tube filled with uncertain energies and strange, pig-faced people from some nightmarish land. I was lost and reeling in self-degradation and some strange warmth that always slips through my limbs when I know something morally irreversible is about to occur. I slumped down in my seat to try and sort the C-drive files in my mainframe when I gazed upon her legs. They were long legs. Long like a one-way street leading to some warped place of intimate viewing.

I knew her naked self from a thousand glossy-paged magazines. The sort that one procures from time to time to pass the never-ending hours of tour-

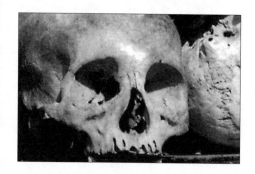

ing. But I was a stranger to her smile. It shocked me that her familiar lust-filled sneer didn't immediately show itself when my eyes made their way to her face. You often think of them one way only to discover that they're either much worse or doctors of astrophysics. This is typical of girls in dirty magazines. I was later to discover that she was in the "much worse" category, but at the time she played me like a bad country song.

She was unlike any woman I had ever met. And even though I was convinced that the devil was now female, I was stumbling to produce some rational dialogue that would endear me to her favour. Maybe it was the alien air in that first-class cabin. Maybe it was the mesmerizing shimmer of the soft lights. Maybe it was simply the fact that I was talking to a woman that would do just about anything in front of a camera for money. I don't know.

We continued talking in whispers and strange advances as the pig-faced people milled about the cabin snorting and laughing their pig laughs. Todd, strangely enough, was nowhere to be found. I would later discover him face down on the floor next to the rear exit with a Polaroid of him and a half-naked Swedish dealer in the bathroom. Memories are important.

Las Vegas: home to tens of thousands of fat people, buffets, superhotels owned by movie studios, and supermodel rejects. Las Vegas is where the low end of normality and botched plastic surgery meet to form something that resembles glamorous euthanasia. The lights of the strip, not unlike the star that led the wise men to Christ, beckon the average to be anything but themselves. Most victims of Vegas end up losers. Eventually everything comes full circle.

It's one of those places that you enter as Superman and leave as the swamp thing. No one gets out of Vegas clean, despite the attempts of late to make the city appear to be something other than what it really is. And what it is, is dirty. The smart realize it. That's why they go to Vegas, for the dirt. It doesn't matter if the mob runs Vegas or if big business runs it. Both are ignorant to its true purpose. A gateway to hell exists beneath Las Vegas. Either that or a river of pure milk chocolate.

As usual we had completely forgotten to secure lodgings. Upon our arrival we found ourselves standing in the airport looking around in bewilderment at our surroundings. It dawned on us that we were actually standing in another city. Maybe we weren't entirely serious back in that alley. Maybe the plane had flown through some kind of vortex that had brought us into a new reality, like teenagers waking up only to realize that the adults had vanished, leaving them in control of the world. Luckily my first-class seating companion spotted us and offered to put us up. She was working a show later that night at a strip

If you've got the guts you can have the glory. You can buy the glory if you want it bad enough. They'll sell it to you. They'll sell it to you for your guts. Remember that always.

I am dreaming of happy pandas. A whole field full of happy pandas. I am beside myself. I am entirely myself. I am going to set myself on fire. Just you wait and see.

club, but assured us that we wouldn't be a bother.

We ended up in a luxury suite high atop the city. Looking down from those huge windows everyone didn't seem so fat. Maybe it was the liquor talking, but I felt like I could drop a bomb and then casually order shrimp cocktail or some other kind of food that people rarely endeavour to make in the privacy of their own homes.

I felt like the god of Las Vegas up there looking down on pitiful creation. The slot jockeys and suburbanites bankrupted by the blackjack and poker tables. The hookers and the street trash, the well to do, the hope to do well, the well done. For a brief moment I saw myself from outside of my own body and was quite pleased for a change.

Todd was sprawled in the middle of the room trying to arm-wrestle a bottle of vodka. He knew he couldn't win. But that hasn't stopped anyone from trying for the past 500 years now has it.

So there we were. Sitting around a room that, in any other city, would be grounds for admittance into a mental institution. And sometime before 3 a.m. a blonde porn star was going to come walking through that door, possibly accompanied by other blonde porn stars, to slap me around. Or at least I hoped that was what would happen. I was perfectly wretched and deviant but completely at peace with it. Maybe that's the secret of Las Vegas.

It wasn't until well after four when she finally arrived. I'm sat on the sofa in one of those robes that expensive hotels have in the bathrooms and Todd was out on the balcony yelling passages from the bible at the miniature fat people down on the street. She looked tired, but tried to act like she was awake. She undressed right in front of us and went into the bathroom to get the other robe. Things were beginning to get weird.

For the first time I began to realized that my counterpart might be somewhat of a nuisance in this particular situation. I sat there on that sofa, my eyes following her across the room, while my brain tried to sort out the details of burying Todd's corpse somewhere in the desert. The demon of lust had complete control over my body, turning me into a fiend of the highest calibre. She sat on the bed and began to roll around and stretch like a cat. By this time I decided to bludgeon Todd using one of the heavier-looking lamps and take her for myself. It's times like this that require tact and unassuming movements. For all I knew Todd could have been planning to bludgeon me to death with the vodka bottle. Luckily, no violent action would be required, because at that moment there was a knock at the door. Enter Debbie, Launa, and the infamous Mr. Tickles.

Some of you might have seen Debbie and Launa do their show, known to most as Feather and Sky in *Taming The Snake*. Though banned from twenty-three states and four provinces, they still do their routine with the snake nightly in a variety of clubs. They're also available for private shows as well (at the whopping rate of $1,000 an hour). I thought about asking them why they called the boa Mr. Tickles but realized that there could only be one reason to call it that.

They put Mr. Tickles in the bathtub and returned to the living room to exchange pleasantries and have a drink. It was then somewhere in the neighbourhood of 5:45.

My self-control was slowly melting into the carpet like a cheap candle as my head snapped between the three trying to get a fix on which one would make the best target. And that was my first mistake. I was sitting in a room with three women that were professional adult entertainers. This was my pathetic high-school mentality; it wasn't a matter of what I wanted. It was more like what they were going to do to me and whether or not I'd survive.

It began to dawn on me that Todd and I weren't the hunters in the room. We were the hunted. We had been brought to this lofty den of promiscuity not by chance, but by a cunning lioness that knew full well what she was doing. There was to be a feast and we were the main course. For an added measure of torture we were made to helplessly watch the three girls launch into one of their threesome routines right in front of us. I have never been so completely immobilized in my entire life.

As a man you assume that, given the opportunity, you would jump right in if a situation like that ever arose. But that's just not the case. There's a good fifteen minutes of shock at first. It was so severe that my counterpart actually lost interest in the vodka bottle and started crawling across the floor to gain a better vantage point. It was like some scene one would expect to find in the depths of hell or in a girl's locker room on the best day of your life.

We sat there motionless while various acts were performed right in front of us. I have never felt real terror like this before. I'm not talking about the kind of fear you feel when you know the school bully is going to be waiting by the bike racks for you after class, but rather the terror you feel when some skinhead that's whacked out on pills and whiskey pulls a .45 out and puts it to your head. And judging from what I remember of Todd's expression, that's what he felt too.

Those fifteen minutes were the longest three days of my life. As if locked inside some terrible dream, I vaguely remember the girls crossing the floor

Steve loves the shopping-cart guy from Uridium 5. You know, we never did get that right. I looked it up and it's not URIDIUM 5, it's URIDIUM 15. Steve says that he does not care, it makes him happy nonetheless. Just like the pandas make me happy. We are all very happy eggs. Yes, indeed we are. Sometimes you've just got to say *"the hell with it all!"* and leave it at that. Sometimes you've got to remember to turn the stove off before you go to bed. It depends.

My father doesn't like it when I use profanity.

Especially when it turns perfectly good sentences into perfectly disastrous sentences.

For example:

example A) *Good try.*

example B) *Holy fucking shit you gimpy fuck, what the fuck was that?!*

Maybe Dad's got a point there.

towards us on their hands and knees. And if my memory serves me correctly, they were hissing. They say that war veterans usually remember the horrors of their ordeal far more clearly and vividly years after they've come home. I believe that to be true. I can only remember bits and pieces of the following twenty-four hours. Rivers of oil, chocolate sauce, and other fluids crowd my mind from time to time when I'm violently awakened by these memories. The cold and terrible images of silvery bindings, leather masks, three speed genies, circus midgets, and Miracle Whip also plague my recollection from time to time. I don't remember the snake. But I've seen Todd's face go absolutely white every time we see one on TV or in a photograph. I can only imagine the horrors that were thrust upon him.

Most of the time I try not to remember.

I woke up on the floor covered in what smelled like gin, though it could have been an antiseptic of some kind. Every muscle in my body felt like it had been removed and then put back slightly out of place. Sitting up, the horror of what had taken place started to hit me. Stumbling around the room I came upon the tattered remains of my clothes, the sofa, several tables, and the mini-bar. I later discovered Todd sandwiched between the bathroom wall and the toilet, wide awake, gazing blankly forward. His eyes were slightly rolled back in his head, like he'd taken a million sleeping pills and was beginning to see the rabbit people slowly encircling him. I hoisted him up and put him in the bed while I tried to figure out what to do next.

Escape was paramount. We would have to make a run for it and soon. Hopefully my counterpart would be up for it. We had little choice.

Swallowing panic every ten feet, I went to the lobby of the hotel hoping to find a clothing store or gift shop. The only thing I was able to get my hands on were two baby-blue Mickey Mouse t-shirts and two pairs of white tennis shorts. Having accepted the fact that insult would have to be added to injury, I headed back to the room and threw Todd in a cold shower. A half hour later he was able to realize that we had to flee before the succubus and her fellow demonettes returned from their daylight raids. Throwing on our clothes, we took the service elevator to the basement, slinked through a series of hallways, climbed a flight of stairs, and found ourselves in sunshine. We grabbed a cab to the airport, then home, followed by years of government-funded therapy.

Everyone in first class on the way back seemed to sense that we didn't belong there. The whole trip was toned down to a semi-decadent level, with a handful of the pig people venturing out of their seats to get down to the disco quietly pumping through the cabin. I was, as fate would have it, seated next to a nun on the return trip. And though considered by most to be a ser-vant of God, and therefore bound by some secret pact to be kind, she could smell my burning flesh and refused to engage me in conversation. My coun-terpart spent most of the flight throwing up in the bathroom, his head held gently over the vacuous receptacle by his lovely Swedish stewardess.

I felt as if I were running from something that I would never fully escape. But as we winged our way back into the bosom of the great Pacific Northwest, I remember thinking that I had survived some kind of test that had prepared me for a greater encounter in the future. And if so, then I was convinced that the future was x-rated. And in it I would remain a spy. As to whose spy. Well, that's another matter altogether.

Where dwells the hangman's hangman? In some forgotten tenement, soaked in the filth of the good Lord's inevitable conclusion, resigned to the ideals of duty where none should admit allegiance? Where dwells the second black mask, those hands of blistered patience steeped in the intimacy of doom brought?

Milton Hadley

There are pessimists in this world and there are optimists. There are the hunted, the hunters, the victims, the victimizers, the fools, the frayed, the genius, the ignorant, the oblivious, the obvious, and the incomprehensible. There are those who must deal with having been dealt impossible hands, those who know only the soft sides of luxury, and those who dwell in the small distance that often separates them. If you stop to consider it there is nothing more important than your life. And by that I am implying that your life is something altogether separate from yourself. Just because you are you does not make you your life. Life is too often misused to be considered the property of someone that never bothered to actually live it. No matter what happens during it, or how it is lived, you will eventually have to give it back. If you spend some time pondering such strange logic you may find yourself not going to work tomorrow morning. You may decide instead to sell the kids, kill your spouse, and head off into the adventure you always said that your life would be. But don't worry. You won't.

There are angry people in the world and there are those who know only the bliss of a simplistic ignorance. There are those who sell and those who buy. At the same instant that a child in some small village in Africa is getting their arms chopped off amidst the turmoil of yet another people's revolution, another of the same age and relative appearance might be nagging their mother to buy them the latest video game halfway around the would. Distraught that they will not get their way in the matter, they may say *"I wish I was dead."* There is quiet in the world and there is the noise of those who are too fractured to let it grow. There is force and there is frailty. There is worth and there is worthlessness.

This is a story about a little boy who was none of the above.

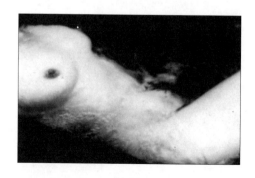

Just The Sky

Milton Hadley was a genius. When he was seven years old he could multiply six-digit numbers in a matter of seconds. His father, who was a retired United States Air Force Captain, sent Milton to a military academy when he was ten. He had hoped that Milton would one day work for the government cracking Soviet codes and such. Thankfully, the following year, both Mr. and Mrs. Hadley were killed by a freak tornado that swept through their suburb on the outskirts of Wichita. Had Mr. Hadley lived, Milton would have most likely remained at the military academy. Which would have been tragic, since the dorm that Milton had lived in was completely destroyed by an artillery shell that one of his classmates had hidden in a footlocker. Everyone on the top floor was killed by the blast. Everyone on the second and first floors were crushed to death by the third floor. Milton, it seemed, was the beneficiary of impeccable timing.

Following the death of his parents, Milton was sent to Bellingham, Washington to live with his Uncle Rex, whom he had never met before. Rex was socially baffling. He lived in a renovated barn with his third wife, Cora, and an assortment of animals that were, for the most part, matted with dirt and permanently smelt of marsh water. His acreage was considerable though, and was home to numerous wrecked cars, buses, and tire fires. It was also home to four very well-constructed ramps, three world-class jumping bikes, two street bikes, and one of the world's ugliest RVs. Since the age of twenty-four Rex had been a daredevil. Hence the name: *Reckless Rex*.

Milton arrived at the bus station still wearing his uniform, expecting his uncle to be the mirror image of his father. As he walked off of the bus he looked to his right and saw Rex and Cora standing there with his name written on a piece of yellow construction paper in purple marker. It was raining lightly and the paper had started to break apart in places. Rex, a cigarette dangling from his mouth, stood there leaning on the seat of his bike, covered in mud from head to toe. Milton was so mortified that he fainted.

Four months after Milton moved into the barn with Rex and Cora, Rex was severely injured during a performance at a monster truck show in the Tacoma Dome. Three days after the accident he would die of complications in hospital. This left Milton in the care of Cora, a borderline alcoholic, who knew very little beyond how to operate a kiln, roll grass, and make instant coffee. Knowing full well that she wouldn't be able to take care of Milton properly, she was left with little choice but to send him to live with Rex's first wife, Anna Hadley St. Claire, who was the nearest thing to a blood relative—as Anna and Rex had two daughters together. Cora gave him some half-assed explanations and put him on another bus.

Some days after his departure, Cora fell asleep while watching television one night and her cigarette, ill-balanced in the ashtray, fell to the floor and started a fire. The flames consumed the barn, killing Cora, the animals, and the majority of the world's Reckless Rex collectibles. Had Milton been there he too would have perished.

Dizzy from the orbit of his life, Milton had no clue what he would have to deal with in Massachusetts. He was about to play a key role in one of the most bizarre happenings in world history. All he wanted was a Coke and a bag of Lay's.

Things I Love To Say But Can't.

1. We are Devo.

2. Chosum.

3. Honey Pants.

4. Disco Dick Tease.

5. That's no moon.

If I were to start my own country I would:

Make it sound like some roller coaster-laden paradise when in fact it would be nothing more than an island laced with high-powered explosives. And, after killing thousands of innocent people, I'd go on *60 Minutes* and tell Ed Bradley that I was the leader of a worldwide death cult.

Just A Calm

Anna Hadley St.Claire met Rex Hadley at Boston College. The daughter of one of the most powerful industrialists in the Northeast, Anna had spent the majority of her life, up until college that is, in exclusive beach and country clubs.

When the unthinkable occurred—being rejected by Harvard—her father decided it would be best to sober her up by making her endure dorm life. Her roommate was a girl named Camille Stewart, the daughter of a Motel 6 maintenance man. Camille, who would—years later—go on to become a world-renowned and award-winning botanist, knew Rex Hadley from a local restaurant where the two of them had worked.

Rex did not attend Boston College. Rex was pretty much an idiot. The type that rich girls use to piss off their fathers.

The first time Anna met Rex he was naked. She had returned to her room following a literature class to discover him standing in front of her full-length mirror, flexing. She immediately began to laugh. After the initial shock of being discovered wore off, so did he. Camille had been allowing Rex to sleep in her bed during the day because he had been evicted from his apartment and was working as a bartender in a nearby tavern to pay off a gambling debt.

The two of them hit it off and the next thing they knew Anna was naked and Rex was flexing elsewhere. Two months later Anna dropped out of school and they eloped to Orlando during spring break. They were drunk, of course. Following their elopement they moved to Bakersfield, California, where Rex got a job working at a garage and began his love affair with jumping motorcycles. Anna, on the other hand, despised the place and everyone in it. She slowly began to realize that her actions were motivated by some need to anger her father. Late one October night, she left Rex, stole his car, and headed back to Massachusetts. When he awoke the next morning, Rex was not surprised when he read the note that she had left. He was somewhat angered that she took his car, but beyond that he didn't care much. What Anna failed to tell him in that note was that she was pregnant. With twins no less. But Rex would never learn of it.

Her father welcomed Anna back with open arms. Overjoyed that she had left Rex, their lifelong feud ended mere minutes after her arrival. And, even though he was secretly disappointed that she was having Rex's child, he realized that regaining his daughter far outweighed the whispers that would fill the locker room at the golf club.

Anna moved back into her parents' house and gave birth to the twins in

June. She named them Emma and Erica. Decades later Anna would be struck with massive bouts of guilt for denying her daughters any sort of relationship with their real father. She had remarried, of course, but not until the girls were old enough to realize that their stepfather wasn't their biological father.

Eleven days after Cora had buried Rex, she received a letter in the mail from Anna asking if Emma and Erica could get to know their real father. And that's where Cora got the idea. She knew that she would most likely deter Milton from becoming anything useful so she decided to write Anna back and work the guilt thing. She told Anna that Rex had recently been killed and that his nephew was now in need of family to look after him. Four days, two postmen, and three phone calls later it was settled. And Milton was packed off to yet another accident waiting to happen.

Just Some Black Clouds

Milton arrived at the St. Claire residence in the middle of an argument. The twins, Erica and Emma, were in front of the house screaming obscenities at each other while they hoisted .38s from time to time in threatening gestures. Anna was nowhere to been seen.

Anna's second husband, Jack St. Claire, had given up on the three of them four years earlier, having met someone altogether younger and far more sexually capitulating. This left the housemaid, Uma, to deal with the girls. An ex-Soviet power lifter, Uma was not the kind of woman to permit such nonsense for very long. Years of steroid use had left her nerves in a very precarious state. Stressful situations caused her head to start twitching uncontrollably, leaving her no option but to wedge her skull between a door and a doorframe until it subsided. Uma feared the twitching more than death itself.

When she realized that the girls were outside with the pistols again she immediately got the house shotgun and fired a shot out one of the windows. This caused several things to occur. The first was to cause the girls to dramatically throw themselves to the ground, where they immediately began rolling about with their guns pointed every which way in search of the illusionary threat. The cab driver that had dropped Milton off decided it best to simply depart the residence at the highest possible speed available him, his fee no longer a concern. And Milton fainted. He would awaken minutes later to discover the twins standing over him, their guns still clutched in their hands. And, before fainting the second time, he heard one say to the other "you get his feet, I'll get the device."

It is commonly thought that identical twins tend to get along better than

If I were allowed to do anything I wanted in one day, I would:

Fly 500 Ethiopian children to North America, give them all tasers, and drop them off in front a Super Value.

Buy the Bud Girls some El Pacifico.

Purchase the *USS Independence* and enter the America's Cup.

Rebuild the Canadarm in the space shuttle so that every time it's deployed it gives the world the finger.

Get the Bat moved from Canada's Wonderland to my backyard.

Buy Arsenal.

Replace every gun on Earth with those plastic guns that fire ping pong balls and proceed to start a world war.

You Can Tell Them I'm Coming. And Hell's Coming With Me.

There's a storm out there making for land. It is like a runaway train. You can feel it when you breathe. Breathing in an absolute silence to produce an absolute exasperation. It'll jab and then it'll use the hook. And it can dance like a ballerina. It has no intentions of allowing you to regain your feet. It prefers you down on the mat wondering what day of the week it is while you fish around in your blood-filled mouth for a couple of free teeth. It didn't come to prove anything to you. It came because it knew that there would be nothing to stop it.

most siblings. There are even those that contend that they share a special telepathic bond, one being able to detect when something happens to the other. This was not the case with the St. Claire twins. Their only aim was to kill each other. They attended school for all of four days before being sent home for their behaviour. They physically attacked four different private tutors, injuring one so badly that she spent three months in hospital. Their crowning achievement, though, was the accidental shooting of the their gardener, Dale Sellers.

Emma had fired several shots at her sister while she had been diving behind a hedgerow. As fate would have it, Dale was also behind the hedgerow, trying to coax a wounded parrot from beneath it. The bullet took him in the forehead. Erica spent a year in a juvenile detention facility, while her sister received three months for her part in it. The girls had attempted to kill each other on seven other occasions.

Fortunately the St. Claire estate was large enough to offer a buffer between the insanity of its occupants and the outside world. The twins hadn't left the grounds in over eleven years, having since moved out of the main house, taking up residences in diametrically opposed buildings on the property. Emma had turned the pool house into a fortress while Erica lived in the basement of the staff house (where she spent the majority of her time mixing volatile chemicals).

It was rare for the twins to work together on anything, so it came as a surprise to Uma when they wheeled Milton through the front door in a wheelchair that had been fitted with restraints. Erica had designed the chair to kill Emma. She had also built a runway from the top of the highest hill on the estate down to the duck pond. Her plan was to surprise her sister, knock her unconscious, strap her in the chair, wait until she came around, and then push her down the runway into the pond where she would drown.

Erica was pleased that she actually got to put one of her inventions to use. Emma just eyeballed the thing, frantically trying to figure a way to break out of it if ever she found herself strapped in. There was never a dull moment at the St. Claire's. Sort of like there was never a dull at Stalingrad.

By the time Milton had regained consciousness Anna had returned from the city. The twins were nowhere to be found by then, as they rarely ventured near the large estate house when their mother was at home. Uma had carried the boy upstairs and put him in bed well before Anna's return. Milton lay there looking up at the shadows on the ceiling, wondering what was to become of him. He counted the spaces between the shadows. There were 210,346 of them.

That night the twins did not sleep. They paced back and forth in their respective dwellings attempting to deduce the meaning behind the arrival of the little boy. And, in their own demented ways, they both came to the same conclusion. Each was convinced that their mother was in league with the other and that the boy had been brought in to replace them. Emma went immediately to her machine gun and fired several volleys into the corner of the staff house. Following this brief outburst Milton drifted off into what would be the last deep slumber of his life. And that night he dreamed of a land of baguette lovers occupied by barrette haters.

Ninny Hawks
In 1951 Colonel Albert St. Claire spent the majority of his time casually walking his estate. A full life of industrial strong-arming comfortably behind him, he favoured wandering the wooded bits of his property flushing out fowl with his dogs and blasting them from the sky. The colonel enjoyed it so much that, when proper game was out of season, he would pay top dollar to have a variety of domesticated birds released around the grounds so that he might continue to spend his days flushing and blasting. Many a cockatoo and parrot met their end in the sights of his shotgun.

Years later his granddaughter would spend her nights wondering from whom her daughters had inherited their instabilities. She had read the appropriate literature, conferred with the appropriate specialists, adopted and abandoned the appropriate religions, and even spent tens of thousands of dollars travelling to the Italian Alps to meet with one of the world's foremost psychics. But try as she might she could never put a finger on it. Her twin daughters, whom she loved, detested each other. And one day their inability to successfully do away with one another would come to an end. What Anna did not know was that her grandfather was partially to blame.

In the summer of 1951 the butler at the St. Claires' was a coloured man by the name of Albert Hawks. Albert hailed from Kentucky. He had come north in search of work as a small boy some thirty-four years earlier. And, since the day he left home, he had neither seen nor heard from any of his relations. Albert started at the St. Claire manor as a yard boy at the age of sixteen. By his thirty-fifth birthday he had become the estate's butler. In his later years the colonel tended to trust Albert more than his oldest friends and even his own family. Albert did the firing and hiring of staff. Albert kept in phone contact with the lawyers and doctors and politicians. Albert kept up the colonel's correspondence. When President Kennedy was assassinated, Albert attended the funeral for him.

The only thing September is good for is the artificial inflation of clothing and stationery prices. Things you could get for maybe half as much in June now put you in the poorhouse until November. The world, by some strange process, begins to revert back into a state of controlled mania, subduing that animalistic anarchy that ran rampant through the streets only weeks before. Everyone is recovering from some kind of abnormality, some kind of euphoric withdrawal, lamenting over vacation photos and letters from that summer fling which will forever represent some absolute, 48-hour perfection at some hotel in Antigua. No pasts, no pertinent details. You were someone else there for a while. But it's September now. Mob rules.

The kids go back to school and sit in those classrooms catatonically staring out the windows into the late summer afternoons. Teachers lecture in alien languages while the managers of various Dairy Queens pore through employee records trying to figure out which summer-staff member is most likely to make a career out of serving ice cream.

The word responsibility takes on a whole new meaning. In July it meant that you made sure you had a good time. In September it means that the universe has got you under its thumb.

I was thinking of quitting music and attempting to ride around the world on a giant, oversized Big Wheel. After checking the most recent edition of *The Guinness Book*

Late one Saturday morning in the summer of 1951 the phone in the staff house kitchen started ringing. Albert Hawks was sitting at the kitchen table drinking a cup of coffee and perusing a copy of *Life* magazine. He got up from his chair and answered the phone. And, to his great surprise, his youngest sister was on the other end. Her name was Ninny.

Ninny Hawks had, up until that week, been the victim of a very violent marriage. Her husband had done time for a variety of crimes during their twelve years together. He had returned home from a three-year term five days earlier and had taken up where he had left off. This meant that he slept all day and beat his wife when he was sober enough to keep his balance. Having just spent the better part of two years alone, Ninny came to the conclusion that enough was enough. She planted an axe between his eyes when he was asleep, packed a suitcase, and walked out of town in the middle of the night. Five days later she arrived in Boston and called the only number that she had for her brother. Albert had sent it in a letter when their mother passed away. He had not been able to attend the funeral and sent a letter to his siblings and aunt in his stead.

Ninny had kept the letter, realizing that she might one day need some way of contacting Albert in the event that the family ever attempted to get together for a reunion or whatnot. As it turned out her reunion with her older brother was not a joyous one. Albert was not pleased with the circumstances surrounding Ninny's arrival. It was one thing to show up unannounced on his doorstep, it was something altogether different to show up with a murder rap.

The first thing that Albert did was put Ninny in his bedroom so that no one would see her. He then went directly to the colonel's study to have a conversation about what to do with her. Despite what most might have thought, the colonel and Albert were the closest of friends. This would explain why Albert looked after the colonel as he did right up until his death.

Albert walked from the staff house to the main house and found the colonel in his study, reading. The two had a brief conversation that was followed by a minute of violent screaming. Albert then left the study, walked back to the staff house, gathered up his sister and her things, put on a coat, and led her out into the woods. To this day, Ninny has no clue what was said between her brother and the colonel. But whatever it was, it ended up with her living in a filthy cabin in the backwoods of Massachusetts.

And, since the 12th of July 1951, Ninny Hawks had not left the St. Claire estate. Even when Albert died she did not venture from the small, self-imposed confines of her time-warped condition. Albert always told her that the colonel strictly forbade it. For all of the 1960s she did not venture further than a half mile from her shack. She kept chickens and goats, a garden, and she fished. And during all that time she went, for lack of a more grandiose term, completely mad. Ninny would inadvertently turn the twins against each another when they were very little.

One evening, during a violent storm, Ninny lost her footing on some rocks and fell off of an overhang into a creek. She landed on her right leg, puncturing her thigh. Realizing how serious the wound was, she decided to do what was for her the unthinkable. The next night she would make her way to the estate house and find something to help prevent infection. It was easy enough, seeing as the doors on the estate were never locked. Once she made it to the house, she simply entered and went about looking for some alcohol or antiseptic. Luckily, in one of the ground floor washrooms, she came across some peroxide. It was during that visit that Ninny met the twins. Erica and Emma caught her red-handed as she limped down the hall between the main foyer and the kitchen.

Ninny, realizing that the girls could quite easily tell their parents about her, decided to do the only thing that she could think of. She sat the girls down in the kitchen and told them this story. It went a little something like this...

A real long time ago there was this little girl that lived in the country. One day, when the girl was walking through the forest, she came upon a small little fella standing on a rock. The little fella didn't say nothing. So the little girl picked up a stick and gave him a little poke. Still the little fella didn't say nothing. So she poked him some more. Finally, after a whole heap of poking, the little fella put his hands on his hips and said "Now little girl! Why in the world would you spend all this time poking at a little fella such as me?"

The little girl just stood there and didn't say a thing. So the little fella jumped off the rock and climbed up into a nearby tree. The little girl thought that he looked real funny up in that tree and she started laughing at him. The little fella inched his way out onto one of the big, overhanging branches until he was right over the little girl, and then jumped off the branch and landed on the little girl's head. The little girl wasn't laughing anymore. The little fella went back to his rock and stood on it as he had been before. The little girl's body eventually rotted away, though some of it was eaten by a fox that came by.

The weeks went by and the little girl's parents were beginning to think that they were never going to see her again. Her pap thought it best to go wandering in the woods to see if he could find her. So he went into the woods and started

of World Records I've discovered that it's never been done before. People have ridden a lot of things around the world, but never a Big Wheel. Now I'm quite aware of how ridiculous I'll look doing it, but there's always a price for glory. Who really cares if you record records, play shows, and make music videos. In this day and age people can put that sort of thing together in a matter of milliseconds. Think of how original it would be as a conversational piece at a party.

"Yeah, I rode a Big Wheel around the world. What did you say you did again? Dentistry?"

This is the kind of thing September should do to you. You should refuse to pay your credit-card bills, eat whatever you want, drink in excess, and throw wild Caribbean theme parties every Saturday night. Life would be like a Tom Robbins novel on uppers and everyone could stop pretending they have somewhere to go.

I don't have anywhere to go. There, I said it. Not one single goddamn place. My name's Matt and I have nowhere to go. Though, come to think of it, Six Flags would be agreeable. Roller coasters, above all things, are my greatest love. They don't really go anywhere either.

It's called melancholia. Supposedly people get this ailment in the fall and winter when everything's bleak and life just isn't worth living anymore. In spring and summer you're a self-contained carnival. Come fall you just can't find the strength to carry on.

calling her name while he searched around. But no matter his calling, the little girl never answered.

One day, while he was wandering, he came across the little fella standing on the rock. And, like before, the little fella didn't say anything. So the man picked up a stick and gave the little fella a poke. Still, the little fella didn't move from his rock. Hours went by and then the little fella finally put his hands on his hips and said "Now sir! Why in the world would you spend all this time poking a little fella such as me?"

The man just stood there shrugging his shoulders. So the little fella got off his rock and climbed up the tree. The man thought the little fella looked funny, and he started to laugh. When the little fella got up onto the branch he crept out on it until he was right over the man's head. And then, while the man was pointing up at him laughing, the little fella jumped on his head and knocked him to the ground. Eventually, his body rotted away just like his daughter's had.

Months went by and the mother of the little girl was beginning to think that she would never see her daughter or her husband ever again. So one night, in a fit, she went running out into the woods and came across a little fella standing on top of a giant diamond.

She said, "My, that's a very pretty diamond you have!"

And the little fella jumped down, took off his little cap, wiped his brow with his sleeve, and said, "Ma'am, you're the first person that ever realized I was standing on a diamond."

And at that wondrous point in the telling, Ninny produced a very large piece of glass from her handbag and slammed it down on the table. And from that moment on both Emma and Erica St. Claire considered Ninny Hawks to be the greatest person they had ever met.

Two Little Rich Girls in a Pot of Stew. Add a Dash of Garlic, Cook Em 'Till They're Through.

The twins viewed their mother as a figure constantly in transit. Occasionally she might dare to put on the mask of motherhood for a while, but for the most part she spent her days in Boston playing bridge and drinking a considerable amount of gin. Their stepfather, to be fair, was even more of a shadow than their mother. He commonly deemed it necessary to personally oversee the completion of whatever project his company was involved in at the time. Of course such things invariably meant travelling to distant parts of the world for extended periods of time. Being as young as they were it seemed to them as if their stepfather was merely a voice that came floating out of a telephone receiver. Surely all fathers were the same, they thought. Perhaps all fathers lived in a far-off land. And there was only one phone in this land. Surely, had his phone time not been limited by the fact that all those other fathers had to call their daughters as well, he would have called more often. But to their credit, the twins dwelled on the absence of their parents for only a brief time in their early childhood. The truth of the matter was that they were far too intelligent to give much thought to it once they realized that their parents were worse off than themselves.

The girls read the paper and watched the news. They realized how well-off their family was. And they also realized that their parents only had themselves to blame for their lives. So it seemed to them that there were better things to do than lament over the absence of love and support. Such as tracking down old ladies that surely dwelt somewhere on the vastness of their estate.

The twins set about finding Ninny in the most expedient way possible. Tapping into the psychosis that would eventually engulf them, they got the Yellow Pages, thumbed through it until they found what they were looking for, picked up the phone, and dialed a number. A rented helicopter arrived at noon the next day.

Discovering Ninny's location was simple after that. Being that it was winter they had the pilot hover high enough to allow Erica to survey the entire estate with a pair of binoculars. All she needed to do was search for signs of chimney smoke. They had the pilot fly to the area where Ninny's shack stood and made sure to note the location on a map. They then had him turn back and return to the house.

You might think this unlikely of girls so young but I assure you that it did occur. Some of you might think that no one in their right mind would rent a helicopter to two young girls. A free-flowing multitude of one-hundred-dollar bills can have that effect on a financially ailing helicopter-rental company though. And, despite the fact that they were preschoolers, they were astoundingly smart for their age. Imagine being confronted by two small girls with fists full of hundreds trying to explain to you that they're looking at various options for a landscaping endeavour that they wish to surprise their parents with for their anniversary. After five minutes of standing there completely stunned I just took the money and kept my mouth shut.

The following morning Erica and Emma set out from the house in search of Ninny's hideout. Having packed the provisions and equipment they considered necessary for the journey, they marched through the rear gardens, past the greenhouses, and into the park. The St. Claire estate was, for the

You've been kidding yourself long enough, you figure. Maybe they can freeze you for half the year so you just have to put up with yourself during the warmer months. That's why I'm riding a Big Wheel around the world.

I've planned the whole trip so I will reside in an endless state of summer. Which should mean that I'll be in a good mood from now on. Which should worry you. Lost in such a euphoric state I'm sure to start penning songs about money, songs about parties, songs about how cool I might look in a rented Ferrari. I'll play shows in Monaco and tour the world in a huge, rented cruise ship. Never knowing that I could feel such freedom, I will willingly become all that I once detested.

Then again, maybe I won't. If you're out

there, if you're seconds away from ordering the Tony Robbins self-help tapes, if you're thinking of rendering yourself helpless because it seems the path of least resistance, just remember what you were taught as a child. 1] STOP, DROP, and ROLL. 2] NEVER TAKE CANDY FROM A STRANGER. 3] there is no 3. I've been sitting here for ten minutes thinking. But there is no 3.

The Boomtown Rats hated Mondays. The world unknowingly hates September. It's like consciously allowing yourself to return to servitude. We do it without knowing, like so many other instances that now offer us nothing but regret and embarrassment. Things like spandex, MilliVanilli, and professional wrestling. You're cringing.

most part, littered with stands of trees separated by small clearings, ponds, and creeks that spread out across a small range of hills. The further one went from the gardens and polo park, the rougher the terrain became. Having underestimated how difficult it would actually become, the twins found themselves faced with a variety of ravines and other impassible terrain that they were forced to circumnavigate. This took time of course. Time that, under such circumstances, slipped by quite unnoticed.

Having walked deep into the wilds of their property, the girls paid little attention to the fact that the afternoon had turned into evening. Things under the spreading trees were clouded by an encroaching darkness that is legendary in the forest. One minute the sun is shining and the next it isn't. An hour after sunset the girls were pushing through underbrush in the dark, unable to see more than five feet in front of them. And it was then that the unthinkable occurred.

Having taken the lead most of the day, Emma had started to cut corners when it came to paying attention to things such as dips in the ground and branches that lashed back to hit her sister. The further they went the more careless and annoyed she became. They were little girls, mind you, which meant that smallish holes were, in fact, medium-sized holes and so on. It also meant that they were somewhat frightened. Geniuses or not, they were still children. It also meant that they spent most of the latter portion of their expedition arguing. About things like who had finished the cream soda or who had allegedly read the map incorrectly. When Emma fell off the cliff the two of them were going on about who was to blame for this adventure.

Ninny Hawks had been following the girls for about an hour when Emma fell off the cliff. Despite the fact that Ninny knew they were approaching the cliff, for it was there that she had fallen and hurt herself only weeks before, she did nothing to alert the girls to the danger. She had doubled back behind them in an attempt to ford the river at a shallow point and then watch them as they argued about how they were going to get across.

Ninny thought quite highly of the twins at first. She was impressed that they did not turn back at the first sign of adversity, nor when the sun went down. They pushed relentlessly forward, which is what made Ninny change her mind about them. In the beginning she thought it sweet that the girls were trying to find her. But it is not like rich little girls to go to such extremes as this. Rich little girls give up after several hours of being lashed in the face by pine boughs, they do not wander further into the woods with night setting in. This made Ninny think that they were up to something. At that moment she decided that the girls must never find her or her house.

Emma fell off the cliff and down into the icy waters of the creek below. She landed flat on her back which, due to her small stature, probably saved her life. Had she gone in head first she would have hit the creek bed and split her head wide open. Had she gone in feet first she would have easily broken both legs. Thankfully she weighed so little that landing on her back, though painful, allowed the shallow water to break her fall.

She cried out in pain, which terrified Erica to no end. Having heard but not seen her sister plummet in the blackness before her, she stood clinging to a tree trunk, paralyzed with fear. Emma, on the other hand, once her crying abated, sobered up to the reality of the situation. It was extremely dark and extremely cold. And, to top it off, her attempts to coax her sister into looking for a way down to her were futile. Erica refused to move. The two talked for a while until Erica was cut off abruptly in mid-sentence. That was all she remembered. After screaming her sister's name in terror for four or five minutes Erica was hit on the head from behind as well.

When the twins regained consciousness they were lying on a wet mattress facing each other, their hands and feet bound with gardening string. The room that held them was faintly lit by a candle and the mattress smelled as if it had been soaked in gasoline. Ninny Hawks was nowhere to be seen, though the girls could hear something or someone moving around in an adjacent area. Their first order of business was to begin wailing terribly, which they did for some time. Following the outburst Emma decided the best thing for them would be to attempt an escape, though she could offer no plan as to how it should be done. They deliberated on into the night or the morning, neither could be sure.

At long last, as the girls were about to admit to each other that, despite their formidable brains, neither could come up with any realistic escape method, Ninny emerged through a rickety door and walked over to them. Too terrified to say anything, they lay there watching her. After standing over them, moving her eyes from one to the other, Ninny reached down, grabbed them by the feet, and dragged them across the floor. The twins started to scream. Ninny stopped dragging them and began kicking them in the back. The twins screamed even louder.

Ninny returned to dragging them across the floor and up a small dirt tunnel into another room. Once inside the room Ninny dragged the girls towards a large pit that was situated in the centre of the room. The pit was about ten feet from side to side and seven or eight feet deep. It smelled of offal and

Have you ever seen pictures of yourself from the past? There's no escaping it. Everyone, at one time or another, buys into something without giving it much thought. For my generation it was parachute pants, pointy leather boots, hair gel, and all those strange dances that Dave Genn knows so well. Some of you out there might have missed all that. Some of you might not be old enough to be considered so stupid. But in fifteen years you'll look back at yourself wearing your ridiculously big pants and wonder what you were thinking. Maybe you'll wonder why your underwear was always showing or your hair was blue and purple. And if those things just happened to be like that in a September, or even several Septembers, won't you look the fool.

The thing I could never understand is why they put October after September. Home to Halloween, October is not only good for treats but provides ample excuse to return to that summer-like non-you. Halloween provides the ultimate release of the year. For one night you get to dress up and act like an idiot. And if you do it correctly you can impersonate someone that you don't like and get them into a shit load of trouble. The Dead Kennedys got it right in that song. That and Forest Fire.

So you're probably asking yourself, as you most assuredly must, does he have a point? Is he going to take this somewhere or be conveniently ambiguous so as to escape some kind of finality. Does he do it on purpose? They're valid questions. Questions that I one day hope to answer for you. But as far as

teemed with flies. Loosening the bonds on their legs, she kicked the girls several more times to subdue them and then tipped them into the pit. The girls fell in tandem, Erica landing squarely on her sister.

The pit was filled with the remains of various animals in varying states of decomposition and what smelled like human waste. Having screamed themselves hoarse, the twins struggled to free their legs and then worked together to loosen their hands. This was easier said than done, as Emma had broken several ribs during the fall and was having difficulty breathing. The girls lay there clinging to each other, their voices spent, tears streaming down their faces. And then, as if the situation couldn't be made any worse, the lights went out.

A Fraction of an Inch Either Way

Ten hours would pass before Uma thought to trouble Mrs. St. Claire with the news that her daughters were nowhere to be found. Having tied one on the night before, Anna dismissed the intrusion with a wave of her hand, adjusted her night mask, and went back to bed. Her instructions on the matter were clear. "They'll turn up," she said.

By nine that night Anna was a nervous wreck, the police had been summoned, and Uma had been fired and rehired a half dozen times. The police were convinced that the twins had fallen prey to kidnappers and were most likely miles away, locked in the trunk of a car. They spared Anna this theory, of course, thinking it best to feed her false hope by convincing her that the girls were just hiding.

The local police did not think to search the St. Claire estate for the twins, nor did they inform other law-enforcement agencies concerning the possibility that the St. Claire girls had been abducted. Instead they sat around waiting for the inevitable phone call that would confirm their theory. But no ransom call would come.

Within walking distance of the twins' location, the police spent the better part of a week trying to piece together what had become of the girls. It wasn't until a junior officer dropped a chocolate bar behind a desk in the foyer that they turned up the receipt for the helicopter rental. Later that day the police came to question me and I returned to the St. Claire estate with my helicopter to show them what I had done with the twins.

You'd think that the police would have been suspicious of chimney smoke rising from the woods off in the distance but it really didn't occur to them that it was out of the ordinary. Another four days would pass before a detective, quite harmlessly, mentioned to Anna that he admired the estate and inquired why the guest house was located so far from the main house, referring to the chimney smoke he'd seen from my chopper. Anna perked up at this of course, telling him immediately that the only other lodging on the property, besides those located within plain view of the estate house, was the stable house.

This confused the detective, who did his best to match up the location of the stable house with the smoke he had seen rising from the woods off in the distance. Anna gave it little thought as well, automatically thinking the man to be one of those Better-Homes-and-Gardens types that loves to find cheap ways to make their paltry suburban houses look majestic.

I won't bore you with the arduous details concerning the eventual realization that there was something odd about that smoke. I won't bother telling you about how they spent the whole night and most of the next morning searching the property in grids. But I will tell you that, when they finally did discover Ninny's shack and kicked in the door, Ninny was dead.

They found her lying on the floor with a fire poker stuck in her stomach. The girls, on the other hand, were discovered at the end of the earthen tunnel that Ninny had burrowed out over three decades of delusion. They found Erica first, crouched up in a ball at the edge of the pit, covered in blood, gripping a large piece of glass. Emma, who had been run through by the fire poker as well, was lying comatose in the pit, barely alive. Thankfully my helicopter was at hand and the police had me fly her to the hospital. Another half hour and she wouldn't have lived.

The days and weeks that followed teemed with innuendo and scandal. Firmly in the hot seat, Anna was badgered by the media day and night about Ninny Hawks and how something of that nature could occur right under her nose. Anna's only option given the circumstances was to drink, sleep all day, and try to forget that her life had turned into a nightmare. The sheer bizarreness of the situation could be easily encapsulated by the fact that Anna's husband, having been contacted and presented with the details, chose not to come home.

In the months following the ordeal the girls were seen by a variety of psychologists in an attempt to help them deal with what had happened. Neither had talked about it though. Nor would they ever.

Once the twins returned home from the hospital the bizarre hatred that now exists between them was glaringly evident. And it was then that the murder attempts began. The first such attempt came when Erica tried to stab

September is concerned let me wrap it up by saying this. Either you do or you don't. You either are or you aren't. You either pump or you slump. Either you have it or you don't have it. And if you don't, is there some kind of class you can take to get it? My name's Matt and I have nowhere to go. I, like the roller coaster, always end in the same place. Right here, it would seem.

That Whole Opium/Talking Animals Thing.

It was in some rat-infested flophouse in Calcutta if my memory serves me correctly. I was lying in a dirty, sweat-soaked bed, dimed on opium, when there came a knock at the door. I got up and went over to see who it was. It's not like I hadn't met talking animals before that night. There was that time in Shanghai when I had a four-hour conversation with two mice and what appeared to be a badger. I later convinced myself that it was all just a dream because it was unlikely that a badger would be on vacation in China with two mice. And then there was that time with Todd in Vegas when we were held captive by a porn star and two strippers. They had a snake. And I'm pretty sure that it could talk.

Emma with a kitchen knife during breakfast, right in front of their parents. Her stepfather was forced to wrestle her to the floor, as Emma rushed over and immediately started kicking her in the head. It's been like that ever since.

And So—The War

Milton awoke to unfamiliar surroundings. Having been at the St. Claires' for only two weeks he was still not used to the place. Replacing the smell of wet hay was the harsh, headache smell of lemon Pledge. And every morning, as he drew air in through his nose, it reminded him that he had been packed off to this place to avoid complication. He was beginning to wonder what exactly the complication was. Him? Or everyone else?

And during those first fourteen days at the estate he had not encountered either of the girls that had set upon him on the front drive. He had spent time exchanging pleasantries with Anna and Uma, but his only formal introduction to the twins came in the small hours of the morning when they exchanged heavy weapons fire and insults at the top of their lungs. No one ever brought it up though, so Milton never bothered to ask. To Milton the only advantage to being at the St. Claires' was the many books that the colonel had been wise enough to collect during his life. His library was extensive. Having spent the majority of his veraciously available reading years living in a barn with a stunt man and the wife of a stunt man, he viewed the St. Claire library as ancient scholars must have the great library of Alexandria.

On the fourteenth day of Milton's habitation there came a knock at the front door that went unanswered. Having been left to fend for himself that day, as Uma had gone into Boston with Anna, Milton had forgotten that there was no one else to answer it. An hour passed before Milton, who was reading in the library, realized that there had been no answer to the knocking. Curious about who it was, he put his book down and started to walk across the room towards the main foyer. As he was walking something caught his eye through the large rear library windows. Walking over to investigate, Milton found himself staring at the most bizarre sight of his young life.

There was a man in a suit dangling over the swimming pool, his arms and legs attached to ropes that had been tied between the pool-house balcony and an upper window of the staff house. The man, who struck Milton as being rather calm, was facing the water, his head moving about in an attempt to survey his bonds. The twins, who had obviously subdued the poor old man, stood facing each other on opposite sides of the pool, both simultaneously slotting 9-mm bullets into handgun clips. Why they had worked together to dangle a stranger above the swimming pool was anyone's guess. Since Milton was not the confrontational sort, he could think of nothing better to do than simply watch. Thankfully the old man had a pretty good idea of what he was going to do. He would melt the guns with his mind and then implore the boy at the window to cut the ropes.

The Incredible Dr. Chalky

It all started in a chair. Ernie Chalky was sitting in the larger of his two living-room chairs flipping through a *National Geographic* when the phone rang. It was not as if he commonly received calls about ceramic dogs that had allegedly attacked and killed human beings. Over the years Ernie had discovered that the clergy, compared to most, almost always tended to blow things out of proportion. So when he found himself talking to a frantic priest he really thought little of it. The fact that the priest was attacked and consumed by a ceramic dog mid-sentence had nothing to do with his inability to take the priest seriously. Granted, once Ernie heard the receiver hit the floor and the priest's screams echo off into the bare-walled corners of the room, he realized there was a good chance that the priest was on the level (and, more than likely, in a basement). It wasn't until the dog picked up the phone and started talking that Ernie knew he was dealing with a very serious situation. Because it is, in the opinion of most, quite odd for ceramic dogs to be able to speak perfect Latin.

For someone in Ernie's profession it is not uncommon to come across inanimate objects that possess the ability to move about of their own free will and speak a variety of languages. For example, four years earlier Ernie had spent the better part of three months tracking a Portuguese-speaking flaming sword all over northern Madagascar. He prevailed, of course, but it was not without anguish. It had been appearing out of thin air and hacking unsuspecting villagers to pieces. You may think it trivial, but it is actually quite difficult to catch something that pops in and out of a standardized molecular constitution. But who are you to call when such abnormalities abound? *Ghostbusters* was just a movie.

Ernie was just a boy when Captain Chalky found him in a ditch in the dead of winter. England was a different place then, having survived German bombs and rockets. Perhaps that's why Ernie's parents decided to leave it. His mother was an Essex girl, but moved to Wales after his father was unable to find work in London. His father was a Welshman, as was Ernie. His mother, being

But there again I can't be 100 percent sure that it actually could. A lot of weird things happened that night and a talking snake wouldn't have been the weirdest

I got out of bed, went over to the door, opened it, and stood there gazing down at a mongoose wearing a safari get-up and tinted glasses. And that's how I know it wasn't a dream: none of the other talking animals I've come across ever had luggage.

His name was Basle. Basle Montcliff the Third. And he was passing through to Southeast Asia on a hunting expedition. Basle was a professional tracker and killer of snakes. The kind of expert that had spent a lifetime doing his job meticulously.

Now I'll admit that I had my doubts about

the entire thing at first. After all, I was so high on opium at the time that my own mother could have come to the door and I probably wouldn't have recognized her. Then again, there was the off chance that the mongoose was my mother.

The strangest thing about the incident was that Basle seemed like the kind of fellow that commonly lodged at far better establishments than the one in which our conversation took place. His refinement dictated better surroundings. I, on the other hand, am at my best whilst doused with shit.

There have been stranger times I'm told. I've been assured by some of my closer friends that, on occasion, I have indulged in far more perplexing behaviour than speaking that she was entirely English, didn't think much of the Welsh. Perhaps that's why she left Wales and returned to England when Ernie was seven years old. After all, it was filled not only with Welshmen but Ernie's father, who was, to his great discredit in her eyes, as Welsh as one could be. Ernie ended up staying with his father. Perhaps she simply forgot him in her haste to leave. Perhaps, realizing that she had, she paused some distance away and considered going back for him. In doing so, she realized that she might wake her husband and thought better of it. So Ernie's mother left him and his father in the dead of night and went back to England with his unborn brother Andrew as passenger. Ernie has never met Andrew. He hadn't really met his mother either.

Ernie's father was not what you would call an intelligent man. His father was a coal miner. The life of a miner is one filled with nightmares of suffocation and collapse. Maybe that is why a great many of them drink as they do. To see if they can destroy their livers before they succumb to the inevitability of black lung. Ernie's father would die from a combination of the two. So Ernie found himself in the care of Father Michael O'Reilly at the Boys School of Holy Seclusion. And during his time there Father Michael repeatedly attempted to convince Ernie that Jesus was ever-present, if only he looked hard enough. But try as he might, Ernie would always come to the same conclusion: the Almighty's picture was everywhere, but He was nowhere to be found.

Five months after his arrival at Holy Seclusion, Ernie came to the realization that his life would be doomed if he were to remain for long. Ernie, not unlike his mother, left Wales in the middle of the night and travelled to England. He would get no further than Lydney before the horrific reality of his actions would set in. He would spend that night in an abandoned barn and would awaken the next morning to find that his toes had turned completely purple. He would then hobble as far as he could in an effort to find help. He made it as far as the roadway. And that's where Captain Chalky discovered him.

Doctor Captain Finnegan Chalky was a Cambridge man. He was also an ordained Anglican minister and a highly decorated RAF fighter pilot. These three things had very little to do with one another, and he would later tell Ernie that each was a foolish pursuit of three goals: 1) knowledge 2) presumed access to the afterlife 3) a vehicle in which to test the boundaries between being smart enough to know better and ignorant enough not to. To the best of Ernie's knowledge Captain Chalky didn't hold a Ph.D in anything except himself, despite the fact that he could speak four languages and knew the answer to every question that Ernie ever put to him. He was, in Ernie's eyes, someone that one would consider to be the perfect representation of a human being. Well, up until the point when he told Ernie that he could bend metal with his mind anyway.

He could melt the fenders of cars, turn doorknobs, open locks, and so on. The first time Ernie ever witnessed it Captain Chalky was attempting to loose some earth under a fence with a hoe. He couldn't get the hoe far enough under the fence so he simply bent the end of it and slid it under. For days Ernie could not believe what he saw. Captain Chalky could in fact bend metal with his mind. And Ernie, as his student, would receive the secret of this gift before the captain's passing.

Ernie lived with Captain Chalky in a variety of places up until his death in 1976. Known in various circles in Europe as paranormal superstars, they were employed by a wide variety of organizations that included such celebrity members as the Pope, the Prince of Monaco, and Salvador Dali. When Captain Chalky died, Ernie decided to carry on their work by himself. He packed and moved to Mexico, where he purchased a large estate near San Carlos on the Baja. From there Dr. Ernie Chalky would conduct the business of dealing with those things that no one else would believe possible.

Ernie Chalky, hot on the trail of a Latin-speaking ceramic dog, has tracked the beast through Central America, up the west coast of the States, and then east to New England. Two days before arriving at the St. Claires' front door he had learned that the dog was camped out on their property. He was oblivious to the added danger of the insane twins that had full run of the grounds. Before he knew it he found himself dangling above a swimming pool, having been hit on the head and knocked unconscious. And, to make matters worse, there was a demonically possessed ceramic dog somewhere in the area that was out for blood.

Good movies...

Having finished loading before her sister, Erica attempted to move towards a nearby retaining wall for cover. But something wouldn't allow her to. Instead she found the weight of the gun change, as if she was no longer burdened by it. She then felt the gun raise her arm, coming to rest in line with her sister's head. And then, without her finger being on the trigger, the gun went off. As if in slowmotion, as all horrific things in this world tend to happen, the shot took Emma in the forehead, ripping her head apart.

What had begun as a promising day had turned suddenly sour. The arrival of the old man had provided the twins with a welcome distraction. As intru-

with animals. As one might suspect, I really have no recollection of such activities and can therefore not comment. But I'm convinced that half of what they tell me is accurate and the other half is crap. But that doesn't mean to say that talking with animals is an irregular thing for me to do. Since my encounter with Basle I talk to them all the time. Like the night I spent in Hanoi with a tiger named Henbob and his elephant friend, Dalafoo. Excellent characters both. Dalafoo, for example, spent most of his life serving the indigenous mountain folk of the interior before escaping into the wilds. An elder statesman of the wilderness community in Southeast Asia, he was a survivor of both the French and American wars. Sadly, he was hit by a vegetable truck some months after our meeting and left lame. Henbob, in an attempt to save his friend, tried in vain to rescue the ailing Dalafoo from the clutches of the poorly equipped Vietnamese Veterinarian Society. But alas, too little too late I'm afraid. Dalafoo died some weeks later, leaving Henbob no choice but to attack some field workers out of frustration and face certain death at the hands of professional wild-game hunters such as Mr. Montcliff. Is it just coincidence that I am able to speak with animals whilst on opium? Maybe. But I firmly believe that if I were to give it up long enough to spend a handful of hours sober I would still have the ability, and privilege, of conversing with my animal friends. Rather, it is the ability that

sions tended to, their fantastic hatred for one another abated long enough for them to subdue the stranger and dangle him above the pool. Then it was back to business. But how this could have happened was beyond Erica. She stood there wobbling, the gun falling from her hand to the pool deck. Her eyes, as if out of focus, searched for some explanation, forcing her head from side to side in a druglike trance. And then she fainted and fell into the pool.

Milton was in shock. His eyes refused to leave the expanding pool of blood on the pool deck. Somewhere in the background he could faintly hear a man's voice yelling, but it failed to register. The contents of Emma's head took a slippery ride from her skull onto the concrete and tiles, filling a near-by pool-filter cap. Milton vomited. Which was, of course, a step up from passing out.

Ernie Chalky stopped yelling. There was no point. He would have to wait there until the boy came to his senses and realized that he was in need of assistance. He hung there casually counting the air bubbles that rose to the surface of the water, after having crept out of Erica's lungs. Almost an hour would pass before the little boy from inside the house would emerge. But unfortunately for Ernie Chalky it was not to aid in his escape.

...end badly.

Milton woke to find himself lying next to a swimming pool. Which was strange since the last place he remembered being was in his bed at home in the loft of a barn. Being that he was a genius, he was quick to come to the realization that he was not dreaming. He was nauseous, though nowhere as profoundly as he would become after pulling himself up to survey his surroundings. In doing so he would discover three bodies. One of an old man hanging above the pool, blood cascading from his body into the water below. A drowned mermaid. And a third on the far side of the pool deck with no head.

After a considerable amount of time, Milton got up, walked the length of the pool, and slumped into a sun chair, where he hopelessly began trying to piece together what had befallen him. He could feel the sun against his face and arms. Despite the gruesome display before him, he felt somehow assured that he had played no part in it. Sitting there he began to laugh. Sitting there, laughing in that sun chair, his eyes came upon the strangest thing.

From the pool-house door there came a dogged little fella carrying an enormous burden. A giant sack slung over his shoulder, the little fella wobbled his way as far as the sun chairs before stopping to take a rest. Removing his tiny cap, he wiped his brow and looked around as if determining which direction to go.

Then he looked up at Milton.

And being that Milton was at a loss for words he could think of nothing better to say than "What's in the sack?"

Replacing his cap on his tiny little head, the little fella lifted the sack and slung it back over his shoulder. Standing there wobbling, he replied "Funny you should ask."

causes the opium. Therein lies the strange balancing act that is my life. Not all things are as easily explained as VCR instructions.

The Night Opus

Somewhere, someone is waiting for a reason. Perhaps a reason for being, or a reason for doing, or reasonable answers. This isn't a story about reason-ability. This is a story about the decay of reason. There are those who would equate such decay with specific strains of mental engineering. I would have to disagree. Only the afflicted can appreciate such conditions, leaving those of us handy enough to express ourselves in want of some greater and altogether elusive quality of paranormal disarray. I would have to say that the decay of reason is nothing more than an inevitability. Human beings have always been destined to be their own undoing. I believe we're just getting to the good bits now. I was in love once. I loved a girl that I had watched love others. I spent years at her side, picking her up when she was too internally disconnected to power herself. Maybe it was this tragic state that drew me to her, I'm not quite sure. There were aspects of this woman that, to me, embodied everything that a woman should be. For some reason I refused to consider her faults when multiplying her numbers. Personal perception of perfection is like that. You see what you want to see. After a while you just see what you need to.

On occasion, for things to make sense, truths have to be bent to suit certain aspects. I am not going to say that this story isn't truthful, on the contrary, it is. But I'm also not going to say that some of it hasn't been tampered with. The reasons for this will remain with me. All you need to know is that I was truly in love with this girl. Years later I would come to the realization that love is nothing more than perspective. As time passes, it has little to do with romance or the heart. It has everything to do with status quo. One day you will wake up and realize that a good portion of your life has been used up. If you're lucky there might be someone lying beside you that will be able to tell you where it went. They, themselves, will appear to be the shadow of an individual you once knew. They will not remember the real you either. Both of you, despite your youthful hopes, will have become lost in a wash of complacency. This is not the decay of reason. It is simply the unconscious deployment of internal countermeasures.

There are instances in every life that will be continuously reviewed as monumental errors in judgment. It is difficult for me to say that my love for this girl was an enormous miscalculation but it's what I'm driving at. I doubt that, no matter my cold aversion, I will ever fully admit that it was a mistake. No one can ever fully do such a thing. Justifying ourselves to ourselves is a talent that we terminal apes have mastered. We're so good at it, in fact, that human history has been profoundly affected time and time again simply because someone, somewhere, refused to face the truth of themself. Instead they justified. Realizing that you're a fool is quite easy. Coming to terms with the realization that you will always be a fool is the difficult part. As a species, we have yet to admit that we are profoundly and prolifically foolish. Who in their right mind is going to admit to such a thing? You will spend your entire life trying to prove otherwise. When you get there take a look around at where it's gotten us.

Let me start by admitting that alcohol had a great deal to do with everything. And when I say alcohol I'm talking about liquor. Not beer or wine or any other such nonsense. I'm talking about good, old-fashioned, four-on-the-floor booze. I was one of those secretive alcoholics that no one ever suspects. Some of my closest friends had no idea that I was a drunk. Come to think of it, it eluded even me for longer than you could possibly imagine. My destructive twirl with the bottle peaked one evening when an old man had the misfortune of driving his car into the back of mine. It had snowed that day and the roads were covered with ice. This did not matter to me. I snapped. I got out of the car, took a rusted nine iron out of my trunk, and proceeded to pound the shit out of his hood and windshield. I would later be arrested for driving under the influence and assault. Thankfully I had yet to use the horseshoes that had been residing up my ass since birth. As it turned out, the old man did not have a license, refused to press charges, and I had played baseball with the arresting officer's son for seven years. So he kept me locked up for a couple of hours and then let me go. That night, the girl that I loved was with another guy. My best friend, to be precise. I would waste my phone call leaving a message on her answering machine. Her mother, who would come to detest me in ways one can barely imagine, thought it best that the message be erased. I have no idea what I said, but I remember it being quite convincing. It would take me years to admit, but that night marked the beginning of my immaculate coercion of Jennifer Dawn Connors.

Hello. Nice to meet you.

Let's talk about Dick because Dick had a lot to do with this. Dick was Jenny's father. Richard Connors, failed architect and lowly car salesman. In the early to mid seventies Dick had his own firm, pulled in almost a hundred thousand dollars a year, and had affairs with younger women. In the early seventies a hundred grand was like a million dollars. It afforded luxuries such as in-ground swimming pools, three-car garages, and expensive vacations. It also meant that Dick could have his very own bar in the basement of his very own house. Dick would spend the better part of seven years in that basement slowly drinking himself into the waiting arms of a General Motors showroom.

For some unknown reason we tend to hold alcohol in the highest of regard. You can go to a bar and get loaded but you can't smoke in one. You can be in bed asleep when your girlfriend starts banging on your window covered in blood, having just been beaten with a lampstand by her drunken father, and no one seems to give a damn. Get caught smoking a joint at school and Jesus Christ himself can't save you. When it comes to alcohol abuse the silent majority tends to look the other way. In the end one of two things always happens: someone dies or someone spends a good deal of their life wishing they were dead. Problems that are easily tackled are always the ones brought to the forefront. Smoking, for example, is such a problem. It's easy to tell people they can't smoke in various locations because the law says they're not allowed. It is not against the law to purchase alcohol. Nine times out of ten the law never finds out what that alcohol precipitates. So smoke up. That way you'll only have yourself to blame when your lungs fill up with blood. Not your father.

When Jenny was very young she used to lie in bed and listen to her father beat her mother. It would go on for hours. Over fifteen years of beatings the neighbours only ever called the police once. Jenny's uncle Ernie always used to tell her mother that he was going to kill Dick if he laid another finger on her. But he never did. Ernie was a big talker and that was about it. When things were good Ernie tended to come around. When things were bad he stayed away. All of them were like that. I used to call them the flying fucking Zelniks. It made Jenny very angry. Anna Zelnik, Jenny's grandmother, was a very quiet woman. She was so quiet that she used to whisper things to Jenny's mom who would, in turn, repeat it to everyone else. Anna's husband, Frank, had died of thyroid cancer several years before I had burst onto the scene. The Connors were another matter altogether. Grandma Connors was a victim of the loving backhand herself. Every time Dick's dad would raise his voice she would go rigid from head to toe. Jenny's mom did the same thing. Come to think of it, so did Jenny. Harvey Connors was one of those gruff types that likes to call Asians "chinks". He found that sort of thing hilarious. Besides Dick Connors I've never met a man I'd like to kill more than Harvey. He used to wander around the house in his underwear when they were down visiting. He was the walking definition of a disgruntled white male. His son was his sidekick.

In the beginning Mrs. Connors liked me, I guess. When I would come by to pick up Jenny I'd sit with her in the kitchen and talk while she knitted. I was half-cut most of the time but to Mrs. Connors it was normal for men to have that hazy look in their eyes. For the most part I always thought she tolerated me because she figured I was a smart kid and Jenny could do with spending some time with a smart kid. I wasn't sleeping with her daughter then, which might be one reason why she was so nice. After Jenny and I started having sex things around the Connors house got tight. Like her daughter, Mrs. Connors eventually came to the realization that I was an idiot. And, on each occasion thereafter, she made it her mission in life to remind me that she'd figured me out.

So there's the pathology. Personally, I had no excuse for my behaviour. And since then I've never tried to offer one up. Jenny, on the other hand, had plenty of excuses. And for all the years she endured her father she never felt the need to use any of them to her advantage. Her time would come. And in her mind there were only two acceptable outcomes: either he would kill her, or he wouldn't.

When I was a young man I used to spend a great deal of time reading. I would read anything I could get my hands on that interested me. My father, to his credit, kept a rather large, though eclectic, collection of books in our basement. So from time to time I'd sneak down there in the middle of the night, grab a book, go back to my room, and start reading. I must have read everything from *Inside The Third Reich* to *Catch-22* before I was fifteen. It was marvellous, but it had its downsides. I was never all that good at making friends. Instead of putting forth any sort of effort in this area I would just sit in my room and redraw maps from atlases. I've drawn the entire planet four times over in my life. From every river to every remote village worthy of being included on a national map. Any idea where Vidz'yuyar is? Didn't think so. I may be the only North American-born person who does.

As it turned out, the key to unlocking my social skills was liquor. In junior high a couple of acquaintances introduced me to gin. My father, it just so happened, was a lover of gin. So these guys would come over after school and we'd raid the old man's liquor closet. By five thirty, around the time my mother got home, I was three sheets to the wind. However, I always had enough sense to drink half a glass of Scope and spend some time convincing myself that I was in control. Most of the time it worked. The rest of the time my mother just thought we were being fourteen, I suppose. Either way, it started snowballing quite dramatically after that. By my sixteenth birthday I was putting away three quarters of a bottle a day. By my seventeenth birthday I had gone beyond the point of no return. As any alcohol abuser will tell you, that's the point where you drink just to feel normal. You're not drunk at all. You're even-up.

That's not to say that drinking made me Mr. Personality or anything. I was still somewhat of an introvert, it's just that I found it easier to deal with strangers than I had in the past. I met Jenny at a house party when I was sixteen. We were both drunk. She came up to me and asked me what my problem was. I said that I didn't have a problem. She said that I did. I said that she was my problem. She kissed me and nodded. It would be the last time that I would touch her until we were almost twenty.

In the weeks that followed Jenny and I became fast friends. We were the kind of friends that rarely spent much time in large groups. Instead, we'd drive somewhere and dissect the world. I had but one thought on my mind; all the while she just wanted to make sure we didn't screw things up by entertaining that thought. As it turned out, Jenny's problems were much too immense for me to handle alone. By the time we were twenty they had crushed me to death and turned me into someone that I no longer recognized.

As an aside, when you're supporting a hefty drinking habit it's always best to have alternatives. One cannot always afford passable liquor, so you end up being creative. We did this by inventing a drink that, to this day, has yet to be surpassed—except, possibly, by a handful of true West Virginians. We called it paint thinner, and for good reason. The drink consisted of the following

- one half bottle of vodka
- one half bottle of J. Walker Red Label
- mix vigorously in large Tupperware container and consume

You might be wondering why vodka and JW's Red Label were the liquids of choice. As funny as it might sound they were the two most common types of liquor found in the discount bins. I needn't say more. On occasion the discount liquor would be changed around, so you might have to put up with rye or whatever they needed to get rid of that week. But vodka was always the constant. There was always vodka. And if you made friends with vodka, it never let you down.

When I graduated from high school I started working full time and suddenly realized that I could afford Jack Daniel's on a daily basis. So that's what I stuck with. Jack Daniel's is made in Lynchburg, Tennessee, by the way. Lynchburg is in a dry county. You have to drive to the next county if you want a drink. America is a strange place.

Besides drinking there was little else to do. Go to school, go to work, go home. Rinse and repeat. Sometimes I would wake up in the morning and decide that the best thing I could possibly do with my day was to conceive of an extremely mysterious method of doing away with myself. It was a good idea for all of about thirty seconds. Thirty-one seconds after the fact I came to the realization that death would hamper my ability to listen to the Police's *Synchronicity*. And that just wouldn't do. I possessed a thirty-second limit of self pity. After that I figured there were better things to do with my time. Like sit around, for example.

If ever one could have a good reason to drink then Jenny certainly did. She got the shit kicked out of her on a regular basis. You'd think she would take solace in the fact that she had alcohol to wash away the uglier side of her existence. Nevertheless, she had a rather bizarre saying that accompanied her flights of boozy fancy. She'd say "Like father, like daughter" with a broken grin on her broken face. She always found it rather ironic that, at the age of seventeen, she drank almost as much as her father did. She also thought it made her a hypocrite. Back then I wasn't much for waxing philosophical so the best thing I could come up with was *you could never be like him*. How thoughtful of me.

The annoying thing about the past is that it remains steadfast in your head, unwilling to capitulate when you decide the time has come to alter it to your advantage. The human brain is a thing of absolute mechanical wonderment. Best to make it sound breathtakingly complicated than admit it causes more grief than good. For I have been of the mind for quite some time that without memory, life would be filled with nothing more than a series of ridiculously happy accidents. There would be no other way to define the past, you see. It would be nothing more than an ensemble of all the days prior to your current state of euphoric ignorance. If only it were that simple. If only we hadn't so many shameful instances of great importance to remember in hopes of deterring sequels. What useless meat we truly are.

I am a cynic. I am a cynic because, like God with his gardening puppets, Jenny fashioned me in her own self-image. You may find it hard to believe but there was a time when I was a care free sort of fellow who could be easily shaken from his bad temperaments by the nonsensical invasions of others. Unfortunately, having spent my impressionable years both intoxicated and in the company of professional degeneration, the boy that I was would not re-emerge on the other side. Only this body, this foolhead, would be left. But I can't rightly blame her for any of it. Try as one might there are only two things in this world that influence decisions, despite what most folks think. The first only affects males of the species. The other, unless you've been in a coma since 1952, is yourself. I realize that you might have been expecting some sociologically long-lived, magical scapegoat to materialize and save what little dignity you thought you had left—but no dice. There's no turning back, I'm afraid. You're stuck with your past selves.

When I think of Jenny now, I try to think of her as she was before everything went horribly wrong with us. After all these years I still try to fixate on one specific image of her, one of which I often think. It is an image of her descending a flight of stairs in a cheap, Italian restaurant. It was the first real date I ever took her on. It was all that I could afford. She left the table, went to the washroom, and as she returned I watched her walk down the stairs. And, in that very brief moment, my mind took a picture. A picture of her smiling at me as she never had before. It was as if, for that one split second, everything in the world stopped. Armies put down their weapons and decided to make war an affair of timed kite flying, the worst teams in every sporting league on earth won by enormous margins, those that had nothing gained everything and I was standing in an openness so vast and spectacular that I was reduced to nothing more than a pickling jar filled with air saved from the beginning of time. It was, in a word, rapture. You may think it sounds unlike me or silly of me to say, but I hope that in your life you will know what I'm getting at.

Besides that, Jenny was short. She was short and round. At the time she was maybe five foot three and weighed about 125 lbs. She always had shoulder length brown hair, blue eyes and crooked teeth. She had worn braces for many years, to no avail. When she smiled she pressed her lips together so that you couldn't see them. She only listened to music when she was alone or driving in a car. When she went swimming she always wore shorts and a T-shirt, never a bathing suit. She liked mushroom soup, those sweet peaches that come in a can with juice and corn chips. Her favourite movie was *A Passage to India*, her favourite band was New Order and her favourite colour was green. She liked dogs not cats, hated eating fish and despised the fact that I used to smoke. The rest is just for me, I'm afraid.

Now, you may be wondering why I keep referring to her as if she were dead. The truth of the matter is that I'm not rightly sure where she is. I have no idea if she's alive, dead, married, a mother, in a cult, or an astronaut. I haven't spoken to her in some years. (I was having a problem with tenses just then. It bothers me to no end when things of that nature seem like they're intentionally working against you. It is the main reason that I gave up on my dreams of one day writing a series of novels about a time-travelling stripper and her arch enemy, Chip Butler.)

As I mentioned earlier, on our first proper date I took Jenny to a cheap Italian restaurant. It was called Alberto's. It was the kind of place that looked like it might be expensive but was actually very cheap. It was a restaurant owned by middle-class people who catered to those who were hanging on to the bottom rung of middle-class status. It was a split-level place with a small balcony. It also had thousands of bottles of cheap wine stuck inside of those red, clay octagon things that Italian contractors (and their clients) find so appealing. Back then it was a big deal for both of us. We even went so far as to dress up for the occasion. This meant that Jenny wore her usual black sweater with a skirt. I wore a white shirt and a tie under my Bones Brigade jacket. Ah, how I loved that coat.

You must remember, by that point in time Jenny and I had been good friends for the better part of three and a half years. We were nineteen when we went out that night, having spent two years discussing whether or not it would be a good idea. After dinner we went to a movie. We saw *Joe vs. the Volcano*. Following that we walked back up the hill, a journey of some two hours, and stopped off at the park and sat on the swings. It was there that we kissed for the second time in our lives. I remember it quite clearly. It was one of those tense sort of unions that ends with one person looking away afterwards and the other laughing. Jenny, who always did have a flare for the dramatic, turned her face away from mine and looked down the road, playing at one of her commonly overused personas. So I laughed—and she hit me with her handbag. (Totally uncalled for.)

That night on the swing set marked the beginning of the end for Jenny and me. After everything that we'd been through the strain of having to put up with each other on a romantic level was just too much to bear. Some months following that night we would make the horrible mistake of moving in together. After that it was all just a matter of time.

Now all of this might have led you to believe that the two of us were somewhat off-kilter. This was not true. Despite the fact that most of the time we looked like we had no clue what was going on, we were actually extremely organized, if not altogether ritualistic. For example, we would only drink at specific times and in specific places on weekdays. Never earlier than our first free block and never if we had to drive somewhere later in the day (which, as you might have guessed, only ever applied to me and never her). Jenny would get very angry if I had started drinking before we met up in free block. To her it was one of the constants in her life, something that never changed. Even if I was sick she would walk down to my house and sit in my room with me. For two years, minus summers, it went like clockwork.

Another thing that was comparable to preordaining time was the ever changing state of Jenny's upper extremities. There were times when even I was surprised that she hadn't been hospitalized because of her wounds. Dick once hit her with a pipe, if you can believe it. He did it right before he left for work one morning. It was lying in the carport and he had tripped on it. He got angry, called her out to the carport, made her pick it up and hand it to him, and then hit her in the forehead with it. The night before I had left it there by accident while we were rooting through some old boxes looking for one of those bicycle tire air pumps.

In our first year of high school, Jenny's counsellor dared to inquire as to why Jenny's face was often bruised. Sarcastically, as if she thought someone with a Cracker Jacks-box psychology degree should know better, Jenny told her that she was a zealous sportsman. As time passed, everyone knew that Jenny's stories and excuses were horse shit but they also realized that she was not the kind of girl that you could lecture. During those years I spent a couple of hours each week talking with Jenny's counsellor, Mrs. Hopkins, about what went on at the Connors house. Mrs. Hopkins believed that I was one of the few things that Jenny had that mattered to her. I would often nod in agreement, wondering secretly to myself if we were talking about the same person. Because if her theory was accurate, then Jenny had a funny way of showing it. Like sleeping with most everyone that I knew, for example.

The night that I was arrested for attacking that old guy's car was a typical example of her behaviour. If I had a nickel for every time I discovered her with some guy—in a bedroom at a party, in a parked car, closet, bathtub, whatever—let me tell you, I'd have a shit load of nickels. You might think that I was a wee bit obsessive about it, busting in on her like that all the time, but that wasn't the case. I was simply making sure that she was alright. On occasion, some of her fuck buddies got a little carried away. Jenny did not fight back. Jenny had learned to take it. I, on the other hand, was frequently on edge when it came to her safety. There might not have been anything I could have done about her father but I wasn't about to let some fucking hump bash her around. I am not a violent man usually. But let me just say that there are some things that I do not stand for. And when such circumstances arise I am not one to play at punches. Just baseball bats and such.

But you see that was the frighteningly weird thing about it. Ninety-nine percent of the time I would simply find her with some guy, make sure everything was okay, and then I'd wait outside until she was finished. I would sit on couches, stairs, the floor, and wait. In a way it almost became my identity. On more than one occasion the guy that she was with would pop his head out the door and tell me that she wanted to go home. This was my cue to either go start the car, call a cab, or figure out which mode of public transportation we would be taking. She would then appear and we'd leave. Most of the time not two words passed between us on the journey home. It was almost as if she knew it hurt me but couldn't bring herself to admit that it was that exact aspect of our relationship that she liked. Some things are better said with the lights out it seems. Just not to me.

So that's the way things went for us. She walked a thin line between physical abuse and causing herself enough emotional harm to ensure that she didn't have to deal with it, and I just kept my mouth shut and did what I thought she wanted me to do. As it turns out, all she ever wanted me to do was take her away from all of it. But you see, when you're young, and not that bright when it comes to girls, you aren't exactly knowledgeable in the ways of double meanings and the behavioral complexities of women. Come to think of it, what man ever is? I'm going somewhere with all of this of course. It would be pointless for me to continue wallowing in such pathetic description. In the future remind me to make sure that I simplify things somewhat. Like this, for example:

Girl - me - booze - bad dad - love - rip off - slut - not her fault - car - kill - accident - haven't seen her since. See. Much better.

So here's the meat of it then. Following a brief courtship the two of us decided to move in together. We had talked about it for almost a year, so it wasn't as if we hadn't worked out the details. These were the details.

1. I would quit college and get a full time job.
2. Jenny would get a full time job.
3. We would buy old second hand furniture and fix up an older apartment that was inexpensive.
4. We would save up some money so Jenny could go back to school.

That was the plan. And that's what we went about doing. For the better part of nine months after graduation the two of us worked our asses off. Besides money for liquor, which was becoming less of a priority in our lives by then, we saved every dollar we made. Neither of us bought new clothes or shoes during that time. We didn't rent movies, go to movies, go to clubs, none of it. We stuck to the plan. And one fateful spring day, the plan paid off. For the first time in our lives we left home. It was a big deal for her. But as I would discover, getting hammered by your dad for most of your life doesn't simply disappear just because you're no longer within striking distance. No matter what, you're always within striking distance of your own mind. For the first couple of weeks everything was what you'd expect it to be. The basics of everyday life accompanied by copious amounts of inter-course. There's just nothing like the first time you find yourself in an environment that is completely void of parental authority. We had so much sex that it was literally a struggle to get out of bed the next morning. It wasn't that it was overly strenuous or anything, it's just that we often did it in intervals, 11:03 pm-1:29 am-3:44 am-and so forth. Not exactly the brightest thing to do when you've got to be at work at 5:30 the next morning. There are a handful of jobs in this world that do not require a great deal of alertness. Let me assure you, unloading shipping containers with a forklift is not one of them. But as time passed we both began to realize that living on our own wasn't all that it was cracked up to be. Besides working impossible hours for slave wages (for that is what newly graduated teenagers get paid when they're limited to a specific job pool), we were forced to spend our weekends doing things like laundry, grocery shopping, botching the simplest of home improvements, while attempting to come to terms with the fact that the birthplace of the world's cockroach population was located somewhere beneath our floorboards. This left absolutely no time for things such as going out, getting loaded and generally having a good time.

Now the one truly remarkable thing about this particular time in our lives was that we were so distracted by the ever-pressing need to keep our financial heads above water that we somehow forgot to be complete drunkards. I'm not saying that we didn't drink, just not every other hour of every day. It was bizarre. I remember waking up one morning and realizing that I hadn't drunk anything in close to a week. But even though our lack of consumption seems like a positive now, back then it was horrible. You see, for the first time in her adult life Jenny was forced to deal with her abusive past as a sober individual. And let me tell you, despite the fact that I loved her, I would have rather been in fucking Antarctica. Either there—or two miles below the surface of the earth in a steel bunker in the middle of a lake of fire guarded by viciously evil manticores. It was gradual at first. She'd do things like toss violently in her sleep and wake up screaming. This led to other things, such as discovering her cowering in the bathtub in the middle of the night. Attempting to approach or talk to her when she was like that was pointless. She would often throw things at me like soap and shampoo bottles. She once gave me seven stitches after hitting me in the head with one of those sharp plastic foot scrubber deals. Those nights were unbearable. She was unbearable. And I was just too young and too panicked to deal with it properly. My only other experiences with her like that were when she'd show up at my house after Dick had done her in. I was used to consoling her after her ordeals. But when it came to being viewed as the enemy I became resentful. I realize now that it was a terrible thing to do of course. It would have been better just to stay close and make sure she didn't do anything stupid. But I never seemed to have enough time to rationalize anything. In the heat of battle, as it were, I just wanted it all to stop. Most of the time it happened in the middle of the night and I was literally semi-conscious. So I did the only thing that I knew would work. I'd get her drunk.

You know, when I was younger my father often left me with a specific phrase after he had finished reprimanding me for some wrongdoing. He would say, "Duffy, I hope one day, when you grow up, you have kids that are just like you. And you'll realize then how little you know now." God damn right, Bob. God damn right.

The night that it happened was just like any other night. I went to bed around eleven, slept for a couple hours and awoke to the familiar sound of running water. So I rolled out of bed with a groan and walked across the hall, all the while looking for indications of how bad a state she was in (as she had an odd habit of scattering clothes all over the place when she was particularly freaked out). So there I was, standing quietly with my hand on the doorknob and my forehead resting against the door, pausing in an attempt to collect my thoughts and come up with a plan.

From what I could tell she wasn't scrubbing herself because she always made whimpering noises when she did that. You see, from time to time I would discover her in the shower rubbing her arms and legs with one of those green scrub pads. You'd be surprised just how much skin they can rub off given the chance. But luckily that wasn't the case. I opened the door to discover her stretched out in the tub, feet resting on either side, a can of Orange Crush resting on her stomach. At first glance I thought she was asleep. So I started to lean over to grab the can when I discovered that she was merely fucking with me. She let out a yelp and started flopping her limbs all over the place, obviously making fun of the fact that I expected her to be freaking out. She laughed a little, flipped the wet hair out of her face, and said "hey there sailor". I responded to this by sliding into the tub, ripping the Orange Crush from her hands and dumping it over her head. So we laughed a while, talked some, and then decided to go back to bed. At that point I thought I was out of the woods. I thought maybe she's taking a turn for the better. We even went so far as to engage in some of the unspeakable contact, which we hadn't done in some weeks. So, after all was said and done, she went into the kitchen to make some tea and I fell into one of those dreamy sleeps that one always hopes will consume them.

When I got up the next morning Jenny was nowhere to be found. Usually this would have concerned me to no end, being that I had turned into a very controlling and possessive asshole by that point who often chose not to believe anything that she told me. You see, she was the one who threw fits in the middle of the night and was on the brink of losing her mind. I was the one in control. For some unexplainable reason I felt that it gave me the right to act as if I were her lord and master. I can admit that now. At the time I figured I was just providing stability and acting accordingly considering that she was prone to a variety of perplexing behavior. But on that particular morning I wasn't at all concerned that she was missing. I knew full well that her friend Alison was over from Courtney and that she had most likely gone over to spend the day. So I spent the morning in blissful ignorance. Then the phone rang and it started raining shit bricks the size of basketballs. I have come to the conclusion that there are six different types of phone calls.

1. Those that are bad and you know they are before you pick up the phone.
2. Those that are bad and you answer the phone like an idiot because you think it's a friend calling you back.
3. Tele-marketing.
4. The kind of call that makes the hair on your arms stand on end because you know it's your mother in law.
5. Normal phone calls.
6. The kind where you don't say anything.

When the phone rang I was sitting in the living room reading the last page of Roald Dahl's *Switch Bitch*. If you have yet to read it, the book is comprised of four short stories, the last of which is simply entitled "Bitch". To this day I can still remember the line that I was reading when the phone rang. It was the following, "A moment later the two of us were millions of miles up in outer space."

Exactly.

Directing your attention to the chart provided in this section, know then that I endured a number 6 phone call with subtle undercurrents of number 4 for good measure. For you see, it was a policeman who rang. And, from somewhere within five hundred feet of his position, I could hear Mrs. Connors wailing in the background. I have been sitting here for fifteen minutes trying to find a way to put this to you, but I can't seem to figure it. So I'll just say this: I dropped the phone.

On July 23rd, 1991, Jennifer Dawn Connors killed her father. She did this by releasing the parking break in her Volkswagen Beetle while parked on a sloping driveway. She steered the ghosting car down the driveway and pinned Dick Connors to the back wall of the carport as he was taking out the trash. The force of the impact was so great that Dick's legs were almost removed at the knees. He died some four hours later at the hospital from a combination of internal complications and blood loss.

When the police and ambulance arrived at the Connors' house Jenny was still in the car. Her mother was banging on the window trying to get Jenny to start the engine and pull away. Jenny just sat there. Some ten minutes after crushing her father Jenny was removed from the car by police. She was not handcuffed. She was taken to the hospital as was the body of her nearly dead father. Mrs. Connors spent the following four hours demanding that her daughter be imprisoned forever. Having lied to the authorities about her vantage point, Mrs. Connors initially told police that Jenny had maliciously driven the car into her father and that the engine was running at the time. Jenny was formally charged later that afternoon. I was contacted just after 11:30 am. I immediately went to the hospital.

I arrived at the hospital only to discover that everyone had left. Having been looked over by a doctor and briefly examined by someone from psychiatrics, Jenny was taken to a police station to be interviewed. I spent close to an hour trying to figure out which station they took her to. The nurses, not having any insight into the years of abuse that Jenny had endured at the hands of her father, refused to help me when I told them that I was the "concerned boyfriend". So I did the next best thing. I called every metropolitan police station in the white pages.

Despite the fact that she had yet to speak to a lawyer or anyone from child welfare she decided to tell the police everything. She told them that she left our apartment at around 4 am, drove over to her parents, parked in the driveway, and sat there. Her mother, having been questioned at the hospital, told police that Jenny had been drinking. This, of course, was a lie. Jenny had not been drinking. She was sober. Unless, that is, someone had unknowingly tampered with the ingredients of that Orange Crush while it was sitting—unopened—in our refrigerator. Beyond that Jenny knew exactly what she was doing. So they charged her with first degree murder. That's murder of the premeditated variety for those of you who are wondering what the difference is. So that's how it happened. Rather unglamorously, I'm afraid.

As the weeks rolled by everything to me seemed a wash of hours spent useless. For all intents and purposes Jenny had gotten away with it. You see, she knew that she would, perhaps even long before she went about doing it. For no one in their right mind is going to send a twenty-year-old girl to prison for killing a man who had beaten and sexually abused her since the age of seven. And that was the shocking part for me. I had no idea that Dick had done anything beyond the clinically violent. I had no idea there was more to the whole affair, altogether vile. When it came to light that there were multiple levels to Dick's abuse, any desire on the Crown's part to pursue a conviction fizzled. Jenny's mental instability at the time could be easily justified. Enough was enough. To make her relive her past in court would most likely have driven her to suicide. So nothing was done.

When she came home she seemed embarrassed about the fact that everything had been revealed and would often leave the house when I tried to get her to talk to me. Sometimes I would yell. I wish now that I hadn't. We spent a couple of months pretending that things between us would go back to the way they were, but her heart just wasn't in it. It was during that time that I came to realize that I had pushed her to love me. As difficult as it was there was nothing left for me to do but admit that she would never look at me the same way again. Maybe, in a way, I was nothing more than a twenty-four-hour reminder of a past that she wanted to forget. But instead of being civil about it I found myself suddenly pride-stricken. You see, I had paid my dues, I had put in my time. All I wanted was a little acknowledgement for the years I spent being the faithful lap dog. Despite the fact that I had, in a way, contributed to her destruction, I was convinced my influence was one of the catalysts that had invited the finality that she had found. But as I've said, I became nothing more to her than a reminder of hell instead of someone who only ever wanted to save her from it.

In the late fall of that year Jenny decided that it would be best if she went to live with her Aunt Rachel on Vancouver Island. I was against it, of course, but there was nothing I could do to stop her. And it was then that I realized that our time together had come to an end. We spent two weeks together before she left, sleeping in different beds, changing clothes behind locked doors. And during that time we came to hate each other in ways that neither of us knew was possible. Everything, all contained within a single perfect sphere in my mind, where had it gone? Good question. Sometimes that's the reality of love and wonderment. It stays with you for a brief time so that you might have something not wholly tarnished to keep you lifted up during the darker trials of your future. And, in some strange way, maybe it's best that such things are typically fleeting. That way they remain the secret of perfection within us, held there as a reserve power source. I will always be reflected in perfection when I think of myself back then. Because even now, after all that I have supposedly gained, I would trade it all for just ten minutes in a lousy Italian restaurant.

The two of us talked on the phone some during the months that followed, but after a while our lives started to get hectic and we lost touch. My current mood of nostalgic recollection aside, I would be lying to you if I said that it ended well because it didn't. It ended badly. It ended with the kinds of words, accusations and untrustworthy thoughts that can never be fully amended or retracted. But that was just us, you see. Being us at our finest.

You know, I have often wondered about her. Sometimes, when I see or hear something that reminds me of the past, images lightning-strike my head and I'm brought to my knees by it all. Like the smell of wet pavement reminds me of the simplicity of childhood. My waking self shows no trace of that which I once was. I am now someone else. I am a grown man and still, though eager for the future's cast, hopeful of nothing to change that which I have known prior. So if death is defeat, or a passage as some see fit, then this will have been my victory. And if that is the only truth I know of myself in this life, then fine by me.

Night kid

The Commoner's Guide To Suicide

And that place which gave you your bearings will always reside within you complete. And of those places and circumstances, only those that offered resistance to one's being will ever produce individuals worth their words.

—Harper Grey

Step One: Life is like bread. It's great at first, but as time passes it gets harder.

Eli was very quiet. And by quiet I'm saying that he never spoke, not that he was soft spoken. In fact Eli didn't utter a word to another living thing until he was almost seven years old. And he did so only to get the attention of a dog so that it did not get hit by an oncoming car. There are events in every life that shape individuality. If that dog had heard Eli in time, it probably would have moved out of the road. But as it happened, the dog did not hear him. And Eli would not speak again until he was seventeen. What was the point?

Eli Lemski was the sort who went undetected by social radar. Raised by his father, an obsessive-compulsive aeronautical engineer, Eli spent most of his childhood sitting in various rooms starring at them. By the time he was twenty-one there wasn't one millimetre of those rooms that he hadn't spent fourteen hours looking at without moving. This, of course, made him one of the most observant people of all time. And though Eli would spend most of his life searching for his one true worldly gift, it always escaped him that his power of observation was it. The downside, of course, is that amazing powers of observation only pay if you decide to count cards at Blackjack tables. Eli's alternative, as it turned out, was much worse.

Due to the fact that Mr. Lemski worked primarily on military contracts, Eli and his father spent a great deal of time moving from one place to another. And as Eli's speech problem worsened it didn't make sense to Mr. Lemski that Eli should attend regular schools. Being the egoist that he was, he assumed that his son had inherited his intellect and wouldn't need to waste his time in the company of troglodytes. So Eli took to getting an education through the mail. It was soon apparent that Eli was not the prodigy his father thought him to be. Eli squeaked through his scholastic career and received his high school diploma in a large manila envelope. And although the water damage to that envelope had turned most of the diploma into an incoherent mess, Eli was still able to make out the two most important words on it. And those were Eli Lemski.

As this story's narrator (and participant), I always find it strange that a man like Leo Lemski (PhD), would have the gall to think his son as brilliant as himself and yet allow him to get an education by correspondence. When I first met Mr. Lemski I realized immediately that this was the kind of man who couldn't care less whether or not Eli did anything at all with his life. He was so entirely self-absorbed that he rarely spoke to his son, let alone give a damn whether or not he excelled at anything. But he used to love using Eli's mediocrity as an excuse to blow off steam. And due to the fact that Eli never raised his voice in his own defense, it just made it all the easier. Neither Leo or Eli were big men. They were slight, gangly creatures with sunken eyes and hands that seemed too large for their arms. But unlike his father, Eli was not an awkward person. He was graceful and moved as though he was trying to elude some unseen force that constantly stalked him. That was the thing I noticed about him when we first met. That and the fact that he could shoot a pistol like no one I had ever seen. And that's where I come into it. I was the one who took Eli to the shooting range that afternoon when we were both twenty-one. My father, unlike Leo Lemski, was not an engineering genius. My father was a test pilot and then later an air force liaison. Before he died he worked with Leo on a couple of projects. That's how I came to meet Eli. One morning my father asked me if I would take Eli with me to the shooting range as a favour to Leo. I was staying with him during spring break and was due back at college a couple of days later. So, since the base was just as boring as every other airbase in the world, I figured it couldn't hurt. My dad warned me that Eli didn't talk much but I wasn't prepared for what I found when I met him. Of all the people in this world and out of it, Eli Lemski only chose to talk to two of them: myself and his mother, Irene. The difference was that I was alive at the time whereas Irene hadn't been for almost nineteen years. Beats me why.

I should clear something up before you start to get the wrong impression. Even though I was taking Eli to a shooting range it does not mean that I am, or was, a proponent of firearms. Truth be told I'd have them all melted down and turned into candleholders given the chance. During my four years at Stanford an ex-girlfriend of mine was killed by a guy at a house party. He thought the handgun that he found in a dresser drawer wasn't loaded. In a haze of cocaine and tequila he squeezed the trigger and sent two bullets through the bedroom wall and into the living room, killing my friend and injuring another. He would serve nine months of an involuntary manslaughter plea. Sometimes having influential parents and lawyers can get you out of most anything. The dead are rarely afforded the luxury of afterthought in such circumstances. The court saw no reason to ruin the boy's life over what they deemed an accident. Had it been their daughter, I'm sure they would have felt different. So let's just say that I'm not fond of guns. Even before that I could never stand them. But growing up in a military family you have little choice as a boy. If your father wants you to learn to shoot, then you shut the hell up and you do it. Because sometimes the fear you have of disappointing your father is stronger than your convictions. So I did what I always did. I went and shot off some rounds at the range so the good o' boys down there could tell my dad that they'd seen me. And on that particular occasion I just so happened to bring along a treat for them. Eli Lemski.

There are certain things in this world that when the right people do them they just seem natural, like driving or cooking or sex. Eli Lemski was a natural marksman. He could hit anything at any range as long as the weapon could perform the task. The day that I picked him up I was initially a little peeved at my father for making me take him. Of course I pictured him as being just another air force brat. But I would understand what my father was talking about the moment that he came out of his front door. He was dressed in a white button-down short-sleeve shirt, dark brown pants, and brown leather shoes. His hair was parted on the side, pasted to his head with pomade, and he wore large-rimmed glasses that were far too big for his face. In all the years I knew him, Eli always wore exactly the same thing, which he owned in triplicate (or at least I hoped he did). But put a gun in that boy's hands and it was like watching God creating and recreating the world. When we got to the range he stood with his hands pressed over his ears as I shot my father's .45. The noise bothered him so much that he went and stood in the parking lot and still would not take his hands away from his ears. But after a while he inched his way back inside and got close enough that I eventually offered him the gun. He meagerly pointed it at the target and looked as if the weight of it would topple him. And then he shot off five rounds right on top of each other without so much as blinking. His body didn't even seem to move. The flurry of reports brought over some of the regulars and we just stood there and watched him fire clip after clip. All afternoon he hit nothing but chests and heads. It was one of the most bizarre things that I have ever witnessed.

That was my first encounter with Eli Lemski. After I finished the semester at Stanford I returned to Texas in the summer of 1982 and spent a great deal of time with Eli. I even got him to talk to me a little. But that summer was the last time that I would see him for almost five years. The next time we'd run into each other would be in a Manhattan alleyway. I was puking and Eli, well, Eli was working.

Step Two: Cancelling yourself because you've been stolen.

After I graduated from Stanford I spent some time working in the Bay area before I realized that I was getting nowhere and didn't like myself much. So I did what every good American kid does. I fucked off. I travelled the country in search of that thing that America is supposed to be. You never find it of course, but at least it made me realize that the "thing" everyone's always talking about never really existed. It's just *Saturday Evening Post* memorabilia bullshit. How in the hell do we have a country where the cradle of our government and historical fortitude exists in a vacuum with the highest crime rate in the union? Figure me that one. The First World is a farce. It's a comedy about a comedy where perfection re-enacts day-to-day life and then feeds itself to the populace and convinces it that it's a reflection of continental reality. Everything's okay. Everything is always okay. I'm sure there will come a time when our greatness resembles that great snake which feasts upon its own tail because there is nothing left for it to eat. We will consume ourselves through consumption. That's what I learned in the two years that I travelled America. That it's kidding itself. That and the fact that I should have just stayed in San Francisco and stopped complaining.

But that's how I ended up in New York. A friend of mine from college was in advertising out there and I looked him up. At the time I was a broke, backpacking, hippie. I explained to him what I'd been up to and it didn't seem to bother him much. You can never tell how people from your past are going to react when you show up penniless on their doorstep and they're well off. He was one of the many who fell victim to the success equals happiness equation. He and his wife had matching Mercedes with signature plates. One was "Jack B" and the other was "Tara B". And despite my disdain at the time for such nonsense I wasn't about to mention it. His sofa was the most comfortable thing I'd slept on in months. Of course he'd changed since school, as most people tend to. There was no point telling them that at the time, mind you, but it's the truth of things. So enjoy your youth while you have it. Because despite your unwavering opinions and views you will change into something later in life that will not understand why music has to be so damn loud.

So there I was. Showered, shaved and ready to hit the town. Jack had made reservations at an upscale place near the park and it conveniently worked out to be Tara's bridge night so it was just he and I. We had dinner and then got drunk at a nearby bar. That's when I began to realize that everything in Jack's life wasn't as perfect as he would have liked it to seem. There were affairs with younger women, borderline alcoholism, flirtations with financial disaster. Tara knew nothing about any of it of course. Wives in situations like that rarely do. They just keep doing whatever it is that they do and don't stop to consider much. Because there's always another Jack out there. And like most, Jack was good for ten years of ignorant bliss. But that's how I ran into Eli again. Puking my guts out in the alley next to the bar.

It's to be expected that people you knew in your youth will become something in their later life that will change your opinion of them. Take Jack. I would have never thought that he'd move to New York and spend his days driving between Manhattan and Jersey, hopelessly grasping for the illusory gold ring. In school he was the sort that spent the majority of his time drinking beer and sleeping. Most things are rarely what they seem. And as for the future, well, it never is. So there I was, puking my guts out in an alley when I caught a glimpse of someone clambering down a fire escape. Now the fact that I was in New York sobered me somewhat. When figures jump from fire escapes in alleyways you tend to get a little wary. It wasn't until I heard my name that I calmed down enough to turn around and see who it was. And of course, it was Eli. He was standing there with a strange grin on his face, and I say strange only because I had never seen him smile or make any other facial gestures of any kind. He was wearing what he usually wore accompanied by a beige trench coat, tied tightly at the waist. At first I thought there was a design on the coat. And then I realized that it was blood. A great deal of blood. So I did what anyone in my position would have done. I puked some more.

Unfortunately Eli wasn't in the mood to stand around while I did. By the time I realized what was happening I was being shoved into the back seat of a car half a block away. Jack was nowhere to be seen; though I would later learn that he had met a young accounting intern and had spent the night wallowing in her arms. Coincidentally, Tara had been doing the same thing back in Jersey. Turns out that she had been sleeping with some famous attorney from Philadelphia for years. But that comes later. At the time I was concerned that Jack wouldn't let me stay with him if I was rude enough to skip out on him. I was lying in the back seat of what I thought was Eli's car when we came to a stop and Eli motioned for me to stay put. Chancing a quick peek out the front windshield, I realized that we were somewhere near the water, but where I couldn't be sure. Some time passed before Eli returned and pulled me from the backseat only to shove me into another car. He then proceeded to pour gasoline in his car and set fire to it. And that's all I remember about that night. When I woke up the next morning I was lying on a sofa in a small apartment somewhere in the Bronx. Eli was sitting at a small table drinking a cup of what I guessed to be coffee and cleaning a variety of handguns.

Oh God. What had I done.

Step Three: Strange things happen to ordinary people and vice versa.

If he had become a cop or a soldier I could have stomached it a little easier. But there was no way that I could ever come to terms with the fact that he actually killed people for money. This was the same guy who hadn't uttered a word in decade in succession. But that's exactly what he did. He killed people for money. He had convinced himself that he'd found his one true worldly gift. And to Eli that was all that mattered. The ridiculous thing about it was that he didn't much like what he did. He didn't enjoy his work and didn't really have the mentality required to forgo the anxieties that came with it. But he had convinced himself that there was nothing else in the world that he could do as well. And, like so many others, he just accepted it. It might sound strange to you but it really isn't all that abnormal. People spend decades doing the nine-to-five thing and hate every second of it. But they never do anything about it because they convince themselves that there isn't anything better within their reach. So they're comfortable with the fact that they know their job and can do it well enough to remain somewhat unconscious day in and day out. The problem with that kind of thinking is that it always ends up creeping into every other aspect of your life. Now I'm not saying that there aren't exceptions. In lower class situations you do what you have to do. Most of the time you just don't have any choice in the matter. That may be difficult for some of you to swallow but it's the truth. Industrialists, social leftists, whomever, can go on about this and that but it matters little. Anyone who can afford the luxury of waxing intellectual on the subject simply isn't in that position. There is no dishonor in spending a life providing for your family. There is no dishonour in doing work that others might consider beneath them or trivial. There are hundreds of millions that do those jobs and are happy that they have them. That's the stoic simplicity of the blue-collar existence. Making the world go round was never that easy. But someone's got to do it.

Everyone gets a turn at bat. Hit anything.

So that's how I found Eli. Trapped in a line of work that he didn't particularly like but was good at. Beside that he hadn't changed much. When work came in someone would give him a call. Sometimes, if he was lucky, there was a reason. But Eli didn't much care about reasons. As far as he was concerned he had found his one true gift and that was good enough for him. But as I sat there I couldn't quite put all the pieces together. How does the introverted son of an egomaniacal engineer go from a life of quite redundancy to one of a hit man? For the life of me I couldn't figure it. So I decided to be blunt and just asked Eli to tell me. Which he did.

It all started the year my father died. Eli was still living with his dad and was working part time at the shooting range. From what I could gather he took the job so that he could shoot after work for free. Later that year Leo Lemski suffered a stroke and Eli was forced to put him in a home. It never ceases to amaze me how things always come around. I'm sure that if Leo had given a damn about his son, then maybe Eli would have taken care of him. But Eli had no reservations about dumping his dad off in some home. As far as he was concerned he was just some stranger that yelled at him. Eli ended up getting a job stocking shelves at a supermarket in Houston and got a small place of his own. At the end of that year he had saved up enough money to buy a used car and decided to give up his apartment in favour of living in the car. He said he did it primarily to save money but I would venture to guess that it was either the apartment or the car. So Eli was working at the supermarket and living in his car. Ain't it just like fate to make that decision seem poignant when it was nothing more than a fluke. One night Eli left work late and was searching for a place to pull over for the night and sleep. He was driving around at about 2 am when he came to a hard stop at a red light. This caused a great deal of crap to come flying up from the backseat and fill the passenger side of the car. So Eli started to throw stuff into the backseat. And that's when it happened. Parked on the other side of the street there was a van. And in the van there was a big guy sitting in the driver's seat. The rear doors of the van were open and just as Eli's eyes came upon them he saw another man hit a woman and then throw her into the back of the van.

Eli's first reaction was to say something. But remembering the whole dog incident from his youth he decided not to bother. Maybe the girl would be alright if he kept his mouth shut. He was good at keeping his mouth shut. Unfortunately, the large guy sitting in the driver's seat of the van noticed that Eli had seen what was going on. So he decided to get out of the van and walk over to the passenger side window of Eli's car. Now, any normal person would have hit the gas and gotten out of there. But Eli just froze. The guy started banging on the window and kept yelling "you didn't see nothin' you little shit!" Now if Eli had simply nodded, his head it might have ended there. But Eli didn't. He just sat there looking from the guy pounding on the window to the other guy standing at the back of the van. And that's when the big guy decided to smash Eli's window. The rest happened so fast that Eli couldn't really go into much detail. All that he could recall was that he went for his gun in the glove box, chambered a round and fired through the broken window. The big guy fell to the ground and the guy behind the van went for something. What that turned out to be was a semi-automatic riffle.

Eli didn't know that of course. He was lost in some strange mental time warp that had taken control of his body, superseding the authority of his rationale. His primary reaction to the man's movement was to get out of the driver's side door and stay crouched behind his car. Luckily it was the right decision. After producing the rifle, the guy emptied and entire clip into Eli's car. But seeing as the guy couldn't shoot for shit, he didn't hit the gas tank. He just took out all the windows and put some holes in the quarter panels. Eli was hit in the leg by a bullet that ricocheted off the pavement under the car and caught him in the thigh. Eli's reaction was to come straight up and return fire through the blown out backseat windows. And like I've said throughout this story, Eli was the best shot that I have ever seen. He took him with two shots to the side of the head and that was that. The light turned green, sirens popped up in the distance and Eli realized that there was a hole in his leg, prompting him to do the decent thing. Pass out.

It doesn't end there, mind you. As it turned out, the girl that had been thrown into the back of the van was the runaway daughter of a New Orleans gangster. It seems that daughter and father had had an argument several months earlier and she had left New Orleans for Houston with some biker. Broke, and accustomed to feeding a hefty drug habit, she soon turned to prostitution and wound up working for the two guys that Eli had shot dead. When the police showed up they questioned the girl, who went to great lengths to make Eli appear her savior. The whole thing was chalked up to self-defense since the cops were familiar with the two dead pimps and didn't really give a damn either way. Eli's gun was conveniently misplaced by an officer and the girl, after being identified, was sent back to New Orleans. So now you've got this gangster who's been reunited with his only child after several months of worrying and wondering where she was, and on top of it all, he learns that some complete stranger saved her life. The fact that she left out the part about being a prostitute had little to do with the fact that the man felt indebted to Eli. So he decided to do something about it. And you know gangsters. When they set their minds to something, well...

The world of crime works in a very specific way. If you've got enough pull you can find out just about anything you need to. A phone call is made from New Orleans to Dallas, from Dallas to an individual on the Houston PD, the chain is then reversed. And, after the delivery of a sound beating to a daughter, a member of the New Orleans mob sends a couple of guys to Houston to pay Eli a visit. It's as simple as that. When Eli was released from the hospital a week later he was met by two men who ushered him into the back of a car. At first Eli was a little concerned that the men were affiliated with the two guys that he had shot and it was curtains. But after one of the men explained the whole thing to him he found it considerably easier to relax. Eli had no thoughts either way about organized crime. During the time that I spent with him it seemed to me that he always gave people the benefit of the doubt, no matter their position in life. So he wasn't all that against the fact that he was being flown to New Orleans mere hours after being wheeled out of a hospital door. After all, we're talking about a guy who stocked shelves at a supermarket and lived in his car. So Eli got on the plane, flew to Louisiana and met the gangster. And that's where his life took a turn for the worse as the gangster's idea of repaying Eli was to give him a job. And because it paid better than stocking shelves, Eli wasted no time in accepting it.

At first Eli did menial things like the opening of car doors, transporting goods, what have you. It wasn't until the summer of the next year that he was invited along to "go see about a guy". It was in Baton Rouge on a rainy night that Eli Lemski took part in his first professional killing. He was only the driver but that's all it would take to get him started. Once his knowledge of guns became apparent to his co-workers he started seeing about more guys. By the winter of that same year Eli was seeing about a lot of people.

As mentioned earlier, the world of crime has specific ways of doing things. There were those in New Orleans that didn't like the fact that an outsider had moved from errand-boy to the guy who saw about people in a little over a year. They were concerned that their superior had become too attached to a kid who, it has to be said, was an outsider. So after the boss was tipped off that someone was going to try and get rid of Eli, he decided to do the decent thing. After all, Eli had saved his daughter's life and that meant more to him than it did to those around him. So he sent Eli to Chicago and set him free.

It was in the Windy City that Eli became an independent, or contract-killer. Because of his affiliation with the mob in New Orleans he got enough work to build up a decent sized clientele. And like any business, that's how the cream rises to the top. Eli was efficient and extremely thorough. And because he tended to keep his mouth shut most of the time those who employed him got the impression that he had been doing this sort of thing for much longer than he had been. Eli's lack of verbalization gave him that whole no-nonsense hit man kind of quality. It made him seem dangerous and unpredictable. Not that anyone in their right mind would ever consider Eli dangerous if they saw a picture of him. But if you knew what he did for a living and met him, you'd understand. His business flourished as word spread, and like some hip new bistro, Eli became the go-to-guy for all the jobs that no one else would touch. And he pulled them off, as if born to it.

So that's how he ended up in New York. After he got too large for Chicago, so much so that the police were watching his apartment, he decided to pack it in and move to New York. And that's where he was when I met up with him. Standing quietly in the middle of a shit storm.

Step Four: There's always something better out there. It's in here that's the problem.

I spent the better part of two weeks with Eli after heading back to Jack's to get my things. He really didn't notice that I was leaving since he and Tara had both decided to simultaneously confess to their affairs. Jack's life went into the shitter and I took a cab to the Bronx to stay with Eli. And it was during those weeks that I found myself for the first time. In a small, lonely apartment in the middle of a mass of humanity. It was there I realized that I, myself, would be the only one accountable for my own happiness. Everything and everyone else just didn't matter somehow. And through that I discovered that eventually I would have to make sure that they did.

Eli spent most of his time just sitting in the kitchen looking out the window. I found it sad that he had lived a life inside himself and surfaced only to find a hideous reality in which he found little comfort. Of all the people I've known in my life Eli deserved the greatest amount of happiness. Simply because he never asked for anything. Simply because nothing was ever asked. There was a time when I used to dream that Eli had settled down and got married. He'd bring his kids over to my place and we'd sit around and talk about sports and politics and life. But I always awoke to the realization that Eli killed people for a living and would never know the simple pleasures of such activities. And you know, somewhere in there I realized that there isn't anything premeditated about us, even though we do our best to convince ourselves otherwise. There's just a long fly ball to center field and the sun's in your eyes. So maybe you come up with the ball, maybe you don't. The only thing that separates us as human beings is the specifics of the play. Everyone's got their concerns. Maybe you're going back for that ball and there are runners in scoring position and your team's down a run. Maybe the bases are empty and it's only the second. It doesn't really matter in the end. It's whether you catch the ball or not that matters. Because that's just you, singularly, tested by both the ball and yourself.

The sun's just in your head. So let it go.

For those two weeks I spent a great deal of time trying to figure out what to do next. Eli's situation, though giving me ample excuses to wax poetic on life and its mysteries, was nonetheless making me uncomfortable. So at the end of those two weeks I decided that my great American adventure had come to an end. I rationalized this by telling myself I had uncovered everything that I had set out to find. It was a lie of course, but then again what isn't these days. I came to the conclusion that I'd head back to San Francisco and give writing a serious go, even though I had a degree in biology and didn't know the first thing about publishing and the rest of it. So I left Eli standing at the door to his apartment block and got in a cab. He waved a slight wave and quickly walked back inside. I continued on to Newark and then home to Austin for a while before returning to the coast. My mother had been kind enough to spring for my flights, so I couldn't refuse a quick stopover at home to appease her never-ending complaints that I rarely endeavour, to visit or call. And that was the last I saw of Eli Lemski. We never crossed paths again.

Step Five: Guts enough to swallow hard and just do what you have to.

As I sit here years later I am comforted by the fact that I took the time to explain myself. My wife often asks me whether or not I'm contented with the fact that I write children's books for a living and I always reply, "it's better than stocking shelves in a Houston supermarket". Of course, she has no idea what I mean when I say that, and I've never told her the whole truth about Eli and what he did. A few years ago I published my first work of adult fiction entitled *Street Oracle*. During my research for that book I decided to look up Eli, as one of the characters was loosely based on him. To my dismay I came across his name in the archives of a New Jersey newspaper. His body had been discovered in a dumpster next to a high school. He had been shot in the head. It's something I try not to visualize but often do. I wonder whether his eyes were open or closed. Because it makes me depressed to think that, even in death, he was robbed of his one true worldly gift. The power of observation. And it seems strange to me that for someone who was so observant he could never see that it was always right in front of him the whole time. Maybe if I hadn't taken him to the shooting range that day he'd still be alive. Blaming myself always seems easier than looking for another reason, even if it's just a blind alley. That way a part of him remains in me and I remember everything. Because remembering is important. Maybe of the utmost importance. The thing that burns me the most is that for someone like Eli there are never any easy roads or happy endings. Life just happens like it's paint by numbers and you only have one colour. So now I write books for kids and my biggest critics are my two daughters. And you know, that ain't so bad. So this one's for Eli Lemski. And maybe a little for me as well.

Once there lived a boy who loved to look outside of his window. And on the other side of that window was a world filled with secrets that only he knew of. He stayed inside his house so that he could watch all the other people stumble over and around all of his secrets. And it made him smile. Because only he could see them.

Rest easy people.

One night, while Francis was asleep, a telecommunications satellite fell from a deteriorating orbit and hit the house that his great, great grandfather had built. Being that it was in the middle of nowhere, Francis could not expect anyone to rescue him or even know that his house had been struck by such a thing. Pinned beneath the smoldering shell of the satellite he watched the sun come up and pour through the hole in his roof that it had made. And then he died.